John Emery Morris

The Bontecou Genealogy

A record of the descendants of Pierre Bontecou, a Huguenot refugee from France,

in the lines of his sons

John Emery Morris

The Bontecou Genealogy
A record of the descendants of Pierre Bontecou, a Huguenot refugee from France, in the lines of his sons

ISBN/EAN: 9783337287733

Printed in Europe, USA, Canada, Australia, Japan

Cover: Foto ©Andreas Hilbeck / pixelio.de

More available books at **www.hansebooks.com**

THE BONTECOU GENEALOGY.

A RECORD

OF

THE DESCENDANTS

OF

PIERRE BONTECOU,

A HUGUENOT REFUGEE FROM FRANCE,

IN THE LINES OF HIS SONS.

COMPILED

BY

JOHN E. MORRIS.

HARTFORD, CONN.:
PRESS OF THE CASE, LOCKWOOD & BRAINARD COMPANY.
1885.

INTRODUCTION.

This work was begun early in the winter of 1882-3, and occupied about two years. During this period over twelve hundred letters were written and sent, many books and records examined, and all known sources of information thoroughly exhausted for data concerning this family. The undertaking has reached such a degree of success that but few names are missing from the record, and the utmost but unavailing diligence has been exerted to obtain some trace of these.[1] Since early in 1884, however, no changes have been noted except those voluntarily furnished to the compiler.

[1] It is not known that *any* have failed of record here, except the *possible* descendants of David Bontecou (104), and William Henry Bontecou (130). These *may*, in part, be accounted for by the following, whom the compiler has been unable to find a place for:

"Bontecou ——, Public house, 66 Lispenard st. (name refused)"— *New York City Directory*, 1828-9.

"Charles Bontecou, son of Daniel and Catharine Bontecou, born March 6, 1851."—*New Haven, Conn., Town Records.*

The name of a Charles Bontecou was given the compiler as a resident of Caro, Tuscola County, Mich., but a search there failed to reveal any trace of him.

Thomas R. Trowbridge, Jr., of New Haven, in a paper read before the New Haven Colony Historical Society, and published in the third volume of their papers entitled *History of the Ancient Maritime Interests of New Haven*, mentions "*Eliakim* Bonticou, an aged mariner, with a face reminding one of the beak of a Roman galley." The compiler has never elsewhere met with this name in his researches, and concludes that Mr. Trowbridge intended to refer to Captain Eliakim *Benham* (See No. 39 in this genealogy), who flourished at the time of the incident in which the name occurs; viz., the celebration of peace, in 1814, at the close of the war with Great Britain.

A John Francis Bonticou resided in Poughkeepsie, N. Y., in 1841-5.

The work originated in the desire of the compiler to trace his lineal descent on the maternal side. Nothing like a genealogy was at first contemplated; but, the discovery of each fact developing a desire for further knowledge, the work continued to grow until its present proportions were reached.

Pierre Bontecou, the emigrant, had three sons, of two of whom we possess some degree of knowledge. The line of *Daniel*, the elder of these, became early extinct. From the other, *Timothy*, most of those appearing in these pages have descended; and it has been thought best to make this a true genealogy of his descendants, rather than the one-sided *paterlinealogy* that is commonly presented. It has been estimated that the proportion of descendants in the female branches of the average New England family, passing through seven generations, is as sixty-four to one in the male branches. The amount of labor required to search out and record the former being in the same proportion, or greater, most genealogists are deterred from the attempt to record them; and this large proportion, having by mere *custom* lost their right to the *name*, though their blood is as thick and kinship as great, are thus barred out and treated as aliens.

Lest the compiler be charged with the errors and deficiencies which must necessarily exist in a work of this character, he asks the reader to remember that he is not the *author*, and is dependent for his information upon others; if therefore he has been furnished with names and dates written in a careless or illegible manner, no

He was a native of France, and came to America when fourteen years old. He was not a descendant of *Pierre*.

The name of " Paul Bontecou, le jeune," a resident of the Isle of Ré, is early recorded in the *Archives Nationales* at Paris, without further comment. Is is quite probable that he was a *brother* of *Pierre*.

The above note contains all mention found of the name *Bontecou*, not having a place in the record.

amount of diligent study will amount to a guarantee that the errors existing in the original manuscript are not perpetuated in these pages.

So far as possible, the ordinary, every-day events in the lives of those mentioned herein have been put down; not that in themselves they possess particular interest (for in the lives of most people no startling or extraordinary events occur), but because there is no reason to doubt that as large a degree of interest towards them will be excited in the minds of those that come after us, as moves us in contemplating the deeds and conditions of our forefathers, which we shall never cease to regret were not more carefully recorded and preserved.

It will be apparent that no effort has been made to render this a work of literary pretensions; the compiler has simply aimed to secure a record of facts. In stating them the language of others has been freely appropriated, derived both from manuscript and printed page. His thanks are due to all who have so generously furnished material for this genealogy, and who have by a kindly interest encouraged him in his work. The cordiality and good-will manifested by *all* with whom it has been his good fortune to come in contact, either in person or by correspondence, have served to cheer his labor, and borne no unimportant part as a means to its completion.

While acknowledging his indebtedness to all, it will not be improper to mention the names of Rev. Charles W. Baird, D. D., of Rye, N. Y., and Rev. A. V. Wittmeyer of New York City, to both of whom he is under great obligations for information furnished, and from whose labors in research he has reaped a much-appreciated benefit.

With these introductory remarks, and without apology for the shortcomings of the work, which of very necessity are numerous, this volume is sent forth in the hope that amongst its readers it may find some share of acceptance.

BONTECOU.

THE FAMILY. — ITS NAME AND EARLY HISTORY.

THE family of Bontecou, while not possessing the acknowledged antiquity of some, is still known to be respectably ancient. I regret that I have been unable to follow the line continuously back to its first known ancestor; but failing this, the record is commenced with *Pierre*, the refugee to America, as the earliest member to whom the lineage of the family can be traced.

The name is of Dutch or Flemish origin, and is undoubtedly derived from a symbolic representation of a brindled or spotted cow, used by some remote ancestor as his business or house sign.[1] Proof of this assumption is offered in the following extract from *Rose's Biographical Dictionary* (Vol. IV. p. 428); and while the individual alluded to is not known to have borne any connection with the family now extant in this country, it is but a fair assumption that the probability of a similar derivation of the name is the case in our family, antedating the one referred to here: "Bonteköe (Cornelius Van), a physician,[2] the son of a burgher of Alcmaer, whose name was (Johan) Gerard Decker, but who obtained the name of Bonteköe from having appended to his house the sign of a cow of many colors."

[1] *Arthur's Dictionary of Family Names* (New York, 1857), derives the name from " *Bonte*, goodness, strength, fruitfulness, and *cul* (pron. *ku*), the bottom behind: denoting, figuratively, the humor or turn of mind." This definition is rather a forced *translation* than the probable *source* of the family name.

[2] "He was born in 1647, and studied medicine at the University of Leyden. Having taken his degree he visited the Hague, Amsterdam,

The derivation of the name is further illustrated. Not far from the village of New Paltz, Ulster County, N. Y., is an insignificant settlement or hamlet called Bontecou Mountain. The name naturally suggests the proprietorship, at some time, of the surrounding land by some one of the Bontecou family; but investigation has revealed the fact that Bontecou was in former years a Dutch tavern, called Buntekau (pronounced Bontecoo), from its sign, which represented a brindled cow.

The change which occurred in its orthography in later years, after the removal of the family to France, was a natural one, and expressed in its French form the same idea as originally conveyed.

During the two centuries that the name has been extant in America, the pronunciation of its terminal syllable has become anglicized to the sound of *cue*, while the mode of spelling it remains unchanged, with but few unimportant exceptions, chief of which is the substitution of the letter *i* for *e* in the second syllable. In this work I have adhered

and Hamburg. Frederic William, Elector of Brandenburg, named him physician to the court; and he repaired to Berlin, where he died Feb. 13, 1685, from a fall which fractured his skull. The Elector honored his memory by a pompous funeral. He was most zealous in recommending the use of tea to neutralize acidity, to which he attributed all fevers; in short, he regarded this beverage as a universal panacea. His enthusiasm on this subject is quite ludicrous, for he went so far as to endeavor to prove that both the physical and moral condition of man would be improved by the use of tea, as in its subtle elements and principles he conceived it to possess properties nearly allied to those of the animal spirits. He proposed the drinking of not less than 100 or 200 cups in the day; and he equally recommended the use of the pipe, which, according to his doctrine, ought to be continuously used during the twenty-four hours. These and other singular opinions entertained by him render his name of no celebrity in the annals of medical science, but rather present him as an example of grave error arising from speculative doctrines, to be avoided by all who desire to exercise their profession for the benefit of mankind." He was the author of a number of books, which were printed at Amsterdam in 1688.

throughout to the orthography as expressed in the signature of the earliest American ancestor of the family.

For the gratification of those who may be interested in
heraldry I will remark that the "coat of arms" of the
Bonteköe family is thus described in *Rietstap's Armorial
General :* " BONTEKÖE. — De sinoplé, au cheval arrête
d'argent," — a white, or silver horse, standing, on a green
ground. Whether or not *this* family is entitled to the use
of this arms I am unable to say. I know of no instance
of its adoption.

The member of the family of whom we possess the
earliest knowledge is Guilliame Isbrand Bonteköe, a
Dutch navigator who lived in the early part of the seventeenth century.

In a volume containing a collection of voyages, by
Thevenot, translated into French from the original Dutch,
published in Amsterdam, 1681, the principal article is
entitled *Journal ou description d'un voyage aux Indes
Orientals commence en* 1618, *et accompli en* 1825, a brief
résumé of which is as follows:

William Isbrand Bonteköe, a Dutch navigator, lived in
the first part of the seventeenth century. In 1618 he
was captain of the "Nouvelle Hoorn," a ship of 1,100
tons and a crew of 206 men, and set sail for the East
Indies. After touching at the then uninhabited island
of Mascaruque, and at Madagascar, he was upon the point
of arriving at Batavia, when a fire broke out in his vessel.
While making efforts to extinguish it, he was deserted
by sixty-six of his men, who escaped from the ship in a
shallop and a small skiff. Being unable to subdue the
flames, he remained upon the vessel until, the fire reaching the magazine, the ship was thrown into the air and
destroyed. Bonteköe, in falling, had the good fortune to
grasp a spar, which supported him in the water until he
was picked up by the shallop, which was fortunately near

at hand. By his bravery and knowledge of navigation this frail bark was brought safely to Sumatra after a perilous voyage of fourteen days, and at a moment when the crew were giving way to despair. At this point Bonteköe and his men endeavored to disembark, but were repulsed by the natives and compelled to make the weary voyage back to Batavia, where they fortunately found a Dutch fleet.

At another time, commanding a ship of thirty-two guns, Bonteköe took part in the expedition in which Cornelis with eight vessels ravaged the coast of China.

The original source of the foregoing accounts is from the pen of Bonteköe himself. These facts have been utilized by *Alexandre Dumas* in a tale entitled *Bontekoe*, being the first in his volume *Les Drames de la Mer*. Unfortunately no record is known to exist relating to this man's descendants, but it was probably one of his sons who crossed the border and settled in France.

The family in France were Protestant, and undoubtedly endured the privations and suffering imposed upon the Huguenots by the Romish Church, both before and subsequent to the revocation of the Edict of Nantes.[1] " By

---

[1] "The revocation of the Edict of Nantes was signed by Louis XIV. of France, Oct. 18, 1685, in the castle of Nantes, which was built in the year 938. The edict was the outcome of the troubles between the Catholic and Protestant factions in France, which resulted in the assassination of Henry III., on the 2d of August, 1559, by Jacques Clement, a Dominican monk. On his death Henry IV. ascended the throne. He was considered a heretic and an apostate, but became a Catholic on July 25, 1593. He put an end to the religious struggles in his dominion by signing and publishing the Edict of Nantes on the 13th of April, 1598. In the preamble of this act the King recognizes that God is adored and prayed to by all his subjects, if not in the same form, at least with the same intention, so that his kingdom will forever merit and preserve the glorious title of Most Christian. The edict was declared perpetual and irrevocable, as being the principal foundation of union and tranquillity of the state. It accorded in brief the following: Full liberty of conscience in spiritual jurisdic-

2

this act of revocation and the consequent flight of those embracing 'the Religion' from her borders, France was deprived of a large population of her most intelligent and useful citizens, and the adjoining states of Holland and Switzerland, as well as the neighboring islands of Great Britain, were correspondingly enriched by the influx of this best blood of France. America, too, became the gainer by a large immigration to her shores of this sterling people, skilled in the mechanic arts."

Among the refugees from France at this time were Pierre Bontecou and his family; tarrying for a time in England, they arrived in America in 1689.[1]

"During the year 1685 there was a large addition of French Protestants to the population (of New York). By the year 1695 they had increased to nearly two hundred families, and were among the most influential of the city. At first they worshiped in a small building on Marketfield Street; then a more commodious chapel was built upon Pine Street, — 'L'Eglise du Saint Esprit' (The Church of the Holy Ghost). It was built of stone, 70 by 50 feet in size, and there was attached to it a burying-ground. They worshiped here for one hundred and thirty years." (*Smiles's Huguenots.*) In this graveyard

tion, the public exercise of religion in all places where it was established in 1597 and in the faubourgs of towns, admission of Protestants to public offices, of their children to schools, of their sick to hospitals, of their poor to a share of the charities, and various other liberties. Henry IV., however, had to sacrifice his life for the signing of this edict, for he was assassinated by Ravaillac on the 14th of May, 1610. He was succeeded by Louis XIII., through whose reign the condition of Protestants became worse; and finally, in the reign of his successor, Louis XIV., on the 18th of October, 1685, a revocation of the edict was signed, which put an end to the exercise of Protestant worship and compelled all those not Catholics to flee to other countries."

[1] This is the advent year of the name in America, notwithstanding that *Washington Irving*, in his *Knickerbocker's History of New York*, uses it in connection with events occurring many years earlier. (Book VI., Chapter VIII.)

the early Bontecous were buried, and their remains were
undisturbed until 1831, when the advancing tide of commercial prosperity demanded their resting-place for less
sacred purposes; so the august remains of all there interred were reverently removed to the churchyard of "St.
Mark's in the Bowery," where for over fifty years they
have lain undisturbed. In the records of this ancient
Church of Saint Esprit is found nearly all that can be
known of the early history of the Bontecou family in
America.

FIRST GENERATION.

1   **Pierre Bontecou,** merchant, his wife (MARGUERITE 2
COLLINOT), and five children, were in 1684 fugitives from
the Isle of Ré to " La Caroline," as we are informed by
records in the *Archives Nationales* at Paris.   The government of Louis XIV., after placing all possible hindrances
in the way of his escaping subjects, and condemning to
the galleys those who were arrested in their flight, still
kept its eye upon those whose efforts had terminated in
success, and their names and destinations became a matter
of national record, to which we are indebted for this
earliest knowledge of our fugitive ancestor.   Although
his departure from France was made from the Isle of Ré,
his previous residence was in La Rochelle, hard by, — a
city of large commercial importance, and a stronghold of
Protestantism.   In this city his son Daniel was born, and
doubtless his other children.

The flight of this family to " La Caroline " (a general
term used to designate the continent of North America)
was by way of England, and it was not until 1689 that
they appeared in New York.   The date of their advent
there is practically fixed by the following extract from the
manuscript of M. du Simitière, now in the possession of

the Philadelphia Library Company: "New York, May 31, 1769. I have been informed by Mr. Buvelot, who had it from old M^{rs}. Bontecou's own mouth, that she came in New York from France *during the time that Leisler had the Government*,[1] that she and her family were well received by him."

It is unfortunate for our purpose that so little relating to our ancestor can be found upon record. In the absence of this we can only conjecture what his history in this new land could have been. That the competence which tradition relates the family enjoyed in their native country, and which his position as a merchant would imply, was lacking for a time in their new home, seems to be proven by the fact that for a few years a pension was paid by the French Church to "Madame Bondecoux," as evidenced by the ancient records of that church. The material attainable for the construction of the subsequent history of Pierre Bontecou is so meagre that I have thought best to present without comment a transcript[2] of such records

---

[1] Jacob Leisler, a German by birth, was, in 1683, appointed one of the judges of the Court of Admiralty in New York. Lieut.-Gov. Francis Nicholson was in command of the colony when Leisler, supported by the mass of the lower orders of the inhabitants, seized the fort and the public funds the last of May, 1689, and assuming the governorship, retained it by force until March, 1691, when, upon the arrival from England of Governor Sloughter bearing the commission of King William, he was arrested, imprisoned, tried for "treason and murder," condemned to death, and executed May 16, 1691.

[2] TRANSLATION OF EXTRACTS FROM THE REGISTER OF THE FRENCH CHURCH IN NEW YORK.

To-day, July 24, 1690, was baptized in this church, Marie, daughter of Pierre and Marguerite Bontecour; born on the 21st of this month, and presented for holy baptism by Daniel Poutrhau and Marie Perdricau.

PEIRET, *Minister*.

D. POUTREAU.
MARIE PERDRIAU.

To-day, July 24, 1690, was baptized Rachel, daughter of Pierre and

containing mention of his name as I have been able to find, and leave the imagination of the reader to construct such account of his career as seems to him warranted by

---

Marguerite Bontecour; born on the 21st of this month, and presented for holy baptism by André Paillet and Judiq Piau.

PEIRET, *Minister*.   ANDRÉ PAILLET.
               JUDHIT PIAUD.

To-day, Sunday, July 2, 1693, after the morning service, was baptized in this church, by Mr. Peiret, minister, Thimotée, son of Pierre and Marguerite Bontecoux; born on the 17th of June last, and presented for holy baptism by Thimotée Archambaud and Elizabeth Hestier.

THIMOTHÉE ARCHAMBAUD.
PEIRET, *Minister*.   ELIZABETH GOURDON.

To-day, Sunday, May 7, 1699, after the evening service, was baptized in this church, by Mr. Peiret, minister, Jeanne Marie Audar, daughter of Daniel Audar and of Marthe Jaufrey; born on the 30th of last April, and presented for holy baptism by Mr. Pierre Bontecoux and Jeanne Audar.

PEIRET, *Minister*.

To-day, Sunday, July 16, 1699, after evening prayer, was solemnly celebrated, by Mr. Peiret, minister, the marriage of Mr. Estienne Perdriau and Miss Marguerite Bontecoux, after the publishment of their banns on three different Sundays.

PIERRE BONTECOU.   ESTIENNE PERDRIAU.
MARGUERITE COLLINOT.   MARGUERITE BONTECOU.
SARRA BONTECOU.   ELIZABETH HASTIER.
H. JOURDAIN.   MARIE PERDRIAU.
ABRAHAM GOUNEAU.   P. JOUNEAU.
              A. BONNIN.
PEIRET, *Minister*.

To-day, Wednesday, January 17, 1698, after morning prayer, was presented for holy baptism, Jeanne Ester, daughter of Samuel Bourdet and of Judith Piaud; born on the 29th day of last December, baptized by Mr. Peiret, minister, and presented by Pierre Bontecou and Marie Ester Charron.

PEIRET, *Minister*.

To-day, Sunday, January 19, 1701, after the evening service, was baptized in this church, by Mr. Peiret, our minister, Marguerite Perdrieau, daughter of Estienne (Perdreau) and Marguerite Bontecou: born on Tuesday, the 14th of the present month, at nine o'clock in the morning,

the few facts recorded. I think it may be safely assumed that he was a man of some prominence among his countrymen and in the church. It will be noticed that no date

and presented for holy baptism by Pierre Bontecou and Elizabeth Perdriau, widow of the late Jean Hastier.

P. BONTECOU.

PEIRET, *Minister.* ELIZABETH HASTIER.

To-day, Friday, September 1st, 1704, died Mr. Pierre Peiret, minister of this church, towards nine o'clock in the morning.

On the second of September, Mr. Peiret was buried in the public cemetery of this city.

To-day, Sunday, September 10th, after the evening service, at the request of the Consistory, the heads of families remained and unanimously resolved to pay the widow of Mr. Peiret, minister, besides the current quarter, which will be due on the next festival of St. Michael, one whole year of the salary which this church paid him.

BONGRAND.	JEAN BARBERIE, *Elder.*
DANIEL GAILLARD.	JEAN DAVID, *Elder.*
JOSUE DAVID.	AUGUSTE JAY, *Elder.*
VINCENT FILLOW.	ELIAS NEAU, *Elder.*
ELIE PELLETREAU.	P. MONTELS.
JEAN PERLIER.	NICHOLAS JAMAIN.
JEAN LE CHEVALIER.	ESTIENNE DE LANCEY.
DENIS RICHIER.	ANDRÉ LAURAU.
JEAN FAJET.	AUGUSTUS GRASSET.
JEAN LAFONT.	F. VINCENT.
JEAN CAZALZ.	ANDRÉ FOUCAUT.
J. GARREAU.	P. BONTECOU.
THOMAS BAYEUX.	D. JAUDIN.
ELIAS BOUDINOT.	LOUMAIN.
BENJAMIN DHARIETTE.	PIERRE MORIN.
JEAN MAYON.	A. BONNIN.
ANDREW STUCKEY.	RENÉ REZEAU.
ABRAHAM GIRAUD.	PAUL DROILHET, *Elder.*
ISAAC GARNIER.	DANIEL MENARD.

To-day, Sunday, September 10th, 1704, the heads of families, being assembled with the Consistory, agreed to write by the first regular mail to Mr. Laborie, in order to ask him whether he is willing to come and preach for us and to administer the sacraments in our present circumstances.

BONGRAND.	JEAN BARBERIE. *Elder.*
DANIEL GAILLARD.	JEAN DAVID, *Elder.*

of death, either of Pierre or his wife, has been found. We only know that the former was alive in 1724. The church-yard of the old Huguenot Church in Pine Street — L'Eglise

VINCENT FILLOW.	PAUL DROILHET, *Elder*.
ELIE PELLETREAU.	AUGUSTE JAY, *Elder*.
JEAN PERLIER.	ELIAS NEAU, *Elder*.
JEAN LE CHEVALIER.	P. MONTELS.
DENIS RICHER.	NICHOLAS JAMAIN.
JEAN FAJET.	ESTIENNE DE LANCEY.
JEAN LAFONT.	ANDRÉ LAURAU.
JEAN CAZALZ.	F. VINCENT.
J. GARREAU.	AUGUSTUS GRASSER.
THOMAS BAYEUX.	ANDRÉ FOUCAUT.
ELIAS BOUDINOT.	P. BONTECOU.
BENJAMIN DHARIETTE.	D. JAUDIN.
JEAN MAYNON.	LOUMAIN.
ISAAC GARNIER.	PIERRE MORIN.
DANIEL MENARD.	A. BONNIN.
ANDREW STUCKEY.	JOSUE DAVID.

ABRAHAM GIRAD.

To-day, October 22, 1712, after the morning service, Mr. Louis Rou baptized Ester Ancherim, born on the 2nd of this month, daughter of Zacharie Ancherim and Anna Naudin, and presented for holy baptism by Pierre Bontecou and Ester Le Conte.

                                       PIERRE BONTECOU.

L. ROU, *Minister.*   ESTHER LE CONTE.

To-day, Wednesday, February 18, 1713, after morning prayer, Mr. Louis Rou baptized Daniel Bontecou, born on the 14th of this month, son of Daniel Bontecou and Marie Machet, and presented for holy baptism by Pierre Bontecou and Jeanne Peltreau.

                                       DANIEL BONTECOU.
                                       PIERRE BONTECOU.

L. ROU, *Min.*   JEANNE PELLETAUX.

At New York, this 27th day of December, 1724. To-day, Sunday, after evening prayer, Mr. Moulinars baptized Elizabeth Hastier, born on the 13th of this month, daughter of Mr. Jean Hastier and Elizabeth his wife, and presented for holy baptism by Mr. Pierre Bontecou and Mrs. Pregente Carré.

                                       JEAN HASTIER.
                                       P. BONTECOU.

J. J. MOULINARS, *Pastor.*   PREGENTE CARRÉ.

du Saint Esprit — undoubtedly received their remains; an l upon its destruction in 1831, to make way for the U. S. Sub-Treasury building, they were removed with all

EXTRACT FROM THE DOCUMENTARY HISTORY OF NEW YORK, VOL. 3, P. 260, QUARTO EDITION.

Morris Nawinhuysen of the City of *New York*, Marriner, being sworn on the Holy Evangelists, saith, that being Master of the Sloop *Constant Abigail*, whereof *John Van Brugh* was Capt., he was taken in the said sloop the 9th of November, 1706, about fifty Leagues of *Scilly*, by a French Privateer. That after he was taken, one *John Thompson*, Boatswain of the Sloop, & one of the French-men belonging to the Privateer, were together in the Cabbin of the Sloop, opening the Letters, in hopes to find a piece of Money, for he could not read. That the said *Thompson* reading the Superscriptions of some of the Letters, found some directed for *France*, whereupon, so soon as the said French-men went out of the Cabbin, the said *Thompson* called this Deponent to come into the Cabbin to him, where there was a Candle burning. That *Thompson* told this Deponent, there was some Letters directed for *France*, which he desired the Deponent to read, because, perhaps, they might find some Bills of Exchange in them; whereupon the Deponent looking on the Letters he found some of them were not signed, and said, he believed there was Roguery in them, because they were not signed. That amongst those Letters there was one pretty near three sides, wherein was something mentioned, according to the best of this Deponents understanding, to this effect, That if the *French* Squadron that took *Nevis*, had come hither, they would have met with less Resistance. That the Letter being writ in *French*, and the Deponent understanding very little of that Language, he could not make out the whole sence of the Letter. That this Deponent told *Thompson* what he understood of the Letter, and said he believed there was more to the like effect, but *Thompson* telling him the Frenchmen were coming into the Cabbin, the said *Thompson* threw the Letters over board for fear there might be something in them that might be prejudicial to *New-York*. That the said Letter was directed to *Rochell*, but does not remember to whom. That the writing of the said Letter was like the handwriting of Capt. *Benjamin Faneuil*, which this Deponent has several times seen, before he saw the said Letter, but cannot say that he wrote it. That this Deponent likewise saw at the same time several other Letters directed to France, which seemed by the character to be writ by several persons, two of which said Letters were signed by *Pière Bontecou*, but that he read neither of the said Letters signed by the said *Bontecou*. This Deponent further saith, That by the said Capt. *van Brugh's* direction, he lookt over the Letters sent

3

others there interred to a vault in St. Mark's churchyard, Stuyvesant Place and Second Avenue, where they continue to repose.

---

from this place, on board the said Sloop, for England, and put them in to a Bag, and the Bag into the said *van Brugh's* chest, but that he did not then perceive any Letters directed to *France.* — That this Deponent, about a day or two after he saw the said *van Brughen* in *France*, he acquainted him with what he had discovered in the aforesaid letter. And further this Deponent saith not.

M. van NIEWENHUYSEN.

Sworn before a Committee of the Council, the 25th of February, 1707.
GEO. CLARKE.

New York, April 19, 1708.

The afore-written is a true Copy of the Original in my Office.
GEO. CLARKE.

SECOND GENERATION.

[1]CHILDREN OF PIERRE AND MARGUERITE (COLLINOT) **1**
BONTECOU.

2 **I. Marguerite Bontecou,** born in France; emigrated to America with her parents, reaching New York in 1689. [2]She married, July 16, 1699, Stephen Perdriau, mariner, freeman of the city of New York. Their children were:

[3]MARGUERITE, born **Jan. 14, 1701.**
[4]STEPHEN, born **March 4, 1703.**

---

[1] It is not at all certain that these are recorded in the order of their birth.

[2] To-day, Sunday, July 16. 1699. after evening prayer, was solemnly celebrated by Mr. Peiret, mini.   marriage of Mr. Estienne Perdriau and Miss Marguerite Bontecoux, after the publishment of their banns on three different Sundays.

PIERRE BONTICOU.   ESTIENNE PERDRIAU.
MARGUERITE COLLINOT.   MARGUERITE BONTECOU.
SARRA BONTECOU.   ELIZABETH HASTIER.
II. JOURDAIN.   MARIE PERDRIAU.
ABRAHAM GOUNEAU.   P. JOUNEAU.

A. BONNIN.

PEIRIT, *Minister.*   — *French Church Records, New York.*

[3] To-day, Sunday, Jan. 19, 1701, after the evening service, was baptized in this church, by Mr. Peiret, our minister, Marguerite Perdriau, daughter of Estienne (Perdriau) and Marguerite Bontecou; born on Tuesday, the 14th of the present month, at nine o'clock in the morning, and presented for Holy Baptism by Pierre Bontecou and Elizabeth Perdriau, widow of the late John Hastier.

P. BONTECOU.

PEIRET, *Minister.*   ELIZABETH HASTIER.

— *French Church Records, New York.*

[4] To-day, March 10, 1703, after service, was baptized Estienne Perdriau, son of Estienne Perdriau and of Marguerite Bontecou, presented

[1] HOSEA, born Jan. 27, 1705.

I have found no record of deaths in this family. It is my purpose to include the descendants of this marriage, should any be found, in a subsequent volume.

3   **II. Peter Bontecou**, possibly one of the *five* children who fled from the Isle of Ré with their parents in 1684. The only mention of him I have been able to find is in *Valentine's History of New York*, p. 398, where "Peter Bontecou" is included among the *schoolmasters* in New York in 1702.

4   **III. Sara Bontecou**, born in France; reached New York with her parents in 1689. Her name appears in the register of the French Church in New York, as a witness at the marriage of her sister Marguerite, July 16, 1699; as sponsor for Daniel Audard, son of Daniel Audard and Martha Joffray, Jan. 17, 1703; and as sponsor for Hosea Perdriau, son of her sister Marguerite, Feb. 4, 1705. [2] She married, Oct. 19, 1709, Alexander Resseguie of Norwalk, Conn. Their children were:

    ALEXANDER, born Aug. 27, 1710; married, Feb. 16, 1737-8, Thankful Belden.

---

for Holy Baptism by Daniel Bontecou and Marie Bontecou. He was born on March 4th, and baptized by Mr. Peiret, minister.

                                  DANIEL BONTECOU.
PEIRET, *Minister.*   MARIE MAYON.
              — *French Church Records, New York.*

[1] To-day, Sunday, February 4, 1705, was baptized Ozée, son of Estienne Perdriau and of Marguerite Bontecou his wife, by Mr. Laborie; born on the 27th of last January, at eight o'clock in the morning; and had for sponsors, Aman Bonnin and Sara Bontecou.

                          STEPHEN PERDRIAU.
                          A. BONNIN.
J. LABORIE, *M.*   SARRA BONTECOU.
              — *French Church Records, New York.*

[2] Mr. Alexander Resseguie took to wife Mrs. Sarah Bontecou, ye daughter of Mr. Peter Bontecou of New York, Oct. 19, 1709.—*Norwalk, Conn., Town Records.*

PETER, born Dec. 19, 1711; probably died unmarried.

JAMES, born Nov. 6, 1713; died in the French
and Indian War.

ABRAHAM, born July 27, 1715; married Jane
——. He left a large line of descendants.

ISAAC, born May 24, 1717.

JACOB, born Aug. 14, 1719; married Mary Curtis of Stratford, Conn. He died Dec.
27, 1801.

SARAH, born July 12, 1721; died May 25, 1753.

Sara Bontecou died in May, 1757. Her husband died
in October, 1752, leaving an estate valued at £8,784. The
compiler has secured a large amount of data pertaining to
their descendants, which it is his purpose to publish in a
subsequent volume.

IV. Daniel Bontecou, born in La Rochelle, France, **10**
in 1681; emigrated with his parents to America in 1689.
He became a merchant, and was an elder in the French
Church in New York; also elected Treasurer of the same
in January, 1751, which office he resigned ¹ in November,
1754.

---

¹ We have received from Mr. Daniel Bontecou the sum of nine hundred and seventy-five pounds, eight shillings, and three and one-half
pence, current money of this city, which sum belongs to the French
Reformed Church of New York, to wit: the sum of nine hundred and
thirty-five pounds, in eight bonds, the interest of which is to be used
for the maintenance of the ministry, with the exception of twenty-eight
shillings a year, which belong to the poor of the said church; and the
sum of forty pounds, eight shillings, and three and one-half pence in
cash, in settlement of his account as Treasurer of the moneys of the
said church and ministry. At New York, Oct. 22, 1754.
£975 8s. 3½d.   VALLADE, *Elder.*
                              JACQUES BUVELOT, *Elder.*
                              CHARLES JAUDIN, *Elder.*
                              JACQUES DESBROSSES, *Elder.*
                              — *French Church Records, New York.*

He married, probably about 1712, Marianne Machet, daughter of [1] Jean and Jeanne (Thomas) Machet, from La Tremblade, France, then living at New Rochelle, N. Y. [2] She was naturalized in New York, June 17, 1726, and was living in 1761.

The most interesting episode in the history of Daniel Bontecou of which we have any knowledge occurred in connection with a difficulty which arose in the French Church in 1763. The following account is from the pen of the Rev. A. V. Wittmeyer, the present pastor of this church:

" On the 23d of May in that year, the Rev. Jean Carle, then minister of that church, resigned his functions in order to return to Europe. At the request of the Consistory, he consented to remain till the following spring, in order to give the church time to secure another minister from abroad.

" At a meeting of the church held on the 30th day of May, Daniel Bontecou and eleven other gentlemen were elected a committee, with the elders of the church, to

---

[1] " Jean Machet, ship carpenter, who settled first in Oxford, Mass., but removed to New Rochelle, N. Y., was a native of the same place (La Tremblade). At the time when the last severities against the Protestants began to be exercised, Machet was pursuing his trade in the seaport town of Bordeaux. ' We left our goods, our furniture, and our clothes,' he writes, ' I and Jeanne Thomas, my wife, and Pierre, Jean, Jeanne, and Marianne, our children, for the sake of our religion, and fled from persecution, only saving our bodies.' "—*The Huguenot Emigration to America, by C. W. Baird.*

[2] At a Council held at Fort George, in New York, June the 17th, 1726. . . . 10th. An Act for naturalizing Peter De Lage, John Zenger, Paulus Deseer, Nicholas Jaboien, Abraham Rodrigos Rivera, Abraham Carcas, Nicholas Van Taerlingh, Matthias Borrell, Johannes Roorbagh, Johannes Lashier, Louis Sacombell, Marianne the wife of Daniel Bonticow, Pierre Elizee Gallaudet, John Draugaud, Michel Berthom, William Crolges, Jean Ballereau the wife of James Ballereau, and Garrit Cornelisen.—*Journal of the Legislative Council of New York,* Vol. 1, p. 536.

enter into a correspondence with the Consistory of the
Walloon Church of Amsterdam, with a view to securing a
new minister; and should their efforts fail there, to address
themselves to the company of pastors and professors of
Geneva. The committee thus appointed wrote, in accord-
ance with the instructions given them by the church, to
the ecclesiastical authorities named, under date of June 5,
1763; addressing at the same time a letter to Mr. Jacob
Henry Chabanel, a merchant at Amsterdam, and a member
of the Consistory of the Walloon Church, in which they
requested him to advance the funds necessary to bring to
New York the pastor to be elected, and to use his good
offices in the selection of a proper candidate.

"In all these letters the church, through its committee,
obligated itself to accept as its minister the person thus
chosen. On the 2d of December came a letter from the
Consistory of Amsterdam bearing the information that,
by a majority vote, the Rev. Mr. Menauteau had been
chosen by them to succeed the Rev. Mr. Carle, in accord-
ance with the powers given them by the church of New
York. On the 27th of the same month came a letter from
Mr. Chabanel, informing the New York church that the
gentleman thus elected was not a proper person for them:
that he was, in fact, of unsound mind, and that he was
preaching in Amsterdam to empty pews; and that in consequence, he (Mr. Chabanel) had refused to advance the
money to pay his passage to America. This second letter became the starting-point of a long, and at times very
acrimonious, correspondence between the church in New
York and that in Amsterdam, and Mr. Chabanel. The
New York Consistory naturally refused, not only to receive Mr. Menauteau, but even to assume the expense
incurred by this election; nevertheless, on the 30th of
March, 1764, the newly elected pastor arrived in New
York, where his conduct soon proved him to be really

insane, and he was sent back on the first convenient
occasion that presented itself. In reference to this matter, and as late as the autumn of 1764, entire harmony
prevailed in the councils of the church; but about this
time Mr. Vallade, who united the offices of elder, Treasurer, and Secretary, was strongly opposed by an influential
party in the church, at the head of which stood Daniel
Bontecou. The grounds of this opposition are not clearly
stated, but the sequel of the quarrel would seem to indi-
cate that the grievance against Vallade had reference to
his management of the finances of the church. Although
he was warmly sustained by the acting minister, Mr. Têtard, and by a large majority of the Consistory and of the
members of the church, he resigned his three offices on
the 13th of December, 1764,—' moved thereto by delicate
scruples,' as the records say.

"Soon after this resignation occurred an event which
enabled the two parties in the church to take up distinct
positions, and which precipitated matters to an unprecedented extent. By a letter bearing date Jan. 6, 1765, a
Rev. Mr. Daller, who seems to have recently arrived, in-
vites the Consistory to determine whether it will receive
him as minister, or not; and if the latter, threatens to
take the matter into court. This candidate was a young
French-Swiss, and seems to have had no other claim upon
the church than a letter of recommendation from Mr.
Chabanel of Amsterdam; at the same time there seemed
to exist no personal objections to him.

"Summoned thus to take definite action, the Consistory
ruled that Mr. Daller had no legitimate claim upon the
church; but that being present they would receive him as
their minister, provided he would consent to be installed
according to the discipline of the Reformed Church of
France, and that he would be bound by such other conditions as the then state of the church seemed to render

necessary. This conditional acceptance Mr. Daller rejected, and now, if indeed he had not already done so, openly joined the party of Mr. Bontecou ; which hereafter sustained his claims *per fas et nefas*. On Jan. 20, Mr. Vallade, who, although occupying no longer any official position, was evidently the head of the party in power, presented to the Consistory a memorandum consisting of four articles, which clearly reveals to what extent the hostility of the two parties had progressed. The first article affirms the present necessity on the part of the Consistory of exercising its disciplinary powers ; and signals out Daniel Bontecou and four others, whom it accuses of spreading scandalous reports, especially against Mr. Vallade, as worthy of severe discipline. Article 2 reproaches Mr. Daller with trying to enter the church by underhanded means, and proposes that the conditional offer made to him should in consequence be withdrawn. Article 3 declares the meeting held on the 16th of January, 1765, by the Bontecou party, at the house of a Mr. Bonnet, a member of the Consistory, to be contrary to the rules of the church, and hence illegal and of no authority ; and Article 4 is a vindication of the acts of Mr. Vallade. These articles were duly voted on and accepted by the Consistory on the 24th of January.

" In this same meeting of the Consistory was read a letter from Messrs. Smith & Scott, two eminent lawyers at that time, in which they informed the Consistory that they had been retained by Mr. Daller, and that they had advised him to submit his differences with the church to arbitration, as a lawsuit would be ruinous to all concerned. To this letter the Consistory replied on the same day, thanking the counsel for their friendly letter, and offering to convince them of the regularity of its proceedings if they would appoint a time for an interview.

" While this matter was pending, Mr. Bontecou and his

4

associates, on the 2d of February, addressed a letter to
Mr. Tétard, minister of the church, requesting him to
allow Mr. Daller to occupy his pulpit on the following
day, which was Sunday, and intimated that if he would do
so they would return to the church. To this letter Mr.
Tétard at once replied, stating that after consultation with
the Consistory, he felt obliged to deny the request of the
petitioners as incompatible with the resolutions of the
Consistory excluding Mr. Daller from the church, which
resolutions were largely based upon the fact that he (Mr.
Daller) openly joined them in their opposition to the authority of the Consistory. On Feb. 7, the interview with
Messrs. Smith & Scott took place in the room of the
Consistory. The church was represented by the Rev. Mr.
Tétard and Mr. Vallade; and Messrs. Buvelot and Verjereau attended the Rev. Mr. Daller. Mr. Vallade gave a
circumstantial account of all that the church had done
since the resignation of Mr. Carle, and the different letters written to Amsterdam and Geneva, and alleged that
Mr. Daller had no manner of claim upon it. This the
lawyers freely admitted, but advised that in the interest
of peace the church should receive Mr. Daller as its minister, on condition of his obtaining from abroad the cer-
tificates which, they owned, he still lacked. To this the
representatives of the church opposed the rules of their
government, which forbade their taking such a step. The
lawyers answered that those rules were here impracticable.
Unable to come to an agreement, Mr. Buvelot arose and
read a most scandalous protest, signed by Mr. Bonnet, and
addressed to the elders of the church. On the 17th, Mr.
Daller presented to the Consistory, through Mr. Verjereau,
a written statement of what he considered his claims upon
the church. This statement was signed by Messrs. Smith
& Scott, and bore, furthermore, the written approbation
of the Rev. Messrs. Ribzema and Ladlay of the Dutch

Church, that of the Rev. Mr. Treat of the Presbyterian Church, and the qualified approbation of the Rev. Mr. Ronde, another Dutch minister. In this statement Mr. Daller offers again to obtain from abroad the necessary papers which he lacked, and concludes by renewing his menace of a suit at law if his proposals are rejected. The examination of this document was postponed by the Consistory to the 23d of February, when the claims therein set forth were finally and definitely set aside. The state of things had now become exceedingly critical. Frequent meetings of the Bontecou party — who assumed more and more to be the true representatives of the church — were held. Mr. Bonnet, at whose house these meetings were usually held, had by this and other acts excluded himself from the Consistory, and Mr. Louis Pintard, who had succeeded Mr. Vallade as elder and Secretary, left this church and joined Trinity Church; this reduced the Consistory to a very small number, and that body itself, according to custom, elected elders and deacons to fill the vacant places, — viz., Messrs. Blanchard, Etienne des Brosses, and Noble. The election of these gentlemen — all, of course, opposed to Mr. Daller and his adherents — brought matters to a climax. According to custom, the names of the new elders and deacons were published from the pulpit without opposition, on the morning of the following Sunday, July 21, prior to their official installation a few days later; but when Mr. Têtard came to church in the afternoon, he saw in the audience Daniel Bontecou and his friends, who had not appeared there for six months. Foreboding trouble, he repeated before the benediction what he had said in the morning; namely, that if any one had any objections to make to the installation of the new elders and deacons, he must reduce them to writing and present them to the Consistory. He then implored every one to leave the church quietly, after which he pronounced the benediction. This was the signal for an attack : making their way to the chancel, Daniel Bontecou and his party evidently stopped Mr. Têtard as he was coming down from the pulpit, loudly protested against the election of the new elders, and created such a tumult that those who had already left the church came back, and even strangers who were passing by, came in. Some of the latter took part in the quarrel; but the majority endeavored to separate the two factions, who were coming to blows, and finally, but with great difficulty, succeeded. This unfortunate occurrence only confirmed the Consistory in its course, and its authors were threatened with a judi- cial pursuit; which threat, however, seems never to have been carried out. But in the mean time the unseemly strife went on. Mr. Vallade, who wished to retire to his farm at New Rochelle, asked to be entirely relieved of his duties as Treasurer, with which he still remained charged, although he had nominally resigned his office long before.

"This was done on the 17th of February, 1766, when Mr. Jacques des Brosses was chosen treasurer of the Poor Fund; but ' in view of the unsettled state of public affairs, and the bad administration of justice,' the Consistory re- fused to elect a Treasurer for the remaining funds of the church, but confided them for safe-keeping to Mr. Elie des Brosses, a member of Trinity Church. In reality this action seems to have been taken in consequence of an anonymous letter signed 'Liberty Boys,' which had been thrown the preceding Saturday into Mr. Vallade's house, by a person who fled immediately afterward. This letter threatened Mr. Vallade with ' great evils,' unless he would hand over the funds of the church to the ' real elders' by the following Monday. In the same letter the acting minister, Mr. Têtard, is treated most indecently, and the opinion is expressed that the church ought to be given to

Mr. Daller. Suspecting its origin, the Consistory ordered that all those who claimed to be elders of the church should declare under oath whether or not they had anything to do with it, and that these declarations should be published in the *Gazette*. The legitimate elders at once complied, declaring that they knew nothing about the matter. The only other persons that responded were Mr. Bonnet, who claimed to be an elder, but whose declaration was a very equivocal one, and Daniel Bontecou, who made affidavit that he had nothing to do with it. On the 31st of March, 1766, each member of the Consistory received a letter signed by D. Bontecou, J. Buvelot, J. Hastier, and D. Bonnet, inviting them as legal representatives of Mr. Vallade to meet the signers on the following Monday at the house of Mrs. Brock, there to make answer to such demands as they, the signers, had to make against Mr. Vallade; and adding that if their request were denied, they should consider it a refusal to give them satisfaction, and take such measures as they considered necessary. The Consistory only saw a snare in this communication, and declined the invitation to meet the signers at Mrs. Brock's, — which was a tavern, — on the very proper ground that church business ought to be transacted, and according to their custom usually was transacted, in the room of the Consistory. It must now have been evident to the Bontecou party that the party in possession of the church was too strongly intrenched in its positions to be legally dislodged, and too wary to be entrapped into any voluntary surrender. Accordingly, on Sunday morning, June 29, 1766, Daniel Bontecou and his friends forcibly took possession of the church, prevented the regular service from being held, and finally closed its doors against its legal occupants. After having tried various means in vain to regain possession thereof, Mr.

Têtard, the ejected minister,' petitioned the governor of
the Province for redress, which petition was read in Council
and referred for further consideration."

It is not difficult for us to foresee the final result of
this quarrel. The Bontecou party, being the weaker,
and doubly so by the illegality of their cause, "went to
the wall." Mr. Daller withdrew from the contest, and

<hr/>

[1] To his Excellency Sir Henry Moore, Baronet, Captain General &
Governor in Chief in and over the Province of New York &c. &c. &c.
The petition of John Peter Tetard, Clerk
        humbly sheweth,
That by an Act of the General Assembly of this Province in the year
of our Lord 1703 as also by the Deed of Purchase, the Property of the
french Church of this City is vested in the Person of the Minister
and Elders of the same for the time being, and their Successors for
ever. That in April, 1764, Mr. Carle, the late Minister of said Church,
returning to Europe, Your Petioner, before his departure, legally succeeded to him in the Ministerial functions of the same; And in
that Station Continued uninterupted till the 29th day of June, 1766
(being a Sunday), when Messrs daniel Bontecou, John Hastier, James
Buvelot, Francis Basset and Frederic Basset, all of the City of New
York, in a riotous manner and contrary to the Peace of our Sovereign
Lord the King, took Possession of said Church, before the usual time
of divine Service, and there by main force opposed the Elders and
every regular officer of the same in their respective Duties, absolutely
refused your Petitioner Admittance into his Pulpit, and after having
different ways profaned that House of Prayer, they then proceeded to
break the locks of said Church, and affixed Locks of their own to
Every door; by means whereof they, to this day, have most unjustly
and illegally kept possession of the same to the inexpressible Detriment
of this Pious Institution, and to the great Scandal of Civil Society as
well as Religion.
    To whom therefore can your Petioner so properly apply for Redress
in so unprecedented a grevance as to your Excellency in Council?
    Your Petioner therefore begs that YOUR EXCELLENCY and the HONOR-
ABLE BOARD will be pleased to take his case under your wise Consideration; And then he is well Assured that he shall obtain the most ample
Justice: For which, as in duty bound, Your Petioner will Ever pray.
                                    J. P. TETARD.
    17. Oct 1767. Read in Council & Referred for further Considera-
tion.

Daniel Bontecou appears no more in connection with the French Church. When we consider his age at this time (eighty-five), we can certainly admire the vigor of mind and body which prompted such a display of energetic enthusiasm for a cause we are bound to believe he considered right, however it may appear in the cold light of history. And we should not lose sight of the fact that our only record of this episode is that written by the winning party to justify its action to posterity; however honestly designed, it could not be expected to set forth the arguments or recriminations of its opponents. Even this *ex parte* statement lets us see that the Consistory was divided against itself; that the expulsion of one member was regarded as illegal, and the minority considered him as still an elder and the remodeled Consistory usurpers; that the Treasurer was so obnoxious that a considerable portion of the church were willing to take desperate measures to dislodge him; and that the quarrel over Mr. Daller was a mere stalking-horse to hide the original grounds of feud. It is difficult to believe that a man in extreme old age would from sheer wantonness maintain for two or three years, with the fury of a hot-brained youth, a quarrel which ended in nearly destroying his own church.

To the manuscript of M. du Simitière, in possession of the Philadelphia Library Company, we are indebted for the following valuable contribution to the history of Daniel Bontecou: "I knew this gentleman very well for many years. In the summer of the year 1770 being in company with him, he told me that he was born at La Rochelle from the descendant of the famous Dutch navigator Bontecoe, that his parents fled from France for the sake of religion when he was an infant, that they went to England, and soon after came over to New York, that he had then resided there 82 years, that about the latter end of the last century he went on a voyage to the Spanish main in the West Indies, but had not been from New York since his return from thence. Mr. Bontecoe was many years an elder of the French Church in New York, and at the above mentioned time he enjoyed a good health, sound judgment and tolerable memory. He complained that his eyesight fail'd him a little."

In the lapse of a century and over, the record of most men's life becomes nearly obliterated: it is fortunate if anything remains to furnish an insight into their character, their work, and the place they occupied. The few items that can be gathered here and there are treasured as of priceless worth, and studied and reviewed with eagerness, that perchance some traits may be revealed therein which may serve as a foundation upon which to rebuild their history. In the scattered records available for this purpose that relate to Daniel Bontecou, we plainly see the adventurous youth, the prosperous merchant, the trusted churchman, and finally the persistent and vigorous old man, standing staunchly by his friends and battling strenuously for his cause. After dwelling for eighty-four years in the city in which his family had found an asylum, he passed away in November, 1773,[1] closing a well-rounded life of ninety-two years.[2]

_____

[1] " A few days ago died aged 92, Mr. Bonticout, a French Gentleman, many years an inhabitant of this city."— *N. Y. Gazetteer*, Nov. 25, 1773.

[2] THE FOLLOWING ARE TRANSCRIPTIONS OF RECORDS NOT ELSEWHERE REFERRED TO, RELATING TO DANIEL BONTECOU.

1. *From the Registers of the French Church, New York.*

To-day, March 10, 1703, after service, was baptized Etienne Perdriau, son of Etienne Perdriau and of Marguerite Bontecou; presented for holy baptism by Daniel Bontecou and Marie Bontecou. He was born on March 4th, and baptized by Mr. Peiret, minister.

DANIEL BONTECOU.

PEIRET, *Minister.*   MARIE MATON.

To-day, Sunday, May 26, 1712, Susanne Forestier, daughter of Pierre Forestier, born on the 20th of last April, was presented for holy bap-

6   V. Susanne Bontecou, probably one of the five children who were refugees from France with their father,
Pierre. The only trace of her that I have been able to find

tism by Daniel Bontecou and Susanne Coutau, and baptized by Mr.
Louis Rou, Pastor.

DANIEL BONTECOU.

L. Rou, *Pastor.*   SUSANNE COUTAT.

To-day, Sunday, Aug. 31, 1712, after evening prayer, Mr. Louis Rou
baptized Thomas Pelletreau, born on the 27th of this month, son of
Elie Pelletreau and Jeanne Machet, and presented for holy baptism by
Daniel Bontecou and Madeleine Vincent.

DANIEL BONTECOU.

L. Rou, *Minister.*   MERI LEDDEL.

New York, September 19, 1714. To-day, Sunday, after evening
prayer, Mr. Louis Rou baptized Mary Anne Odard, born on the 11th
of this month, daughter of Daniel Odard and Marthe Jeffroy, and presented for holy baptism by Daniel Bontecou, and Anne Many.

DANIEL ODART.
DANIEL BONTECOU.

L. Rou, *Min.*   ANNE MANY.

To-day, Wednesday, March 9, 17$\frac{18}{20}$, after prayers, Mr. Louis Rou
baptized Anne Ballereau, born on the 8th of this month, daughter of
Jacques and of Jeanne Ballereau, and presented for holy baptism by
Daniel Bontecou and Anne Many.

JACQUES BALLEREAU.
DANIEL BONTECOU.

L. Rou, *Pastor.*   ANNE MANY.

To-day, Sunday, February 18, 1724, Mr. Louis Rou baptized Jeanne
Pelletreau, born on the 6th of this month, daughter of Elie and Eliza
beth Pelletreau, and presented for holy baptism by Daniel Bontecou
and Elizabeth Pelletreau.

DANIEL BONTECOU.

L. Rou, *Pastor.*   ELIZABETH PELLETREAU.

To-day, Sunday, April 18, 1736, after the second service, was baptized in this church by me, the undersigned minister, Samuel Pintard,
born in New York on the 5th of last April, son of Mr. Jean Pintard
and Mrs. Catherine Carré, his wife, and presented for holy baptism by
Mr. Daniel Bontecou and Miss Susanne Boudinot, in the name of
Miss Marie Catherine Boudinot.

JEAN PINTARD.
DANIEL BONTECOU.

L. Rou, *Pastor.*   SUSANNE BOUDINOT.
5

is in Vol. III. of the *Documentary History of New York*, p. 283 : "An act of opposition to that which was passed on Sunday last, the 20th of September, 1724, in the French

By virtue of a license granted by Cadwallader Colden, President of the Council of New York, dated March 12, 1761, being the first year of the reign of George Third, our legitimate sovereign, I celebrated the marriage of Guillaume Lucy and Elizabeth Hatier, on March 12, 1761, at seven o'clock in the evening, in the house of Mr. Hatier, in the presence of the Hatier family, of Mr. and Mrs. Bontecou, Basset, son-in-law of Mr. Hatier, and Mr. Rivet, officer in the American Royal Regiment.

Registered on July 7th, 1761.

JEAN CARLE, *Pastor.*

To day, July 22, 1764, towards eight o'clock in the evening, I married Mr. Jacques Buvelot and Marie Bonnet (widow) both of this city and members of the French Church. I celebrated the said marriage by virtue of a license granted by the Lieutenant-Governor of this Province, dated the 9th inst., and in the house of the said lady, Marie Bonnet, in presence of Messers. Daniel Bontecou, Jean Hastier, Daniel Bonnet, and Mrs Elizabeth Basset.

Done in New York the said 22nd of July, 1764.

J. P. TÉTARD, *Pastor.*

2. *From Journal of the Legislative Council of New York.*

At a Council held at Fort George in New York, May 17, 1723. Present — His Excellency Wm. Burnet, Esqr., &c.

CAPT. WALTER.   MR. BARBERIE.
COLL. BEEKMAN.   MR. HARISON.
MR. VAN DAM.   DOCTOR COLDEN

MR. MORRIS, JUN'.

His Excellency communicated to this Board the address of the General Assembly of this Province.

Ordered, that Capt. Walter, Mr. Harison, and Doctor Colden be a select Committee to Join a Committee to be appointed by the House of Representatives to prepare the Draft of An Address to be presented to his Majesty from the Governour, Council, and Assembly of this Province, and in order thereto the said Committee will meet tomorrow at the hour of three in the afternoon at the House of Mr. Bonticow in this city. (Vol. I. p. 496.)

At a Council held at Fort George in New York, June the 28, 1723.

A message from the Assembly by their Speaker acquainting this Board that himself together with Coll. Morris, Mr. Phillipse, Capt.

Reformed Church of the City of New York, and signed
afterwards by some members of said Church." This "act
of opposition" disapproves the action of the Consistory

Jansen, Col. Provoost, or any three of them, are appointed a Committee
by that House to Meet and Make their observations upon a Act passed
in the Colony of Connecticut the Ninth of May last, Relating to the
Division Lines between that Colony and this, and Desireing his Excellency that he will be pleased to appoint a Committee of the Council to
joyn thereon.

Ordered, that Capt Walter, Mr. Clarke, Mr. Harison, Doctor Colden,
and Mr. Morris, Junr, or any three of them, be a Committee to Join a
Committee of the House of Representatives for the purposes in the
said Message, and that the said Committee do meet to morrow at three
in the Afternoon at the House of Mr. Bonticow in this City. (Vol. I.
p. 503.)

At a Council held at Fort George in New York, Sept. ye 2nd, 1725.
Ordered, that Mr. Van Dam, Mr. Barberie, and Doctor Colden, be a
select Committee to Join a Committee of the Assembly in Examining
the Accounts of Coll. David Provoost, late Tonnage Officer.

Ordered, that Mr. Bobin, the Deputy Clerk of the Council, do Acquaint
the Assembly that this Board desires them to appoint a Committee of
that House to Join a Committee of this Board for that purpose, at the
House of Mr. Bonticow in this City, at ffour in the afflernoon on Thursday, come sevennight. (Vol. I. p. 518.)

3. *From the New York Gazette, Revived in the Weekly Post Boy, Feb.
5, 1750.*

To be Sold. The five following Lots of Ground in this City, *viz.*:
One Lot fronting *Nassau-Street*, near *Gold-Street*, 30 Feet and a half
Front, and 69 Feet back: One other Lot fronting *Ann-street*, right
back of the other, and is 22 Feet front, and 60 feet back; Two other
Lots fronting *Gold-street*, 20 Feet front each, and from 49 Feet and a
half to 48 Feet deep; And one other adjoining to the Two last, 20
Feet front on *Gold-street*, and 47 Feet deep, fronting Ann street. Any
Person inclining to purchase any of the said Lots, may apply to Daniel
Bounticon, in the Smith's Fly, who will dispose of the same on reason-
able terms.

4. THE LAST WILL AND TESTAMENT OF DANIEL BONTECOU.

In the name of God. Amen. I, Daniel Bontecue of the City of
New York, Gentleman, being in good state of health and of sound
and disposing mind, memory, and understanding—thanks to God for
the same—but calling to mind the uncertainty of life and certainty of

in dismissing from the pastorate the Rev. Louis Rou, "contrary to the Rules of our Discipline, to the Word of God, and Equity," and bears the signature of sixty male members of the church, after which, " Here followeth the names of the widow, women, and others, members of the same church, which have signed the same act." There are twenty-five of these names, among which is that of Susanne Bontecou.

Death, Do therefore make and ordain this my last Will and Testament in manner and form following, that is to say, first and principally I commit my soul into the Hands of Almighty God my Creator, and my Body to the Earth to be decently interred at the discretion of my Executors hereinafter named, hoping for a Resurection to eternal Life thro' the Satisfaction and Righteousness of Christ my Redeemer, and as to such temporal Estate as God hath been pleased to bestow upon me, I dispose thereof in Manner following: that is to say, I will and desire that my just Debts and funeral Expenses be paid and satisfied within some Convenient Time after my Decease. Item. — I do hereby give, devise, and bequeath unto Timothy Bontecue, Jun', the son of my Brother Timothy Bontecue of New Haven, in New England, the Sum of one hundred Pounds, with the Payment of which sum I do hereby expressly charge my real and personal estate. Item. — All the rest, Residue, and Remainder of my Estate whatsoever and wheresoever both real and personal, I do hereby give, demise, and bequeath unto Mary Bassett, the wife of Francis Bassett of the City of New York, Pewterer, and to her Heirs, Executors, Administrators, and Assigns forever. Lastly, I do hereby nominate, constitute, and appoint the said Francis Bassett, Executor of this my last Will and Testament, hereby revoking, Annulling and making void all former and other Wills and Testaments by me at any Time heretofore made, declaring this and this only to be my last Will and Testament. In testimony whereof I have hereunto set my hand and seal this twentieth day of August in the year of our Lord, one thousand seven hundred and seventy two.

DANIEL BONTECOU. [L. S.]

Signed, sealed, published, pronounced, and declared by the Testator, as and for his last Will and Testament in the presence of us who subscribed our names hereto as Witnesses in his presence and at his request.

CORNELIUS BLANCHARD.
WILL HARTSHORNE.
GILBT BURGER.

(This will was proved in New York, Nov. 30, 1773.)

7   VI. Marie Bontecou, born in New York, July 21,
1690. and baptized in the French Church on the 24th
of the same month. She appears, March 10, 1703, as
sponsor for her nephew, Stephen Perdriau. son of her sister Marguerite. No further trace of her is found, unless
we may consider it possible that she became the wife of
Francis Bassett, who was associated with her brother,
Daniel Bontecou, in the troubles in the French Church,
in 1763–6, and was the Mary Bassett to whom Daniel,
in his will, bequeathed the greater part of his estate.
(See Daniel Bontecou's will, pp. 35, 36.) No record of
such a marriage, however, appears in the Registers of the
French Church.

8   VII. Rachael Bontecou, born in New York, July
21, 1690 (twin with Marie). She probably died young, as
nothing further is found relating to her.

9   VIII. Timothy Bontecou, born in New York, June   11
17. 1693, and baptized in the French Church on the 2d of
July. His boyhood was undoubtedly passed in that city,
and when he became of sufficient age to think of taking
an active part in the affairs of life, he repaired to France,
to acquire the trade of a silversmith.[1] From the time of
his leaving America until the year 1735 (a period of probably more than twenty years), we have no positive knowledge of his history.[2] It is quite likely that he remained

[1] This fact was related to the grandfather of the writer over fifty
years ago by his cousin, Polly Storer, who was for eighteen years an
inmate of Timothy Bontecou's household, and is beyond question re-
liable. It was recorded at the time, and the paper containing the
statement is in the possession of the writer.

[2] A tradition exists which by some is thought to relate to Pierre
Bontecou, the refugee, while others claim that it has reference to
Timothy. We have such intimate knowledge of Pierre's arrival in
this country, together with that of his family, that it may be set down
as untrue so far as he is concerned. Whatever foundation in fact may
have existed to base such a tradition upon, it must be conceded that
in its *entirety* it is untrue, also, as relating to *Timothy* Bontecou, with

38

BONTECOU FAMILY.

abroad long enough to lay the foundation of, if not to have fully acquired, the comfortable fortune which he subsequently possessed. He probably, also, married in France, for his wife *Mary* died in New Haven, Conn., Nov. 5, 1735, at the age of thirty-three years, as evidenced by her gravestone now existing in the old cemetery of that city, removed from the still older burying-ground in the public square. We have no knowledge of the time of his return to this country, but it was probably not long previous to the above event.

He again married, Sept. 29, 1736, Mary Goodrich, daughter of Colonel David and Prudence (Churchill) Goodrich of Wethersfield, Conn. Col. Goodrich was an officer in the army during the French and Indian War, a prominent citizen in his town, and a justice of the peace, and in the latter capacity performed the ceremony of his daughter's marriage. She was born Dec. 15, 1704, and died about 1760, aged fifty-six years. Timothy Bontecou

---

the possible (and most probable) chance of its being of a similar nature to the story of the three black crows.

THE TRADITION.—Timothy Bontecou, a refugee from France for the sake of his religion, left behind him in his flight a wife and two infant sons. Years rolled by, and Timothy, having in all this time received, from his retreat in the New World, no news of his family, and concluding that his wife had perished in some one of the terrible massacres of the day, again married, and became once more the father of two children. One of these died in infancy, the mother herself not long surviving ; the other in course of time became a sailor, and dying at sea in his early manhood, was buried at St. Thomas in the West Indies. Some *twenty* years after Timothy's advent in New York, while one day walking on the street in that city, he met a lady whose familiar appearance impressed him ; closer scrutiny revealed her as the wife he had left in France, and who, hearing nothing from her husband in all these years, had crossed the sea in search of tidings of him. With her were her two stalwart sons, now grown to manhood. The recognition between husband and wife was mutual, and the reunited pair thereafter lived happily together. The situation is quite romantic, as well as embarrassing. The reader is at liberty to believe so much of it as he chooses, but will undoubtedly find it difficult to reconcile the claims of the tradition with the known facts of Timothy's history.

resided on the west side of Fleet Street in New Haven,
not far from the water-side. He was a considerable owner
of real estate, both there and in New York. His religious
affiliations were with the Church of England, and in the
absence of a church of that denomination in New Haven
he became a member of the one in Stratford, being registered there Oct. 12, 1735; and some years later, when
a new church was to be erected, he contributed £15
toward the building of it[1] and became the owner of a
pew. Undoubtedly he was a regular occupant of this pew
on the Sabbath; the distance of fourteen miles to Stratford being no great obstacle to the privilege of worshiping
in his own church. His wife, Mary, is registered as a
communicant there May 25, 1740. When Trinity (Episcopal) Church in New Haven was established, he was
one of the founders, and its first recorded warden, in
1765. He was also a member of the committee appointed
to purchase a site for the church edifice.[2] He owned and

----

[1] "The Episcopal Society built a house also in 1743; but on the
principle of stock ownership, and not by a public tax." . . "It
was unanimously voted y⁰ 1st day of January, 1744-5, that the
proprietors of y⁰ church should chuse their ground for their pews
according to what they have given towards building the same."
— *History of Stratford, by Rev. Samuel Orcutt.*

[2] To all people to whom these presents shall come — GREETING:
Know y⁰ that I, Enos Alling of New Haven, Town and County and
Colony of Connecticut, for the consideration of two hundred and
seventy-one pounds five shillings lawful money, rec⁴ to my full satisfaction of Timothy Bonticou and Isaac Doolittle, Church Wardens,
and Christopher Kilby and Stephen Mansfield, Vestrymen of Trinity
Church in s⁴ New Haven, and y⁰ rest of y⁰ members of y⁰ s⁴ Episcopal Church, do give, grant, bargain, sell, and confirm unto y⁰ s⁴ Timothy Bonticou, Isaac Doolittle, and y⁰ rest of y⁰ Professors of y⁰ Church
of England and members of s⁴ Trinity Church, for y⁰ time being and
to their successors, a certain piece or parcel of land, containing one
acre and a half, more or less, situate and lying at a place called Greg-
son's Corner, in y⁰ town plat, in s⁴ New Haven, bounded Northerly
on the Market Place or highway, Easterly on highway or Town street,
Southerly by land in possession of Sam¹ Cook, and Westwardly by

occupied a large square pew in this church, prominently located.

At the time of the British invasion of New Haven, in July, 1779,[1] he was an old man eighty-six years of age, a resident of the household of his son Peter, on the corner of Olive and Wooster Streets. On this occasion he was the victim of outrage by the British troops. A mob of soldiers visited the house, and the old gentleman was

land in possession of Ralph Isaacs, together with y⁰ dwelling house, barn, and other buildings thereon. To have, and to hold y⁰ s⁴ bargained and granted premises, with all and singular the appurtenances unto them, y⁰ s⁴ grantees, and their successors and assigns, forever to their own proper use, for the support and maintenance of s⁴ church, and I, y⁰ s⁴ Enos Alling, do for myself and my heirs, Ex⁰ and Adm⁰⁰, covenant with y⁰ s⁴ grantees, their successors and assigns, that I shall not nor will, nor shall my heirs and assigns, or any of them, ever have, challenge or claim any right, title, or interest in or to y⁰ same, or any part thereof, but thereof and therefrom shall and will be ever barred and secluded by these presents. In witness whereof, I have hereof set my hand and seal, this 31st day of October, 1765.

ENOS ALLING. [SEAL]

Signed, sealed and delivered in presence of
JERE⁰ TOWNSEND, JR.
ROBERT BROWN.

— *New Haven Land Records, Vol. XXVII. p.* 369.

[1] "New Haven was invaded by a British force of twenty-six hundred men, under Governor Tryon of New York and Brig.-Gen. Garth, in the summer of 1779. They were conveyed from New York in two ships-of-war and forty-eight transports and tenders, commanded by Commodore Sir George Collier, and sailing up New Haven Bay on the night of the 4th of July, landed the next morning in two divisions, one at East and one at West Haven. They advanced upon the town from both directions,— opposed, however, by the inhabitants, but without avail. The shipping drew near and menaced the inhabitants with bombardment. Before night the town was completely possessed by the invaders, and the soldiery committed many excesses and crimes, plundering houses, and murdering some citizens. . . . It was the intention of Gen. Garth to burn the town; but the rapid increase of the militia, who flocked in from the surrounding country caused him to retreat to his ships, and he sailed away, carrying with him some forty citizens of the town." — *Lossing's Field Book of the Revolution, Vol. I. p.* 422.

robbed of his silver knee and shoebuckles,—his daughter-in-law, the wife of Capt. Peter, being ordered to pull them off. Personal violence was offered; and on an attempt by the soldiers to bayonet him, she interposed herself between them and saved his life. Infuriated at being baffled in their murderous design, they were ripe for any degree of iniquity, and the daughter of Capt. Peter unfortunately presenting herself at this juncture, she was seized by the soldiers, and her abduction attempted; but her mother with great tact and courage interfered, and while entertaining the soldiers with food and drink, secretly sent for assistance, which speedily arrived in the form of a guard of soldiers, obtained through the efforts of an influential royalist neighbor. This put a stop to their outrageous conduct; but they had well-nigh succeeded in their designs upon old Timothy, for he was found by the guard with a rope around his neck, the other end thrown over a beam of the house, and the mob evincing a diabolical disposition to pull him up, which was prevented by the officer in charge.

The once ample estate of Timothy Bontecou was undoubtedly greatly depreciated and diminished during the war, and what remained of it was deeded by him to his son Peter in 1778, in consideration of support during the rest of his life.[1]

---

[1] COPY OF BOND GIVEN BY PETER BONTECOU.

Know all men by these presents, y' I, Peter Bontecou, of the Town and County of New Haven, in the State of Connecticut, am holden and do stand firmly bound and obliged unto my Hon'd father, Timothy Bontecou of s'd Town, in the just sum of Two thousand pounds, Lawfull money, payable to my s'd father, his heirs, Ex', Admin'', unto the which payment well and truly to be made and done I bind myself, my heirs, executors, administrators, firmly by these presents, signed with my hand and sealed with my seal. Done in New Haven, Oct. 6, 1778.

The condition of the above obligation is such that whereas s'd Tim° Bontecou hath by Deed herewith of even date conveyed unto s'd Peter Bontecou, one certain house and home lot, and two lots of land in the oyster shell field, and it being their agreement that in consideration of

He died in New Haven, Feb. 14, 1784, aged ninety-one years, and was buried beneath Trinity Church. He is known to have been a prominent and useful citizen, a zealous churchman, and a good man.

---

s^d lands being conveyed unto s^d Peter, he was to become under obligation to support and maintain his s^d father from the day of the date hereof during his natural life. Now, therefore, if s^d Peter, his heirs, executors, or administrators, doth from the day of the date hereof, Provide for his said father with every thing needfull and necessary to make the life of his s^d father comfortable, and support and maintain him in sickness and health, During the Term of his natural life, then the foregoing bond to be void; but, if otherwise, then to remain in full force.

Signed, Sealed, & Del^d
in presence of   PETER BONTECOU. [SEAL.]
    SAMUEL BISHOP, JR.
    WILLIAM P. CUYMERT.

THIRD GENERATION.

CHILD OF DANIEL AND MARIANNE (MACHET) BONTECOU.   5

10   I. **Daniel Bontecou, Jr.,** born in New York, Feb. 14,
1713; baptized Feb. 18, 1713.   Very little is known about
him.   In 1737 he was a member of the military company
commanded by Capt. Cornelius Van Horne.   He married
Marquise le Boyteulx, whose name appears as a signer
of the petition in opposition to the act of the Consistory
dismissing the Rev. Louis Rou from the pastorate of the
French Church in New York, Sept. 20, 1724.   From this
circumstance it would appear that she must have been
much older than her husband.   The date of this marriage
is unknown.   They were both living in 1744, but no later
trace of them is found.   They had no children.

CHILD OF TIMOTHY AND MARY BONTECOU.   9

11   I. **Timothy Bontecou, Jr.,** born in 1723, probably   17
in France.   He was a silversmith, and resided in New
Haven, Conn.   He married, Nov. 5, 1747, Susanna Prout,
daughter of John Prout, Esq., of New Haven, and Sibbyl
Howell of Southampton, L. I.   She was born April 1,
1718, and was drowned Oct. 9, 1755, with five others, by
the upsetting of a ferry-boat, while returning from the
ordination of Rev. Nicholas Street, in East Haven.   He
married for a second wife Susan Gordon;[1] she died in
November, 1805.[2]   He died in May, 1789.[3]

[1] From information given, I have assumed that her family name was
Gordon, but this is not positive.

[2] "Died — In this city, Mrs. Susan Bonticou, widow of Mr. Timothy
Bonticou, æt. 69." — *Connecticut Journal*, Nov. 21, 1805.

[3] "Died — In this city, Mr. Timothy Bonticou, aged 66." — *Connecticut Journal*, June 3, 1789.

CHILDREN OF TIMOTHY AND MARY (GOODRICH) BON- 9
TECOU.

12   I. Peter Bontecou, born in New Haven in 1738.   27
IIe was married Nov. 14, 1762, by the Rev. Chauncey
Whittlesey, to Susannah Thomas, daughter of Jehiel and
Mary Thomas of New Haven. She was born Sept. 9, 1739,
and died in New Haven,[1] Sept. 20, 1799. Peter Bontecou
was captain of the barque " Hawke,"[2] of 47 tons, trading
to Ireland, and returning *via* the West Indies In order
to secure storage for his cargoes of rum and molasses,
he built a house, with a large cellar, now standing on the
corner of Olive and Wooster Streets, and known as the
" Wooster House." This building remained in an unfin-
ished condition, as to its interior, at the time of the Revolution, although occupied by the family. Capt. Bontecou
on one of his homeward voyages entered the harbor of
New York, which chanced to be at that time in possession of the British, and was captured and confined on the
prison-ship " Jersey "; but afterwards escaping and making his way homeward through Long Island, was seized
with the small-pox (undoubtedly contracted in prison),
and died at a tavern in Huntington, in 1779. Letters of
administration were granted to his widow March 5, 1781.
IIis estate inventoried at £600 10s. 0¾d.

13   II. Daniel Bontecou, born in New Haven, Sept. 9, 36
1739. IIe graduated from Yale College in 1757 ; then repaired to France to pursue the study of medicine. About
1760 he was appointed surgeon in the French Army, and
undoubtedly served in that capacity a number of years.
IIe returned to New Haven and announced himself as

---

[1] " Died — In this city, Mrs. Susanna Bonticou, aged 60 years, relict
of Capt. Peter Bonticou." — *Connecticut Journal*, Sept. 25, 1799.
[2] Capt. Bontecou commanded also the brig " Mansfield," the brig
" William," and undoubtedly others.

follows, in *The Connecticut Journal and New Haven Post Boy* of Feb. 1, 1771 :

" The subscriber takes this method of informing the Public that he proposes to pursue the practice of Physick in this Place. Likewise Surgery in all its branches, as Bone Setting, &c., and Midwifery.

" DANIEL BONTECOU.

" New Haven, January 25, 1771."

He married, Sept. 12, 1775, Mrs. Rebecca Rohde, widow of Dr. John Rohde[1] (a native of Prussia), and daughter of Joseph and Sarah (Southmayd) Starr of Middletown, Conn. She was born June 8, 1733. Dr. Bontecou was a prominent member of Trinity Church, New Haven, a vestryman in 1774–5 and 1777–8, and for the last two years clerk of the vestry. He died Aug. 20, 1778. The *Connecticut Journal* of Sept. 2, 1778, contained the following obituary notice : " On Thursday, the 20th inst., departed this life for a better, Dr. Daniel Bontecou, of this Town, in the thirty-ninth year of his age ; a gentleman of liberal education in his profession to which he was regularly bred, he was truly respectable, was prudent and judicious in his practice ; possessed many good and useful qualities, was modest and benevolent and just ; a worthy citizen and an excellent Christian. In him the several relations of husband, parent, and friend, shone with dignity and honor. He was beloved through life, and his death is sincerely lamented. May his virtues excite an emulation in others, and provoke them unto love and good works." His death was the occasion of a sermon by the Rev. Bela Hubbard, rector of Trinity Church.

In common with many who died during the disturbed and critical days of the Revolution, Dr. Bontecou left but

[1] " Yesterday afternoon, departed this life, Dr. John Rhode, for many years a noted physician and surgeon in this town." -- *Connecticut Journal*, Jan. 25, 1775.

little estate, the principal item of value in the inventory being a silver tankard valued at £11 10s., the next being "one negro woman, Flora, value, £10." This woman he had rescued from a brutal master by purchase, and she long survived him, and is remembered by persons now living (1883). It is related of her, that upon the approach of the British in their raid upon New Haven in July, 1779, she saved the valuables of her mistress by burying them in the garden.

Dec. 23, 1787, Dr. Bontecou's widow married Capt. Ephraim Pease,[1] a prominent citizen of Enfield, a magistrate and member of the General Court; removed thither with her children, and died there April 6, 1802, at the age of 69.[2]

In the old cemetery in New Haven, stands a tablet with the following inscription:

---

[1] "Married—last Sunday, Captain Ephraim Pease of Enfield, to Mrs. Rebecca Bonticou of this city."—*Connecticut Journal*, Dec. 26, 1787.

[2] "Died at Enfield, Mrs. Rebecca Pease (formerly of this city), relict of Mr. Ephraim Pease, in the 69th year of her age. Mr. Pease was her 4th husband."—*Connecticut Journal*, April 22, 1802.

NOTE.—Rebecca Starr is said to have been a remarkably beautiful woman. She married (1st), July 27, 1753, Thomas Tyler. He died Nov. 7, 1754, leaving one daughter, *Miriam*, born May 17, 1754, who married Capt. William Powell of New Haven, Oct. 28, 1773, and died March 12, 1808, leaving no children. She married (2d), Sept. 23, 1756, Dr. Johan Rohde, a physician of New Haven, who was born in Heiligenbad, Prussia, in December, 1723. They had the following children: I. John, born March 4, 1757. II. Frederick, born Jan. 14, 1759, died Nov. 22, 1759. III. Thomas, born Sept. 10, 1760. IV. Joseph, born Nov. 12, 1763, died Jan. 3, 1776. V. William F., born Jan. 24, 1766. VI. Andrew Southmayd, born April 9, 1768. He married and resided in Charleston, S. C. VII. Catharine, born Jan. 27, 1770, died Jan. 14, 1773. VIII. A son, born and died July 8, 1772. She married (3d) Dr. Bontecou; and (4th) Capt. Pease.

Dr. Daniel Bontecou,
Son of
Timothy & Mary (Goodrich)
Bontecou,
& a descendant of a French
protestant, who left his country
at the revocation of the edict of
Nantes. He was born in New Haven
Sept. 9, 1739.
graduated at Yale College 1757,
Died Aug. 20, 1778,
& interred in the ancient bury-
ing grounds of the public square.
This monument is erected to his memory
By his only Son Daniel Bontecou of
Springfield Ms.

14   III.   David, born 1742, died 1766 ; unmarried.

15   IV.   James, born 1743; died Nov. 8, 1760.

16   V.   A daughter. Nothing is known of her, except
that she married a Mr. Lathrop, a cabinet-maker of New
Haven, and had no children. An oil portrait of her, torn
and defaced, is in the possession of Mrs. Elisha Peck (92)
of New Haven. Its dilapidated condition was thought by
its possessor to be due to ill-treatment by the British in
their raid on New Haven in 1779, but old Capt. Peter
Storer (86) confessed to the compiler that he and "Tom
Bontecou" (54) found it in the garret when they were
boys, and used it as a target for their arrows.

17   **I. Timothy Prout Bontecou,** born in New Haven, **38**
Aug. 20, 1748. He married Elizabeth Upson, daughter
of Daniel Upson of New Haven. He was master of the
sloop " Delight," engaged in trade between New Haven
and New York. He died Nov. 28, 1785, in the same
house, on Water Street, in which he was born. His
widow married Jacob Morgan of Amity (in Woodbridge),
May 22, 1789.

18   **IV. Eleanor Bontecou,** born Dec. 25, 1749–50.
She grew to womanhood, and was engaged to be married;
but the groom failed to appear at the appointed time, and
was never heard of afterward. She became insane, but
recovered. The date of her death is unknown.

19   **III. John Bontecou,** born in 1751, baptized Dec. 1,
1751. He was a tailor. He married, Aug. 7, 1784, Lois
Dunwell of New Haven; removed to New York, and died
there about 1818. They had no children.

20   **IV. William Bontecou,** baptized Aug. 12, 1753.
Died young.

21   **I. William Bontecou,** born in New Haven in 1763. **45**
He married, Nov. 13, 1784, Hannah Storer, daughter of

John and Hannah (Brown) Storer of New Haven. She was born in 1764, and died in New Haven, June 20, 1842. William Bontecou resided on Water Street, occupying, with his brother Thomas, a house on the south side of the street, immediately west of the site of the present engine-house. He was a manufacturing tailor, and had a partner in New Orleans who sold out the business and absconded with the proceeds. After this loss, he removed to Troy, N. Y., but returned again to New Haven, where he died of consumption, Sept. 29, 1807.

22   II.   Thomas Bontecou, born in New Haven in 1766.   54
He married, Feb. 13, 1790, Ruth Storer, daughter of John and Hannah (Brown) Storer, and sister of his brother William's wife. The ceremony was performed by Rev. James Dana. She was born in New Haven, Sept. 13, 1769, and died in New York, Jan. 20, 1852. Thomas Bontecou was a master mariner, chiefly engaged in the West India trade. During the Revolutionary War, he was captured by the British. Through the latter part of his life he was engaged in trade between New Haven and New York. He died Sept. 8, 1805.[1]

23   III.   Elizabeth Bontecou, born March 20, 1770.   60
Married, July 31, 1790, William Hood of New Haven. He was born April 16, 1766, and died Dec. 26, 1842. She died April 11, 1837.

24   IV.   Samuel Bontecou, born in New Haven, March 2,   68
1773, married Phebe Tallman, daughter of ——— and Hannah (Brush) Tallman of Long Island. She was born Jan. 16, 1776, and died May 16, 1847. Samuel Bontecou removed to Lansingburg, N. Y., about 1794. He was a

---

[1] "Died — In this city Mr. Thomas Bonticou, late master of one of the New York Packets, aged 39 years." — *Connecticut Journal*, Sept. 12, 1805.

tailor by trade, and for a number of years postmaster of Lansingburg. He was a man of energetic disposition, and was looked upon as the head of the family by his immediate relatives, whom he treated with great kindness and liberality. He died in Lansingburg, May 3, 1850.

25   V. Susannah Bontecou, born in New Haven in   76 1775. She married, Dec. 1, 1793, Marcus Merriman, Sr., of New Haven, as his second wife. He entered the army at the age of 17, and assisted in the defense of West Bridge when the British attacked New Haven, July 5, 1779. He lay under the cannon at Cedar Hill all night, and contracted a cold from the effects of which he never fully recovered. In 1780 he enlisted as a regular soldier, and remained in the service until the close of the war. He died Feb. 20, 1850, aged 87.[1] She died Jan. 11, 1807, aged 32.[2]

26   VI. Roswell Bontecou, baptized Sept. 18, 1784. He was a silversmith, and died in Charleston, S. C., unmarried.

CHILDREN OF PETER AND SUSANNAH (THOMAS) BON-   12 TECOU.

27   I. Polly Augusta Bontecou, born in New Haven,   81 Aug. 13, 1763. She married, July 22, 1781, Capt. Nathaniel Storer, son of John and Hannah (Brown) Storer, and brother of the wives of William (21) and Thomas (22) Bontecou. She was a remarkably handsome woman,

[1] "ANOTHER PATRIARCH GONE.—Marcus Merriman, Esq., aged 87 years, a well-known and highly-respectable citizen, was released from earthly trials, this noon, after an illness of a week. His demise, though he had long passed the space allotted to man, will cause sincere sorrow in many an attached circle. He leaves an untarnished reputation to his children, and will be long remembered as a pure, just, and upright man."—*New Haven Register*, Feb. 20, 1850.

[2] "DIED.—In this city, Mrs. Susannah Merriman, wife of Major Marcus Merriman."—*Connecticut Journal*, Jan. 15, 1807.

possessing the French type of beauty : tall and erect. with
brilliant and expressive dark eyes, and carrying herself
with quiet dignity and grace. She retained her mental
faculties to a remarkable degree in her old age. Her
memory was unimpaired, and to it we are indebted for
many incidents in the family history which she related to
its younger members. She was the young girl whom the
British attempted to abduct, as related in the account of
her grandfather, Timothy Bontecou (9). She died in New
Haven, March 28, 1849. Capt. Storer served as a private
in the War of the Revolution, until its close. He went to
sea, and became master of a vessel; made several voyages to China ; succeeded to his father's business as ship-
builder. and at the same time carried on mercantile trade.
In the latter he was unsuccessful, and again went to sea.
In 1811, on a voyage to China in the ship " Huntress,"
which he commanded, he was lost, with his son Nathaniel,
his nephew Thomas Bontecou, Jr., who was his mate, and
all hands. The vessel was owned by John Jacob Astor,
and had loaded with seal fur in the Pacific, and started
on her way to China. but was never heard from.

28 II. James Bontecou, born in New Haven, Aug. 6, 91
1766. He entered upon a seafaring life at about fifteen
years of age, setting out upon his first voyage from
Philadelphia. He rose to be master of his vessel. He
married, June 2. 1803, Joanna Clark, daughter of Samuel
and Anna (Hawley) Clark. She was born Oct. 13, 1781,
and died Jan. 8. 1872. He died of yellow fever on board
the brig " Freeman," on his passage home from Berbice,
July 12, 1806.[1]

[1] "Died on the 11th inst., of a fever, on his passage from Berbice,
Captain James Bontecou, master of the Brig " Freeman," of this port,
æ. 40. A wife and two small children, and numerous friends and
acquaintances have most sincerely to deplore his death. As a tribute
of respect to the deceased, the vessels in the harbour set their colors
at half-mast." — *Connecticut Journal*, July 31, 1806.

29   III.   David Bontecou, born 1767 ; baptized Aug. 23, 1767 ; died 1767.

30   IV.   David Bontecou, born Sept. 9, 1768 ; died Jan. 26, 1769.

31   V.   Susannah Bontecou, born 1769; baptized July 23, 1769; died 1769.

32   VI.   Susannah Bontecou, born 1770 ; died Dec. 25, 1777.

33   VII.   Peter Bontecou, born 1770 ; died June 12, 1794, of consumption.

34   VIII.   Sarah Bontecou, born 1775; baptized July 30,   93
1775. She married in 1795, Justus Trowbridge, son of William and Rebecca (Painter) Trowbridge of New Haven. He was born May 4, 1774, and died in New Haven, March 2, 1810. He was a hatter. She died Jan. 9, 1861.

35   IX.   David Bontecou, born March 17, 1777.   He   99
married. Oct. 1, 1796, Polly Clark, daughter of Samuel and Anna (Hawley) Clark, whose sister Joanna married his brother James (28).   The ceremony was performed at the house of his cousin William Bontecou (21).   His wife was born April 11, 1776, and died in Troy, N. Y., Jan. 17, 1861.   David Bontecou was a shoemaker by trade.   He lived in New Haven for a number of years after his marriage, and several of his children were born there.   He then emigrated to Cocymans, N. Y., on the Hudson, the journey being made all the way by sloop.   The latter part of his life was spent in Troy, where he died May 5, 1854.

CHILDREN OF DANIEL AND REBECCA (ROHDE) BON-   13
TECOU.

36   I.   Rebecca Bontecou, born in New Haven, March 13,   109
1777 ; she married in Enfield, Conn., July 5, 1795, Rev.

Menzies Rayner, son of Benjamin and Mary Rayner of
Long Island. He was born in Hempstead, L. I., Nov. 23,
1770, and died in New York City, Nov. 22, 1850. She
died in New York, March 22, 1862. They are both buried
in Greenwood Cemetery. Rev. Menzies Rayner obtained
his education principally under the direction of private
instructors. When quite young he became a member of
the Methodist Society, and before he was twenty-one years
of age was received as a preacher in the traveling connection of that denomination. Two years later he was
ordained in Lynn, Mass., by Bishop Francis Asbury. He
continued in this connection for two years longer, when,
receiving an invitation to settle over the Protestant Episcopal parish of St. John's in Elizabethtown, N. J., he accepted
the same, and was accordingly ordained as minister of the
church by the Right Rev. Bishop Provoost of New York.
He continued pastor of the Elizabethtown church for
about six years, when, July 12, 1801, receiving a call to
the rectorship of Christ Church in Hartford, Conn., he
removed thither and remained for ten years in this connection. He was the first pastor settled over this parish.
At the expiration of this time (Oct. 14, 1811) he accepted
an invitation to St. Paul's Church in Huntington, Conn.,
and became rector of the two parishes of Huntington and
New Stratford (now Monroe). Here he remained seventeen
years, when, after careful inquiry and examination, he em-
braced the doctrine of universal salvation, and answered
a call to become pastor of the Universalist Church and
Society in Hartford, to which place he removed Nov. 1,
1828, just seventeen years from the time he before left it.
He remained here about four years, and then took charge
of the Universalist Church in Portland, Me., remaining
there four years also. At the end of this time he
removed to Troy, N. Y., and spent the period of four
years there, and at the neighboring village of Lansing-

burg. In the latter part of August, 1840, he removed to New York City, continuing there until his death, and serving for a time as pastor to the Universalist Society in Bleeker Street. Of his literary efforts the following published account is given: "Mr. Rayner has written much and with acknowledged ability upon religious subjects; of some of his works large editions have been sold. During his last residence in Hartford, he edited and published a weekly paper entitled *The Religious Examiner*, which was continued several years, and was conducted with distinguished candor and ability. At Portland he also aided in the publication of a periodical called *The Christian Pilot*. A few of his numerous works have been stereotyped, and all bear intrinsic evidence of sincerity, moderation, intelligence, and industry."

While he was Universalist minister at Hartford, he printed a letter written in verse, addressed to the wardens and vestry during his rectorship at Christ Church, asking for payment of arrears of his salary. As a matter of interest, it is here appended.

" THE DUNNING LETTER.

" For ten years, commencing in 1801, I was the Minister (commonly called Rector) of the Episcopal Church, in the city of Hartford, called ' Christ Church.' During the summer and fall of two successive years, after preaching twice in Hartford on the Sabbath, I used to travel twelve miles and preach a third time, at a place called Warehouse Point, in East Windsor; where an Episcopal Society was soon collected and organized, and subsequently a handsome building was erected for their accommodation, the Corner Stone of which I had the satisfaction of laying, with appropriate religious services.

" It happened at a certain period in my ministerial labors above named, that I became afflicted with a troublesome

complaint — not very unusual, it is said, with the Clergy
— it was the want of what has been denominated the
'NEEDFUL.' There was due to me from the parish in Hartford, some two or three hundred dollars; but — owing
to my *natural diffidence*, I suppose — I could hardly sum-
mon sufficient resolution to disclose the necessities of the
case. The Vestry of the Church were in the habit of
having frequent meetings, to consult together upon the
affairs of the Parish. Such a meeting they were to have
on the ensuing Sunday evening, at the house of a Mr.
Olcott, but my appointment at the above-named place
would not allow me the opportunity to meet with them.
I therefore concluded that I would communicate what I
wished to say in the epistolary form, and avail myself of
the license which is always allowed in poetry. I ought
to add that whatever may be thought of the merit or de-
merit of the article, it had the effect to relieve me at once
from the afore-named embarrassment, for the very next
day the amount due was handed over. Here follows the
epistle — subsequently called the DUNNING LETTER."

TO THE WARDENS AND VESTRYMEN OF CHRIST'S CHURCH, HARTFORD.

GENTLEMEN:

On Sunday evening next you will attend
At Mr. Olcott's, my esteemed friend.
I much regret that such my engagements are
As will prevent my meeting with you there.
At Warehouse Point I must give my attendance,
The brethren there say I'm their sole dependence.
The sheep, they say, will scatter wide and stray,
If hireling-like the Shepherd flee away.
To lead them into pastures fresh and fair,
And guide them to the fold, shall be my care.
But still, my chief attention must be due,
And shall be given, my HARTFORD flock to you.
Wolves, greedy of their prey, around you roar
With cruel rage, impatient to devour;
They frown, they flatter, every art employ,
That some unwary sheep they may decoy.

Let not their numbers nor their rage alarm,
Your heavenly Shepherd will preserve from harm,
And shield you still with his Almighty arm.
Meanwhile his under Shepherd will not cease
His labors to preserve the flock in peace;
To explore the lost, the wandering sheep direct,
And in his Master's strength the fold protect.

What now I have to add you must forgive;
The shepherd also with the sheep must live.
He makes the feeding of the flock his care,
And must have food to eat, and clothes to wear.
Nor will it do if he alone's supplied,
His growing household must not be denied.
Three little babes — I'd almost said 'twas four,
And, if in time, there be as many more,
They every one, and their dear mother too,
Must still depend on me — and I on you.

A cold and barren winter's drawing near,
A season which the sons of want may fear;
To lay in stores, and for that scene prepare,
The little ant may teach should be our care;
The fire with fuel must be closely tended;
An hundred dollars here are soon expended;
And to withstand the force of every storm,
The back, and other parts, should be kept warm;
For men and women proper clothes be had,
And children in soft flannels should be clad;
And if you'd have your household round you smile,
The well remembered pot must daily boil.

More items of expense I might disclose,
But why repeat what every body knows ?
Farmers and Merchants each their claims will make,
And these must all be paid — and no mistake —
Physician, Surgeon, Cobbler, Tinker, Tailor,
All want their fees — perhaps at last the Jailor —
All want their fees, in full, and without failure.

But now, to be more serious, and conclude —
(For hitherto I fear I've been too rude.)
My wants are pressing, my resources few,
And for relief must look alone to you.
The sum is small which I've a right to ask,
But to collect it, doubtless, is a task.

The times are dull, cash not in circulation;
And each can scarce "work out his own salvation."
A part of what is due my turn may serve,
I hope that better days are in reserve.
I urge no more; I will be no complainer;
    I am
        Your humble servant,
            MENZIES RAYNER.

37   II. **Daniel Bontecou,** born in New Haven, April 20,   **120**
1779. His father having died previous to his birth, and
his mother within a few years marrying, and removing to
Enfield with her children, he was brought up under the
guardianship of his stepfather Capt. Ephraim Pease. He
married, March 16, 1798, Sybil, daughter of Rev. Elam
and Sybil (Pease) Potter of Enfield, Conn., and granddaugh-
ter of his stepfather. When a young man he established
himself in mercantile business in Enfield; he was also
active in the militia, and held the rank of Sergeant in
the 31st Regiment. About 1806 he removed to Springfield, Mass., and formed a copartnership with Col. Solo-
mon Warriner in the dry-goods business. His wife died
in Springfield, May 5, 1810, aged 29. He married again,
Nov. 13, 1816, Harriet Bliss, daughter of Hon. Moses
and Abigail (Metcalf) Bliss of Springfield. She was
born March 23, 1782, and died Nov. 10, 1853. In 1817
the partnership with Col. Warriner was dissolved, and
after continuing alone for some years, Mr. Jonathan Hunt
(now of Oakland, Cal.,—1882) was admitted into partnership, and they continued together until 1835, when Mr.
Bontecou sold out his interest and retired from mercantile
pursuits. He represented Springfield in the Massachusetts
General Court in 1820. He was elected deacon in the
First Congregational Church March 5, 1833, continuing
in the office until May 2, 1845, when he removed his relations to the South Church, then a new and struggling ‘
society, and was shortly afterward elected deacon, which

8

office he continued to hold until his death. In 1815 he purchased of Col. Warriner a homestead upon Main Street where Fallon's Block now stands, and his house was always a hospitable home for his friends. In 1846 he removed to the corner of Main and Howard Streets, where the remainder of his life was passed. After retiring from active business, he employed his leisure in cultivating several pieces of land which he owned in the outskirts of the town, and took great pleasure in this occupation. He died in Springfield, Nov. 24, 1857, aged 78. The *Springfield Republican* said of him, "He has lived long, sensibly, and usefully; his name is associated with no brilliant deeds, but honor, integrity, and piety belong to it. Useful and faithful in his day and generation, he is called home fully ripe for its immortality."

FIFTH GENERATION.

38   **I. Daniel Upson Bontecou.** I have been able to learn   **129**
but little about him. His wife was Mary ——— (family
name not positively known, but probably Sheering); she
was of Irish descent. He was a seaman, mate of a vessel, and was lost at sea in August, 1816. His widow died
in 1822, and was buried in Trinity churchyard, New York.

39   **II. Susannah Bontecou,** born Jan. 24, 1774, mar-   **133**
ried Capt. Eliakim Benham of New Haven, who was born
Feb. 1, 1773. He was a sea captain, and died in the West
Indies, March 30, 1816. Having sold his vessel in the
West Indies, and purchased a smaller one, he was still in
possession of a considerable sum of money, for which he
was murdered by his mate, and his body thrown overboard and never recovered. The British minister (the
United States being unrepresented) made an unsuccessful
effort to bring the murderer to justice. It is related as a
singular coincidence, and for the gratification of those
superstitiously inclined, that on the same night upon which
he was killed and thrown into the sea his family in New
Haven were startled by a great *splash* in the washtub,
which had been filled for the morrow's washing, and the
morning revealed the water splashed over the floor, but
by what agency has never been explained. His widow
removed to Smithfield, Isle of Wight County, Va., and
resided there with her daughter, Mrs. White, until her
death, which occurred May 11, 1848.

40   **III. Elizabeth Bontecou,** born February, 1777. She **138**
married, June 22, 1802, Amos Hall of Cheshire, Conn. He
. was a descendant of John Hall, one of the first settlers of
Wallingford, and was born in the west part of Cheshire (then included in Wallingford), May 21, 1773. She
died in Cheshire, June 13, 1829. Mr. Hall married (2d)
Mrs. Orilla Bradley (*née* Ives) of Cheshire. She was
the mother of Hiram Bradley, who married her step-
daughter, Nancy Hall (140). She survived her husband several years. Mr. Hall died in Cheshire, Feb. 18,
1848.

41   **IV. Julia Bontecou,** born 1778; died Feb. 24, 1788,
of small-pox.

42   **V. George Anson Bontecou,** born 1779; died Sept.
11, 1794.

43   **VI. Polly Bontecou,** born June 4, 1784. She married **145**
in 1801 Daniel Benedict, son of Francis, and a descendant
of Thomas Benedict of Nottinghamshire, England, who
emigrated to New England in 1638. He was born in Norfolk, Conn., December, 1774; removed to Vermont, and
was admitted to the Chittenden County bar in September,
1800. In 1824 the family removed to Western New York,
settled on Tonawanda Creek, and in 1838 removed to Clarence, Erie County, where he died in 1842. She died June
5, 1845.

44   **VII. Nancy Bontecou,** born in New Haven, year **149**
unknown, married Thaddeus Rice, a lawyer of St. Albans,
Vermont. When crossing Lake Champlain on the ice
to attend court at Plattsburg, his team broke through and
he was thrown into the water. He escaped, but sat in his
wet clothes in the court-room, and contracted a severe
cold which resulted in consumption. He died in 1808 in

New Orleans, where he had gone for the beneficial effects of the climate. His widow removed to Buffalo, N. Y., with her children, and died there in 1848.

CHILDREN OF WILLIAM AND HANNAH (STORER) BON- **21**
TECOU.

45 I. **Clarissa Bontecou,** born May 23, 1785. She **151** married, March 9, 1806, James Dougrey of Lansingburg, N. Y. He was born in Ireland, April 26, 1781, on a farm near the city of Donegal, and in 1790 emigrated with his father to this country, and settled in Lansingburg. He commenced early to earn his living by teaching, and clerking in the store of John Rutherford & Co. About the year 1803 he commenced business for himself, but abandoned it after a year or two, returned to Mr. Rutherford, and was admitted as a partner. He continued with him until the latter's death in 1812; then with John Kennedy as a partner until 1819, when the firm dissolved, and Mr. Dougrey built and moved into a larger store, and in 1829 admitted his son James as a partner. About this time the firm of Dougrey & Son and Matthew Vassar of Poughkeepsie purchased the Topping distillery property, and changed it into a brewing and malting establishment; this business was carried on until the death of Mr. Dougrey, which occurred Oct. 10, 1838. He was an honest man, a kind husband and father, and a good neighbor, beloved by all who knew him. He was a strong churchman, and a vestryman in Trinity (Episcopal) Church. His widow survived him until June 15, 1850. They are both buried in Trinity Church cemetery.

46 II. **William Bontecou,** born Feb. 25, 1787. Seaman and captain's mate. He was accidentally killed in the port of New York, " while the anchor was being got out," Dec. 15, 1806. He was unmarried.

47   **III. Julia Bontecou,** born July 13, 1789. She   **157**
married, June 13, 1809, Anthony Bristol, son of Nathan
and Annie (Lambert) Bristol of Milford, Conn. He was
born in Milford, July 16, 1778, and died June 15, 1867.
He was a merchant tailor, and for a few years carried on
a country store in connection with his tailoring establishment. His wife died in Milford, Oct. 27, 1862.

48   **IV. Timothy Bontecou,** born May 10, 1791. He
was a silversmith, and died unmarried, in Savannah, Ga.,
Oct. 2, 1815, of fever, after an illness of eleven days.[1]

49   **V. Polly Bontecou,** born July 22, 1792. She mar-   **169**
ried, Nov. 2, 1812, Captain Richard Hanford of Lansing-
burg, N. Y., who was born Jan. 9, 1784. He came from
Connecticut, and settled in Lansingburg at a time when
it was one of the most important places on the river for
country produce of all descriptions, requiring the employment of a large number of vessels in the freighting business; in this and the lumber business he embarked, own-
ing two of the largest vessels on the river, the "Royal
Oak" and "Hope," one of which he himself commanded.
He continued in this line until the advent of canals and
railroads turned the business in other directions, when he
sold out and engaged in mercantile business. He lived
greatly respected by all who knew him, and died June 5,
1844. His widow died April 11, 1857.

50   **VI. Henrietta Bontecou,** born Jan. 8, 1794. She   **174**
married, July 17, 1822, Anson Smith of New Haven. He

---

[1] "Timothy Bounticue, 26 years, died Oct. 2, 1815, of Fever, was a
silversmith, and came from New Haven, Conn.; was sick eleven days
at Marquand, Paulding, and Penfield's, died there, and was buried
from there."— *Savannah, Ga., Register of Deaths.*

"Died lately in Savannah, Mr. Timothy Bontecou, aged about 25
years, a native of New Haven (Conn.), but for several years past a
resident of Savannah."— *City Gazette and Commercial Daily Adver-
tiser, Charleston, S. C., Oct. 5, 1815.*

was a shoemaker. He was born in 1797, and died Aug. 2, 1855. She died Jan. 24, 1862.

51   VII. Hannah Elizabeth Bontecou, born April 2, 1797; died Nov. 8, 1862, in Milford, Conn., unmarried.

52   VIII. James Bontecou, born Aug. 25, 1799; died July 22, 1800.

53   IX. Nancy Bontecou, born March 13, 1802. She   **182** married, Oct. 14, 1821, William B. Thomas, a cabinet-maker, and lived in Bridgeport, Conn. She died July 17, 1835. After her death he went South and resided in Georgia before the war, but returned North, again married, and subsequently died in Brooklyn, N. Y.

CHILDREN OF THOMAS AND RUTH (STORER) BONTECOU.   **22**

54   I. Thomas Bontecou, born July 30, 1791. He was a seaman, and mate of the "Huntress," commanded by his uncle Nathaniel Storer. The vessel and all on board were lost in 1811, while on a voyage to China.

55   II. John Bontecou, born Dec. 15, 1793; died Jan. 8, 1794, of cholera.

56   III. Susannah Bontecou, born May 2, 1796. She married, Aug. 9, 1827, Benjamin Hood (60) of New Haven. He was a tailor, and resided at one time in Statesburg, S. C. They had no children. She died Oct. 4, 1842. He died Sept. 30, 1871.

57   IV. Harriet Bontecou, born June 25, 1798. She   **183** married, Jan. 14, 1816, Capt. Menemon Sanford, son of David Stebins and Olive (Johnson) Sanford. He was born in Pawlet, Vt., Nov. 15, 1789. About 1798 his parents removed to South Britain, Conn. When about seventeen years of age he went to sea, his first voyage

being to Liverpool, England. In 1813, on a voyage from
Turk's Island, his vessel was captured by the British near
New London, Conn., and burned ; he was placed on board
a prison-ship, where he was confined for some time. After
his marriage he made his home in New Haven, but continued to follow the sea as master, making voyages to the
Pacific and Europe up to 1822, when he engaged in the
steamboat business; at first in boats running between
New York, New Haven, and Hartford, and afterwards to
various other places. In the spring of 1835 he moved to
Hartford, Conn. In 1840 he removed to New York City,
where he died June 24, 1852. His widow died in Oakland, Cal., Oct. 11, 1883.

58   V. Maria Bontecou, born Jan. 17, 1801. She married, in 1818, Capt. Edward Huntington, who was born
in New London, Conn., May 13, 1791. When a child his
parents moved to Albany, N. Y. At an early age he went
to sea. In 1813 his vessel was captured by the British,
and he was confined in the same prison-ship with Capt.
Sanford (57); was taken to England and discharged.
After the war he commanded a ship in trade between
Havre and New York, up to 1828, when he retired. After
his marriage his home was in Brooklyn, N. Y. In 1828-9
he removed to Hudson, N. Y., and engaged in the manufacturing of carpets up to 1839, when he removed to New
York. In 1848 he moved to Matawan, N. J., where he
died Dec. 13, 1881. She died Aug. 16, 1875. They had
no children.

59   VI. William Higby Bontecou, born March 22,
1803; died Nov. 12, 1825, unmarried.

CHILDREN OF WILLIAM AND ELIZABETH (BONTECOU)   23
HOOD.

60   I. Benjamin Hood, born Jan. 27, 1791; married,
Aug. 9, 1827, Susannah Bontecou (56), his cousin, daugh-

ter of Thomas and Ruth (Storer) Bontecou. She was born May 2, 1796, and died Oct. 4, 1842. He served an apprenticeship to the tailor's trade, with his uncle, Samuel Bontecou, in Lansingburg, N. Y., and established himself as a merchant in Statesburg, S. C. During the War of the Rebellion he had charge of a hospital in Sumter, S. C. He died in Brooklyn, N. Y., Sept. 30, 1871. They had no children.

61   II. **Susan Maria Hood,** born about 1792. She never married, and died July 5, 1873.

62   III. **Elizabeth Hood,** born Jan. 27, 1794. She **195** married, May 11, 1820, Zacheus Maples, who was born in Norwich, Conn., Aug. 14, 1793. He learned the shoemaker's trade, and removed to New Haven, where he pursued it for a time, and then took up the trade of locksmith. In 1855 he gave up business and removed to Brooklyn, N. Y. She died there Feb. 28, 1858, and he died Dec. 17, 1863.

63   IV. **Nancy Hood,** born about 1796. She married, Dec. 18, 1855, Marcus Merriman, Jr., as his second wife. He was born in New Haven in 1792. He was a politician of the old Whig school; represented New Haven in the State Legislature in 1844, and was a member of the State Senate in 1846–7; was also an officer in the Custom House in New Haven for some years. He died Dec. 11, 1864. She is living (1882) with her nephew at 77 William Street, New Haven.

64   V. **James Hood,** born in 1798. He was a seaman, and died at sea on a voyage from the West Indies, being mate of the vessel at the time. He was unmarried.

65   VI. **Harriet Hood,** born in 1802; died Aug. 3, 1879, unmarried.

9

66   VII. Charles Bontecou Hood, born in 1803. He was a merchant in Alabama, but afterwards settled in Washington, Ark. He married, Aug. 31, 1843, Eliza, daughter of William and Ann (Whelan) Sale of Brooklyn, N. Y. After his marriage he gave up business and established his residence in Brooklyn, where he died Dec. 24, 1871. His widow resides (1882) at Richmond Hill, L. I. They had no children.

67   VIII. Roswell Hood, born in 1806; married, June   202
19, 1839, Abby Meeker Beach. She died Nov. 25, 1852, aged 36. He afterwards married Mary Beach, the sister of his first wife, by whom he had no children. She died November, 1873. He died Jan. 7, 1875. Mr. Hood learned the tailor's trade of his uncle Samuel Bontecou.

CHILDREN OF SAMUEL AND PHEBE (TALLMAN) BON-   24
TECOU.

68   I. Charles Hubbard Bontecou, born Jan. 6, 1798.   203
He married, Jan. 28, 1826, Sarah Keeler, daughter of Stephen and Margaret (Pyncheon) Keeler of New York. She died March 7, 1869. He commenced his business life in 1816, as clerk in the dry-goods trade in New York. After a time he associated with himself, William Israel, and they commenced business under the firm name of Bontecou & Israel. Eventually this proved to be an unprofitable venture, and he took the road as a traveling salesman. He now (1884) resides in Lansingburg, N. Y.

69   II. Hamlet Bontecou, born Dec. 23, 1799. In 1816 he began as clerk in a hardware store in New York, and continued clerking until 1820. when he shipped on the "Henry" from New Haven, for a four-years' whaling voyage. He reached New Haven, on his return, Nov. 12, 1824, and the following year obtained a situation as clerk in the

Troy House, Troy, N. Y., where he remained seven years. The following four years were spent in New York and in Lancaster, Mass., in the same business. He was clerk in the Lansingburg post-office at the time his father was postmaster. He died in Lansingburg, Feb. 26, 1883, unmarried.

70   III. William Bontecou, born April 4, 1802; died Dec. 23, 1805.

71   IV. Harriet Bontecou, born Jan. 6, 1805; died Jan. 15, 1830.

72   V. William Bontecou, born March 22, 1808. He was a grocer in Lansingburg; then removed to Wells-town, Hamilton County, N. Y. In 1882, he was living somewhere in Vermont.

73   VI. Roswell Bontecou, born July 1, 1810; died April 25, 1851.

74   VII. Cecelia Bontecou, born May 9, 1813. Resides (1884) in Lansingburg.

75   VIII. Elizabeth Bontecou, born Aug. 5, 1819; died Oct. 5, 1846.

CHILDREN OF MARCUS, SR., AND SUSANNAH (BONTECOU)   **25**
MERRIMAN.

76   I. John Merriman, died aged three months.

77   II. Sally Merriman, died aged eighteen months.

78   III. Infant.

79   IV. Infant.

80   V. Sarah Parmalee Merriman, born April 27, 1799.   **204**
She married, Aug. 27, 1817, Eben Norton Thomson of

Goshen, Conn. He was a man of more than ordinary ability, and it was designed that he should be liberally educated; but being prevented by circumstances from entering college, he turned his attention to mercantile pursuits and became a merchant in New Haven. He was generous, genial, and affable, and a universal favorite. He died July 18, 1856. She died Aug. 12, 1869.

CHILDREN OF NATHANIEL AND POLLY AUGUSTA (BON-   **27**
TECOU) STORER.

81   I. **Samuel Storer,** born March 1, 1782. He was drowned " in Mr. Broome's fish-pond," June 22, 1787.[1]

82   II. **Susannah Storer,** born Oct. 28, 1783; died Aug. 13, 1872, unmarried.

83   III. **Nathaniel Storer,** born March 5, 1786; died Dec. 18, 1793.

84   IV. **Samuel Storer,** born May 11, 1787. He fell out of a boat in New Haven harbor and was drowned, Aug. 29, 1798.[2]

85   V. **Polly Storer,** born July 1, 1789. She married,   **211** July 15, 1807, Capt. George Miles, son of John and Mary (Bill) Miles. He was born in New Haven, Nov. 24, 1784. They removed to Erie, Pa. Capt. Miles followed the lakes for a long term of years, having been in command of some of the first steamboats on Lake Erie. He died in Erie, April 10, 1863. She died Oct. 31, 1840.

---

[1] "On Friday last a boy about six years old, son of Mr. Nathaniel Storey of this city, was drowned in Mr. Broome's fish-pond."— *New Haven Gazette, June* 28, 1787.

[2] "Wednesday last, a son of Capt. Nathaniel Storer, about 11 years old, fell out of a boat in our harbor, and was drowned; his body was taken up, after being in the water about an hour and a half."— *Connecticut Journal, New Haven, Sept.* 5, 1798.

86   VI. **Peter Storer**, born Aug. 6, 1791. He married,   218
Sept. 12, 1813. Hannah Eliza Woodruff, daughter of Nathaniel and Abigail (Cooper) Woodruff of New Jersey.
She was born April 8, 1791, and died Aug. 13, 1864. He
commenced a seafaring life when less than nine years old,
making a voyage to China in the ship "Sallie," with his
father. He continued to follow the sea for over sixty
years. His first command was the brig "Shepardess,"
when about twenty-six years old. The latter part of his
sea life was spent in the United States Revenue service.
About 1860 he made his home at Westville, near New
Haven, and died there March 28, 1883. The following is
taken from a New Haven paper: "He was a prominent
man and a thorough Christian. His father was captain
of the ship "Sally," which sailed from this port to China,
and he made the trip with him in 1799, when only nine
years of age. Since that time he had followed the sea
continuously until his retirement. He was not in the
War of 1812, but stood at the Fair Haven draw in 1815,
when the "Eagle," improvised for the occasion, went out to
capture a British gunboat which had destroyed the packet
"Susan" of this port and committed other waste. Her
decks and rigging were crowded with men and boys. He
was invited to go, but owing to an injury received while in
the woods was unable to do so. Instead of capturing the
English gunboat, the "Eagle" herself was captured. She
was run aground, and the motley crew were permitted to
escape. Capt. Storer was afterward in command of one
of the West India brigs, and then for thirty years in the
United States Revenue service. He was commander of
many revenue cutters, proving himself fearless and vigi-
lant in the discharge of his duties."

87   VII. **Nathaniel Storer**, born Aug. 28, 1794. Lost
at sea in 1811, in the ship "Huntress," commanded by his
father. All on board perished.

88   **VIII. Hannah Augusta Storer,** born Jan. 31, 1797.   **222** She married, Nov. 19, 1820, Chauncey Ives, and died Dec. 14, 1868. Mr. Ives was enrolled and did some duty in the War of 1812. He was for many years connected with the Sun Mutual Insurance Company of New York. He died Feb. 2, 1879.

89   **IX. Lydia Storer,** born May 12, 1799. She married,   **227** April 13, 1822, Grove Smith of New Haven, and died Nov. 23, 1838. Mr. Smith was born in Ridgefield, Conn. He was a shoemaker, or in the shoe trade, was a member of the Episcopal Church, and belonged to the Masonic Fraternity. He died Oct. 13, 1830.

90   **X. Harriet Elizabeth Storer,** born in 1805; died Sept. 26, 1871; unmarried.

CHILDREN OF JAMES AND JOANNA (CLARK) BONTECOU.   **28**

91   **I. Jane Bontecou,** born in New Haven, April 24,   **231** 1804. She married, Nov. 18, 1833, Charles Parsons Bishop, son of Charles and Phebe Bishop of Whitesboro, N. Y. He died in New Haven, Oct. 26, 1869. His widow resides there (1882), at 11 Fair Street.

92   **II. Grace Bontecou,** born in New Haven, Aug. 9,   **233** 1805. She married, June 14, 1831, Elisha Peck, son of Henry Peck of New Haven. He was born May 5, 1790, and died June 11, 1866. She resides at 129 Wooster Street, New Haven. The following account of Capt. Peck is from the *Army and Navy Journal,* of July 7, 1866 :

"At thirteen years of age Capt. Peck first went to sea, as a cabin-boy in the brig 'Argus,' on a voyage from his native town, New Haven, Conn., to the West Indies, and he continued in the merchant service till the year 1813, with the exception of two years forced service on board English men-of-war. Being at London in August, 1812, mate of

the embargoed ship 'Ann,' war having been declared by
the United States against Great Britain, he was arrested
and detained as a prisoner of war on board the prison-ship
'Nassau' in Chatham River till the following March, when
he was paroled and sent to Newport, R. I., in the American ship 'Robinson Potter,' a cartel [ship of truce]. Having
been exchanged, in July, 1813, he entered as master's
mate in the United States Navy for twelve months, and
joined 'Gunboat 92' at New London; in May in the following year was transferred to the frigate 'Macedonian,' and
on re-entering after his discharge, he was attached to the
frigate 'United States,' at New London; in December, 1814,
he was appointed acting sailing master, ordered to the
'Macedonian,' in a few months transferred to the 'United
States,' and in September, 1815, sailed in the latter frigate as acting midshipman and acting sailing master from
Boston for the Mediterranean, continuing upon that station
till November, 1820. He served from 1821 till 1824 as
acting sailing master of the line-of-battle ship 'Franklin'
in the Pacific; in the 'Brandywine' when she took Gen.
Lafayette to France, and on her cruise in the Mediterranean in 1825 and 1826; was promoted to a lieutenancy in
1826; served from 1827 to 1830 in the frigate 'Java' and
line-of-battle ship 'Delaware' in the Mediterranean; from
1831 to 1834 in the sloop 'Falmouth' and brig 'Dolphin' in
the Pacific; from 1836 to 1838 in the sloops 'Natchez' and
'Vandalia,' and in command of the schooner 'Grampus' in
the West Indies; and from 1840 to 1843 as senior lieutenant of the New York Navy Yard. Being commissioned
a commander in 1843, Capt. Peck from 1849 to 1851 commanded the sloop 'Portsmouth' on the coast of Africa,
and from 1852 to 1855 was in command of the receiving
ship 'North Carolina' at New York. In September, 1855,
he was placed on the reserved list with leave pay as
commander, and in 1863 was promoted to captain.   Dur-

ing three years of the late war he was in command of the
Naval Rendezvous at Portsmouth, N. H.

"In January, 1807, being then a seaman on board the
American ship 'John.' from New York, bound for the
north of Europe, the vessel was boarded off the coast of
Holland from H. B. M. sloop-of-war 'Ariel,' Commander
Joseph Olliver, and the late Capt. Peck was impressed as
an English subject and taken on board the English vessel ;
and though he showed a genuine American protection and
asserted that he was a native of New Haven in the State
of Connecticut. the English commander chose to regard
the protection as spurious and the statement regarding
nativity to apply to New Haven, England, and refused to
release his acquisition.   After serving on board the 'Ariel'
till 1808. during which time he was once disabled by a
splinter in action, he was transferred to the 'Trident' of
64 guns, then fitting out for the flag-ship of Admiral
Ball at Malta, and he went to Malta in her in July of
that year.   While on board the 'Trident,' 'promotion to
the quarter-deck' was offered to him as a reward for
jumping overboard and saving the life of a boy who had
fallen overboard at sea, an honor he declined 'because
he was an American'; and he was rated captain of her
maintop at eighteen years of age, an evidence of his pro-
ficiency at that early age as a seaman.   In January, 1809,
when on shore from the 'Trident' as coxswain of a boat,
he availed himself of a favorable opportunity and deserted,
shipping under a fictitious name on board the hired armed
ship 'Lord Eldon,' then ready for sea.   The efforts made
to obtain men for the 'King's ships' rendered officers of
vessels sailed on private account little disposed to regard
without compulsion the King's prior claim, and interest
impelled them to shield from apprehension those men of
their crews suspected of desertion from men-of-war.   In
consequence of precautions taken on behalf of the deserter,

the officer and party from the 'Trident' were foiled in their
search, and Capt. Peck reached Gibraltar in the 'Lord Eldon,' where, once more, by deserting from her and crossing to Algesiras, he was enabled to place himself under
the somewhat precarious protection of the United States
flag, by entering on board the American ship 'Alpha,'
whose captain showed him much kindness in taking
such precautions that he escaped detection and capture
by English searching officers; and he reached London in
July, and in August returned to the United States in the
ship 'Ann.' . . .

"Every person associated upon duty with Capt. Peck
will recollect with a smile the many evidences of a quaint
sense of humor that was a characteristic of his mind, and
all will remember with pleasure how careful he was that
these eccentricities of pleasantry should never wound the
feelings or offend the prejudices of others, or mar the
harmony of intercourse with associates. Always honest,
single-minded, and courteous, a man of generous impulses,
with a delicate sense of honor, of warm feelings and kindness of heart, he was esteemed most by those who knew
him best.

"The decease of this genial, cheerful, humor-loving gentleman will bring sadness to the hearts of many friends
in the Navy, a pleasant, cheerful, respected companion
having passed from their midst; and the Navy at large
will receive with regret the fact that another officer of
the old school, whose education was essentially practical,
a thorough and accomplished seaman, of diversified experience, eminently conscientious, zealous, and intelligent
in the discharge of his duty, is lost to the service for the
future. Unfailing cheerfulness of disposition and unself-
ish consideration were especially obvious in his last illness:
deprived of speech, rendered, to a degree, helpless by disease, he seemed to endeavor, with his accustomed tender-

10

ness, by avoiding complaint, to spare the feelings of those dearest to him, — to wish to alleviate, as it were, to their hearts the poignancy of the bereavement that was inevitable. Solaced by the presence of his wife and children, it seemed at last when his active spirit took its flight that in truth it had found rest."

CHILDREN OF JUSTUS AND SARAH (BONTECOU) TROW- **34**
BRIDGE.

93   **I. James Trowbridge,** born August, 1796; died Oct. 23, 1798.

94   **II. Rebecca Trowbridge,** born Nov. 8, 1798. She **236**
married, March 11, 1832, William Townsend of New Haven, Conn., as his second wife. He is the son of Timothy and Hannah (Alling) Townsend, was born in New Haven, Jan. 16, 1799, and is living (1883) at the corner of Dixwell Avenue and Charles Street: is a carpenter and master builder, and has resided in New Haven and vicinity all his life, with the exception of one season in South Carolina. He has been senior warden of Christ Church for over thirty years. His wife (Rebecca) died in New Haven, Sept. 1, 1881.

95   **III. James Trowbridge,** born June 27, 1800. He **240**
married, March 5, 1826, Charity Cannon, daughter of James and Mary (Burritt) Cannon of Stratford, Conn. She died Feb. 10, 1860. He learned the trade of an umbrella maker, and carried on that business on Chapel Street, New Haven, until 1832, when he removed to Catskill, N. Y., and entered into the employ of his brother Charles, in the chandlery business. He is still living in Catskill (1883), and has always been remarkable for physical health, never having had occasion to employ the services of either physician or dentist.

96   IV. Susan Trowbridge, born in 1802; died in 1826, unmarried.

97   V. Charles Trowbridge, born Aug. 28, 1805. He **243** married, Sept. 15, 1829, Emily Scott, daughter of Samuel and Melinda (Hurlbut) Scott of Farmington, Conn. He early learned the printer's trade in New Haven ; did not, however, adopt it as a profession, but removed to Cats- kill, N. Y., and bought into the tallow-chandlery business, continuing in it till his death, which occurred Dec. 21, 1880. He was connected with St. Luke's Church, Cats- kill, for nearly fifty years ; first as vestryman, and after- wards for many years as senior warden. He held various village offices, and had a high reputation for honor and integrity ; he was intrusted with the settlement of many estates. His widow is still (1883) living in Catskill.

98   VI. Henry Trowbridge, born in 1807 ; died in May, 1815.

CHILDREN OF DAVID AND POLLY (CLARK) BONTECOU. **35**

99   I. Peter Bontecou, born in New Haven, Jan. 26, **249** 1797. When quite young his parents removed to Coey- mans, N. Y. He went to Troy, N. Y., when a lad, and obtained employment in a shoe store, of which he after- wards became proprietor, continuing the business until his death. He married, April 29, 1823, Semantha, daugh- ter of Reed Brockway of Troy. She was born Feb. 23, 1803, and died in Troy, May 9, 1824. He married (2d), Aug. 6, 1828, Sophia, daughter of Stanley Thompson. She was born Nov. 23, 1806, and died in Troy, June 9, 1850. Mr. Bontecou was cold and austere in manner, and strictly honest in all his dealings ; a member of the Methodist Episcopal Church, and a great student of theo- logical works. He died March 20, 1868, in Troy.

100   **II. Elizabeth Bontecou,** born Oct. 14, 1798. She married, in September, 1820, Leonard Witbeck, son of John Witbeck of Lansingburg, N. Y., and died at Cocymans, N. Y., Jan. 22, 1824, leaving no children. Mr. Witbeck married again and died at Cocymans, leaving a large family by the second marriage.

101   **III. Susannah Bontecou,** born in New Haven, July **259** 25, 1801. She married, Oct. 28, 1820, at Cocymans, N. Y., Moses Northrup. He was a harness-maker, shoemaker, and tanner. From the time of his marriage until 1834 he resided in New Baltimore, Greene County, N. Y., in which place his wife died Jan. 15, 1829. He removed from there to Cocymans, Albany County, and in 1837 to Danby, Tompkins County. Nov. 13, 1830, he married Eve Wolf, and by her had three children. He died in Danby, Nov. 14, 1847.

102   **IV. James Clark Bontecou,** born in New Haven, **264** July 11. 1803. In his infancy his parents removed to Cocymans. N. Y., and he lived there till about sixteen years of age, when he removed to Troy, and entered the employ of his brother Peter, in the shoe business. An attempt to establish himself in an independent business a year later resulted in failure through the dishonesty of his partner. who finally absconded, leaving the debts of the firm to be faced by the boy he had deceived. Although as a minor he could not be held responsible by the creditors, yet as a matter of personal honor he shouldered the burden. He returned to his brother's employ as foreman of the manufacturing department; and at the end of seven years, by dint of unwearied industry and the closest economy, succeeded in paying the last debt of the firm. While undergoing this severe discipline he became active in the work of his church; and as soon as the incubus of debt had been lifted from his

shoulders, he entered the ministry of the Methodist Episcopal Church, in the year 1827. He was ordained deacon in 1829, and elder in 1831. Transferred to the New
England Conference, he traveled several circuits, and
afterwards served as pastor of churches in Sag Harbor,
Charlestown, Martha's Vineyard, and Bristol. While
stationed on Martha's Vineyard in 1835, in conjunction
with others he inaugurated and conducted the first camp-
meeting held on the island,—an institution that in the
succeeding half-century has become famous. He married,
July 22, 1836, Abby Connable, daughter of Joseph and
Mary (Maxwell) Connable of Bernardston, Mass. She
was a woman of remarkable strength of character and
fine culture, whose quick sympathies and exquisite tact
greatly added to the success of her husband, both as
preacher and pastor. Mr. Bontecou filled, after his marriage, successful pastorates at Worthington, Circleville,
and Athens, Ohio, at which latter place his wife died,
June 27, 1846.

He married (2d), Aug. 1, 1849, Mary Ann Goode, of a
Virginia family. Subsequent to this marriage he was
stationed at Franklin, Oxford, Sharon, Greenfield, Love-
land, and North Bend, Ohio, and for ten years lived in
Cincinnati, being pastor of Pearl Street and York Street
Churches and Wesley Chapel, and financial agent for the
Wesleyan Female Seminary. In 1870 he withdrew from
the active work of the ministry, and after a year spent
in revisiting the scenes of his early labors, settled in
his home at Xenia, Ohio, and died there, Oct. 14, 1875,
aged 72. His widow still (1883) lives near Xenia. As
a preacher, Mr. Bontecou was methodical in statement,
clear and logical in argument, with somewhat of disdain
for meretricious ornament and the mere graces of rhetoric. As a pastor he was of great value to the church,
and throughout his ministry his fine administrative tal-

ents were employed in healing divisions, overcoming
financial difficulties, and looking after the temporalities
of the church. As a man he was of undaunted courage,
strong convictions, and inflexible integrity. From the
beginning of the anti-slavery agitation, his voice and pen
were constantly employed on' the side of freedom, and
never quailed or faltered before the storm of opposition
and obloquy which he was sometimes called to face in his
defense of human rights. At a time when the church
lent the mantle of respectability to cover the liquor curse
and crime, his voice rang out with no uncertain sound;
and upon every moral and politico-moral question of the
last half-century he was invariably found in the front rank
of earnest and practical workers for humanity.

103   V. Sarah Bontecou, born in Coeymans, N. Y., May   267
19, 1805. She married, Feb. 18, 1834, Gilbert Dean
Golden, son of Joseph Golden of Troy, who was born
July 17, 1810, and died in Troy, Feb. 18, 1872. He was
an undertaker, and proprietor of the chief establishment
in this line in Troy. She died there, April 12, 1882.

104   VI. David Bontecou, born Oct. 25, 1807. He left
home when a young man, and was last heard of in Texas
about 1840. During the War of the Rebellion the existence of a Bontecou family in that State was rumored, and
the natural conclusion reached was that it was the family
of David ; but a recent search through every county in the
State fails to reveal the existence of such a name, neither
do the land records show that a patent to land has ever
been issued to'one of the name of Bontecou. It is possible that he or his descendants may be living, but we know
nothing of them.

105   VII. Samuel Storer Bontecou, born Jan. 23, 1810,
died July 11, 1812.

106   **VIII. George Bontecou,** born in Coeymans, N. Y.,   **273**
June 23, 1812. When he was thirteen years of age his
parents removed to New Baltimore, N. Y. In 1830 he
went to Troy, learned the trade of a shoemaker, and married, Sept. 6, 1838, Lydia Ann Whipple, daughter of William W. and Hannah (Adams) Whipple of Troy. She
was born in that city, May 28, 1818, and died there, Feb.
20, 1864. In 1849 Mr. Bontecou relinquished his trade,
and from that time until 1866 was engaged in the lumber
business, as clerk, inspector, and principal; a portion of
the time in New York City. In 1866 he removed to
Vineland, N. J., where he still resides, engaged in farming and fruit culture. He married (2d), July 1, 1869,
Margaret Dustin, daughter of Ananis and Margaret
(Hunter) Dustin of Waterford, Erie County, Pa.

107   **IX. Edward Bontecou,** born Jan. 13, 1815. He   **285**
married, Sept. 2, 1842, Mrs. Cornelia Keifer, widow of
Baltue Keifer, and daughter of Garret and Maria (Pal-
mater) Whitbeck of Coeymans Hollow, N. Y. She died
there in September, 1877. Edward Bontecou passed the
years 1846 and 1847 in Texas, but returned to Coeymans,
remaining there until 1852. In that year he departed
by steamer for California, located in Weaverville, Trinity
County, and was for a number of years interested in
mining enterprises there and elsewhere. In 1878 he
removed to Newhall, Los Angeles County, and engaged
in building roads for the Pico Oil Company. He died
in Newhall, May 4, 1883. At the time of his death he
held the offices of school commissioner and justice of
the peace, and was a member of the Methodist Episcopal Church.

108   **X. Francis Bontecou,** born in Coeymans, N. Y.,   **288**
Nov. 17, 1819. He married, Jan. 25, 1844, Clarissa Maria
Landon, daughter of Gardner and Mary (Bissell) Landon

of Troy. About this time he established himself in the
lumber trade, conducting it for six years in Troy, then
for a year in California. In May, 1851, he removed to
New York City, and continued in the same business until
May, 1878, when he removed to Toronto, Woodson County,
Kan., where he now resides, engaged in farming and stock-
raising.

CHILDREN OF REV. MENZIES AND REBECCA (BONTECOU)   36
RAYNER.

109   I. Miriam Powell Rayner, born in Elizabethtown,
N. J., Dec. 3, 1796; died in Westborough, Mass., Oct. 31,
1881, unmarried.

110   II. Caroline Starr Rayner, born in Elizabethtown,   293
N. J., April 2, 1799. She married, Jan. 2, 1827, John
Peck Burritt of Newtown, Conn. He was a comb-maker
by trade; was born in Newtown, Dec. 10, 1800, and about
1830 removed to Wappinger's Creek, now Wappinger's
Falls, N. Y., and established himself in the manufacture
of those articles. He was shortly after seized with rheu-
matism and confined for six months, and there being no
one to attend to his business, the enterprise failed. He
soon afterward returned to Newtown. He was drowned,
Sept. 20, 1842, while crossing the Housatonic River in a
row-boat. The family removed to New York, and resided
with grandfather Rayner at 22 First Avenue. In 1860
they removed to Stoughton, Wis., where Mrs. Burritt
died, Sept. 21, 1882.

111   III. Daniel Bontecou Rayner, born in Elizabethtown, N. J., Jan. 14, 1801; died in Hartford, Conn.,
Dec. 1, 1801.

112   IV. Benjamin Lester Rayner, born in Hartford,   301
Conn., Sept. 7, 1802. He married, May 10, 1835, Nancy

Merrill, daughter of Benjamin and Dorothy (Currier)
Merrill of Portsmouth, N. H. She died in New York,
July 6, 1866. He studied law at Washington College
(now Trinity), Hartford, and practiced it as a profession,
but combined some literary work with it: besides editing
a newspaper, he wrote a eulogistic life of Thomas Jefferson, which was published in Hartford by subscription, and
is said to have been the *first* of the subscription books of
which that city afterwards became so great a center of
publication. After his marriage he removed to New York
City, and owing to deafness gave up legal practice. He
died in that city, Nov. 29, 1862.

113   V.   **William Charles Rayner,** born in Hartford, Sept.
5, 1804; died there, Dec. 10, 1805.

114   VI.   **Daniel Olcott Rayner,** born in Hartford, May   **302**
26, 1806. He married, Aug. 22, 1834, Frances Case,
daughter of Harlow Case of Windsor, Conn. She died
July 20, 1872. At present he resides with his daughter,
Mrs. Vincent, at Sioux Falls, Dak.

115   VII.   **Rebecca Bontecou Rayner,** born in Hartford,
June 19, 1808; died in Westborough, Mass., Oct. 12, 1881,
unmarried.

116   VIII.   **Menzies Rayner, Jr.,** born in Hartford, Conn.,   **304**
March 20, 1810. He commenced his business life at the
age of 14, as clerk in a grocery store in Bridgeport,
Conn. After a trial at this, both in Bridgeport and New
York, and at other business in Hartford, he removed to
Portland, Me., with his parents, about 1832, and estab-
lished himself in the book trade and printing business; the
Christian Pilot, edited by his father, was issued from his
establishment. He married, Nov. 14, 1833, Ann Elizabeth
Stevens, daughter of Capt. James and Elizabeth (Trum-
bull) Stevens of Portland. In 1835 he removed to Troy,

11

N. Y., and shortly after to New York City. After a trial and failure in the bakery business, he obtained employment as book-keeper in Peter Cooper's rolling and wire mill, and when his works were built in Trenton, N. J., removed there, and remained over twenty years in different departments. His wife died in New York, Nov. 30, 1843. He married (2d), Aug. 6, 1844, Mrs. Susan Nodine of New York, daughter of Joseph and Hester (Brown) Prindle of Sandgate, Vt. She died at Trenton, Feb. 28, 1858. He married (3d), March 13, 1859, Mrs. Rebecca Jane (McClure) Starr, from whom he was divorced in 1874. In 1870, he went West, remaining eleven years in Wisconsin, and then returned to Trenton, where he now resides at 341 Fair Street.

117   IX. **Mary Martha Rayner,** born in Huntington, Conn., April 10, 1812. She married, Feb. 9, 1831, Lucius Bonaparte Allyn, eldest son of Nathan Allyn of Hartford, Conn., and died at Washington, D. C., Oct. 18, 1866. She had no children. Mr. Allyn was born in Hartford in 1809. He engaged with his brother in the drug business, but about 1835 sold out his interest and removed with his wife to Wisconsin, with a view to settling there. Not meeting with success, they returned to Hartford, and in 1848 removed to Washington, where he obtained a clerkship in the Navy Department which he filled for nearly twenty years: he was then called to a responsible and arduous financial position in the Treasury Department, which he filled creditably to himself and with marked advantage to the Government. Mr. Allyn married (2d), Oct. 31, 1867, Mary Jane Burritt (295), niece of his first wife, and died in Washington, Aug. 7, 1876. He held high rank in the Order of Odd Fellows; was a large-hearted, benevolent man; sympathetic and kind, and extremely courteous in manner. His widow resides in Washington, at 610 M Street, N. W.

118   X. Jane Elizabeth Barry Rayner, born in Hunt-   311
ington, Conn., May 19, 1815. She married, Feb. 24,
1840, in Lansingburg, N. Y., George Gilman Warner of
Walpole, N. H. He was born in Holden, Mass., and at
the age of 16 entered the employ of a house dealing in
West India goods at Roxbury; at 21 he went to Troy,
N. Y., and commenced business for himself, but after two
years removed to Walpole, N. H., and opened a dry-goods
and general merchandise store, which he continued until
1848. He then removed to Westborough, Mass., and continued in the same line for nine years, at the end of which
period he sold out and retired from active business. He
shortly after removed to Philadelphia, but in 1860 returned
to Westborough, where he now resides. Mrs. Warner died
July 25, 1885.

119   XI. William Charles Rayner, born in Huntington,
Conn., April 17, 1817. He commenced his business life
in a music store in Troy, N. Y. Having a strong musical
taste, he became under able instruction a proficient, and
for many years made musical instruction his business.
He has resided in Whitehall, N. Y., Pittsfield, Mass., New
York City, and Janesville, Wis. Making a specialty of
organ music, he has usually filled a position as organist
in each place of his residence; in New York he served in
this capacity in the North Dutch Church and the Lafayette
Place Dutch Reformed Church. In 1863 he removed from
New York to Janesville, and taught the piano for about
eight years, since which time he has been engaged in
tuning pianos, traveling in the States of Wisconsin and
Iowa. He has never married, and calls Janesville his
home.

119 a. XII. Cornelia Shelton Rayner, born in Huntington, Conn., Jan. 12, 1820; died there, July 4, 1824.

CHILDREN OF DANIEL AND SYBIL (POTTER) BONTECOU.   37

120   I. Catharine Rhodes Bontecou, born in Enfield, 313
Conn., Dec. 26, 1798. She married, Nov. 12, 1819, Wells
Lathrop of Springfield. He was born in Becket, Mass.,
Feb. 25, 1795, and died in South Hadley, Mass., April 12,
1871, thirty-five years after a 'second marriage. Mrs.
Lathrop was a lady of superior intelligence and piety.
She died Dec. 24, 1832.

From the *Springfield Republican* of April 12, 1871 : —
" Wells Lathrop, who was prominently identified with
the business interests of Springfield half a century ago.
died at his home at South Hadley Falls, on Wednesday,
in his 77th year. He was a native of Wilbraham [error :
he was born in Becket, but his parents removed to Wilbraham when he was a child], a son of Capt. Joseph Lathrop, and a grandson of the famous Rev. Dr. Lathrop of
West Springfield. with whom he passed the winters of his
boyhood in study. He came to Springfield when sixteen
years old, and served as an apprentice in Warriner & Bontecou's store, which stood on the site of the present First
National Bank. In 1816 he joined his fortunes with
those of Charles Howard, who is still living, and the
firm of Howard & Lathrop for eight or nine years kept a
miscellaneous store in the old style. In 1824–5 the same
firm built, at South Hadley Falls, on the site of the present Glasgow Mills, the first paper mill erected in Hampshire County, and during more than twenty years Mr.
Lathrop ran it, Mr. Howard remaining here. The enterprise was not successful, however, and in April, 1846, the
firm went into insolvency. The next month a fire swept

---

[1] He married, Sept. 12, 1836, Mrs. Lydia Washburne, widow of Dr.
Lewis Washburne of Bridgewater, Mass., and daughter of Benjamin
and Relief (Dunbar) Ager of Acton, Mass. They had two children:
Wells Lathrop, born Aug. 14, 1844, died young; *Mary Lathrop*, born
Feb. 15, 1847, now the wife of Prof. Fernald of Williams College.
Mrs. Lathrop resides in Williamstown, Mass., with her daughter.

away the mill and its contents. The site was purchased by Joseph Carew, who had been for twenty years their clerk, and who then laid the foundation of his present fortune. Mr. Lathrop became subsequently a landholder in South Hadley (though not himself a practical farmer), and was largely interested with his brother Paoli Lathrop in stock breeding. . . . Politically Mr. Lathrop was formerly an old Whig, but became a Democrat in the " 15 gallon law " times of 1838, along with Ex-Mayor Bemis and many other Whigs of those days; and he was afterwards an active and prominent Democrat, and frequently a delegate to the State and National Conventions. He was one of the founders of the Chicopee Bank; and of one hundred and fifteen corporators of the Unitarian Church he was one of only three who survive, the remaining two being Charles Howard and David Barber. Subsequently, however, he was converted to orthodoxy under the preaching of Rev. Dr. Osgood. A man of positive qualities and strong convictions, he was earnest and enthusiastic in religion, politics, or whatever he undertook; and some of the sharpest and sauciest of the political handbills which were so freely used to fire the hearts of voters thirty and forty years ago were from his pen. For many years past he has been an invalid, and of late has entirely withdrawn from active life. His funeral will take place at South Hadley Falls to-morrow afternoon."

121   II.   Daughter, born Nov. 4, 1803 ; died same day.

122   III.   Daniel Boutecou, born Oct. 23, 1804. He was a sailor, and died in New York of cholera, Aug. 20, 1852.

123   IV.   Martha Potter Boutecou, born in Springfield, 317 Mass., Oct. 10, 1806 ; died in New York City, April 30, 1855. She married, Nov. 25, 1836, Oliver Ellsworth Wood, son of Joseph and Fanny (Ellsworth) Wood of New Haven, Conn. He was born in Stamford, Conn.,

April 14, 1812. Mr. Wood married (2d), Oct. 22, 1863,
Catharine Bontecou Lathrop (315), daughter of Wells
and Catharine Rhodes (Bontecou) Lathrop, and niece of
his first wife. He died at Westport, Conn., Dec. 18, 1883.

From the *New York Herald*, Dec. 20, 1883: — "Mr.
Oliver Ellsworth Wood, a well-known merchant of this
city, died on Tuesday, at Westport, Conn. He was nearly
seventy-two years of age, and was born in Stamford,
Conn. He was a son of Joseph Wood, late judge on
the Connecticut bench, and his grandfather was Oliver
Ellsworth, Chief Justice of the United States Supreme
Court by appointment of President Washington. Mr.
Wood came to New York fifty years ago, and took a position as clerk in the house of Starr & Hoffman, dry-goods
jobbers. In 1836, and from that date until 1844, he was a
member of the formerly well-known firm of Stone, Wood
& Starr, in Cedar Street. About 1844 he formed the
firm of Baldwin, Willard & Wood, a dry-goods commission house, which carried on business until 1861, when
he retired from business, and since that time has been
occupied as a negotiator of securities. In addition to his
business affairs, Mr. Wood found time to attend to the
interests of various benevolent and religious societies.
He was an officer of the Old Brick Church many years
ago, and afterwards a deacon in the Church of the Puri-
tans, Rev. Dr. Cheever's, on Union Square. Of late he
was an elder of the Madison Square Presbyterian Church.
When the Home Insurance Company of this city was
in process of formation in 1853, Mr. Wood acted as
chairman of the preliminary meetings, and on the organization of the company he was elected chairman of one
of the standing committees of the board of directors,
a position which he retained for more than thirty years."

124   V. **Sybil Pease Bontecou,** born in Springfield, Mass.,   **319**
March 31, 1808. She married, Sept. 10, 1828, Richard

Darius Morris, son of Edward and Lucy (Bliss) Morris of Wilbraham, Mass. (South Parish). He was born Aug. 30, 1797. She died in Springfield, Nov. 22, 1851. "Mr. Morris was a member of the Hampden County bar previous to 1837, when he became connected with the Western Railroad (now Boston & Albany), as agent to procure for them the right of way. After the completion of the road he continued in their employ as wood agent, and became well known to all the farmers of Western Massachusetts; and ' 'Squire Morris ' was being constantly called upon to arbitrate between the farmers in their disputes with one another. On the morning of June 21, 1870, he arose in his usual health, passed a half-hour in his garden, came in and lay down on a sofa, and shortly after died. At one time he served on the governor's staff and held the rank of major."

125 **VI. Mary Bontecou**, born Feb. 16, 1810. She married, Feb. 25, 1828, James Worthington of Springfield, a hotel keeper. He died Dec. 15, 1838, aged 33. She afterwards married Charles C. Machette, and died in Springfield, in July, 1846, leaving no children.

CHILDREN OF DANIEL AND HARRIET (BLISS) BONTECOU. **37**

126 1. **William Bontecou**, born Aug. 28, 1817; died Sept. 14, 1817.

127 II. **Harriet Bontecou**, born in Springfield, Mass., **323** Oct. 9, 1818. She married, Aug. 23, 1842, Capt. Henry Morris, son of Edward and Mercy (Flynt) Morris of Wilbraham, Mass., born Feb. 25, 1819. At the age of 15 he entered upon a seafaring life, and was master of a vessel before he had attained his majority. His earlier voyages were made to various parts of the globe, but he finally settled down in the West India trade, and made many voyages between New York and the West India

islands. He was lost at sea early in March, 1844, in
the "Mary Bright," of which he was part owner, though
not in command at the time. His widow married (2d),
Dec. 1, 1859, ¹ Charles Morris, a brother of Henry, as his
second wife. He was born June 6, 1812. He was a
merchant tailor, and resided in Keeseville, Essex County,
N. Y., where he died Jan. 25, 1875. Harriet Bontecou
possessed many admirable traits of character : gentle in
manner, pleasing in conversation, combining the qualities
considered desirable in cultured society with a natural
sweetness of disposition, she made and retained many
friends. A fond wife and loving mother, with strong
domestic attachments, she was early called to mourn the
loss of her husband; which sorrow, combined with the
uncertainty of his fate for a time, proved too great a
strain upon her health, and it gave way and was never
fully recovered. For the last few years of her life she
was a great invalid, but bore her sufferings with fortitude,
meekness, and resignation. She died in Keeseville, Jan.
28, 1872.

128   III.   William Ely Bontecou, born in Springfield,   324
Nov. 1, 1823. He married, Oct. 23, 1849, Caroline Cod-
dington Thayer, daughter of Abraham and Abigail (Bow-

---

¹ Charles Morris was first married in New York City, April 6, 1837,
to Sarah Maria Smith, daughter of Isaac and Lydia (Rogers) Smith.
She died in Keeseville, N. Y., Jan. 26, 1852. Their children are:
    I.   Sarah Maria, born March 22, 1838. Married, Aug. 25, 1863,
         at Keeseville, Charles Clinton Adams of Warren, Ohio,
         a merchant. Their children, born in Warren:
             1.   Jenny Morris, born April 2, 1866.
             2.   Mary, born Aug. 26, 1869.
    II. Charles, born Oct. 12, 1842, married, Aug. 31, 1865, at Fair-
         haven, Vt., Fannie Haywood Cox, daughter of Edward B.
         and Arvilla (Brace) Cox. They reside in St. Louis, Mo.,
         where he is a book-keeper and cashier. They have an
         adopted daughter, Minnie (Daniels), who was born in Alton,
         Ill., Dec. 25, 1867.

ditch) Thayer of Weymouth, Mass., born Jan. 14, 1832.
He commenced his business life in a drug store in Boston,
and afterwards established himself in the same business
in Springfield. This eventually proving a failure, he
subsequently followed the business in New York, Buffalo,
Toledo (Ohio), and San Francisco. He served during
the Civil War as an assistant surgeon in the Navy, and
participated in the battle of Mobile Bay. In the spring
of 1867 he removed to California, and has ever since
remained there, following his profession at times; but,
compelled by ill health to seek open-air pursuits, he has
chiefly engaged in "ranching." He resides at Santa
Rosa.

CHILDREN OF DANIEL UPSON AND MARY BONTECOU.   **38**

129   I. **George Sheering Bontecou,** born May 25, 1796.   **327**
He married, March 28, 1827, Mrs. Martha Baisley, widow
of Abraham Baisley.   She died June 5, 1864.   He was
a baker, and pursued his trade in New York City until
about 1831, when he removed to Newburg, Orange County,
being a portion of the time in business for himself.   He
died there, Jan. 1, 1861.

130   II. **William Henry Bontecou,** born in 1802, and
baptized in Trinity Church, New Haven, July 18, 1804.
He is said to have been a mariner, and lost at sea.   It is
not positively known that he ever married, but the probability is that he did.

131   III. **Mary Bontecou,** born in New Haven in 1804.   **331**
When a child she was adopted by Capt. John A. Thomas
of New Haven, who was subsequently given charge of
Fort Hale, on the East Haven shore of the harbor.   She
married, in 1825, George Washington Bradley, son of
Samuel and Sarah (Bradley) Bradley, who was born in
East Haven in 1797.   He was a sailor by profession, and
sailed as mate between New Haven, Branford, and the
West Indies.   While he was absent on one of his voyages,
his wife died of consumption, March 29, 1827.   He died
(also of consumption) in East Haven, May 16, 1833.

132   IV. **Harriet Bontecou,** born in New York City in   **332**
1812.   She was adopted by a Mrs. Sing of Sing Sing,

N. Y., and brought up there, her parents having died when she was a child. She lost all knowledge of the whereabouts of her brothers and sister, but discovered her brother George after his settlement in Newburg, and went to live in his family. She married in Newburg, May 22, 1836, James Hamilton, born in County Antrim, near the village of Antrim, Ireland, Oct. 10, 1814. His father's family emigrated to America in 1832, and settled in Newburg, where Mr. Hamilton was brought up to the trade of mason; but in 1844 he entered the grocery business, continuing in it as clerk and proprietor for twenty-six years, when he was elected sheriff of Orange County. When his term of office expired, he took up his trade again; but in 1878 was elected coroner, and also holds the office of constable. He resides (1883) at 169 Lander Street, Newburg. His wife died in Newburg, April 5, 1876.

CHILDREN OF ELIAKIM AND SUSANNAH (BONTECOU) BENHAM.   39

133   I. **Julia Elizabeth Benham,** born Oct. 11, 1793.   **340**
She married, March 11, 1813, Norman Hayden, a merchant of New Haven, who was born March 2, 1786, and died March 17, 1820. In 1825 she removed to Smithfield, Isle of Wight County, Va., and engaged in teaching, in which profession she was very successful. She married (2d), Dec. 15, 1831, in Smithfield, Sampson White, a merchant of that place, and died there, Dec. 15, 1865. She was a strict Episcopalian, a most pious Christian, and a woman of great benevolence. Mr. White died April 20, 1867.

134   II. **Susan Clarinda Benham,** born Feb. 11, 1796.   **344**
She married, May 9, 1818, Cleveland Jarman Salter, a merchant of New Haven (son of Daniel Salter), and died Oct. 14, 1820. Mr. Salter afterwards removed to Illinois,

where with several others he founded the town of Waverly. He married (2d), Eliza Cotton of New York City,
and by her had a number of children. He died Jan. 27,
1878.

135   III.   Elisha Mandeville Benham, born in New   346
Haven, Sept. 12, 1800. He married, Aug. 5, 1821, Abby
Kimberly, daughter of Horace and Huldah (Kimberly)
Kimberly of New Haven. She was born in April, 1804.
He was a mariner in early life, and afterwards connected
with mercantile pursuits. On a visit to Virginia under-
taken for the benefit of his failing health, he died in
Smithfield, April 29, 1854. Mr. Benham was a strong
temperance advocate, and member of the popular temperance orders of his day. His widow resides with her
daughter, Mrs. Childs, in Providence, R. I.

136   IV.   Louisa Walter Benham, born in 1802. When a   350
young woman she removed from New Haven to Norwich,
Conn., and opened a school, in which she was assisted
by her sister Harriet. She married, Jan. 21, 1822, Capt.
Francis Wells Bushnell of Norwich, and they went to
housekeeping in what is known as the "Spooner House,"
opposite Breed's Hall on Church Street. He was born in
May, 1796. He was bred a cabinet-maker, but turned
hotel keeper, and was the proprietor of a hotel known as
the Thames House, by the water-side. He afterwards
owned and commanded vessels coasting between Norwich
and New York. Mrs. Bushnell died Sept. 28, 1833, and
Capt. Bushnell again married. He died in Norwich of
consumption, Aug. 22, 1859.

137   V.   Harriet Augusta Benham, baptized July 8,
1804. She was remarkable for her small size when an
infant: her father's finger-ring could be slipped over her
hand and up to her shoulder; but she attained to ordinary

size as she became older. She assisted her sister Louisa in the care of a school at Norwich. She never married, and died at Smithfield, Va., Sept. 3, 1844.

CHILDREN OF AMOS AND ELIZABETH (BONTECOU) HALL.

40

138   I. **Eliza Ann Hall,** born Sept. 21, 1804. She married, June 16, 1824, William Pritchard, son of David and Anne (Hitchcock) Pritchard of Waterbury, Conn., where he was born, March 20, 1800. He was brought up a farmer and stock dealer. In 1831 they removed to Canandaigua, N. Y.; the next year to Ohio, where he bought a farm in Brunswick, Medina County. He continued to deal in stock, shipping to New York by lake and canal, and sometimes driving through on foot. Mrs. Pritchard died in Brunswick, Aug. 18, 1857. After his wife's death he removed to Iowa, and married, Aug. 25, 1859, in Des Moines, Mrs. Delia E. Gordon, as her third husband. He was a member of the Congregational Church. He died in Jefferson, Iowa, Oct. 27, 1884.

355

139   II. **Charles Hall,** born in the western part of the town of Cheshire, Conn., Oct. 12, 1806. He was brought up on his father's farm, and married, Sept. 13, 1830, Amy Moss, daughter of Asahel and Amy (Andrews-Hitchcock) Moss. She was, through her father, a descendant of John Moss, one of the first English settlers of Wallingford, Conn., who died at the age of 103. In May, 1834, Mr. Hall and his wife joined the Congregational Church. In the fall of 1838 he removed with his family to Brunswick, Ohio, and in connection with his brother Amos bought a tract of nearly wild land, which they were obliged to clear of heavy timber before they could put in their first crop of wheat. During his stay in Brunswick he was clerk of the Congregational Church, and connected

364

with the Sabbath School as teacher. In the fall of 1843
he returned to Cheshire and settled on the old homestead,
where he now resides. In 1832 Mr. Hall was commissioned by Governor Peters of Connecticut as a captain in
the 22d Regiment of Militia. He has always been highly
respected in the community, and known as an industrious
and upright man. At the age of 79 he enjoys good health.
Mrs. Hall died Aug. 13, 1875.

140　　III. Nancy Hall, born in November, 1808; mar-　373
ried in 1829 Hiram Bradley of Cheshire. Conn., a manufacturer of wagon materials. He was born in Cheshire,
Oct. 3, 1809, and died April 1, 1876. She died May 4,
1873. They are both buried in Cheshire cemetery.

141　　IV. Amos Hall, Jr., born Feb. 18, 1811. He was　374
a farmer. He married, March 31, 1834, Arpatia Doolittle, daughter of Enos and Millie (Preston) Doolittle of
Cheshire. She was born in 1811, and died Jan. 1, 1876.
He died Aug. 16, 1861. Both are buried in Cheshire
cemetery.

142　　V. George Anson Hall, born in Cheshire, Jan.　377
31, 1814. He married, June 5, 1838, Sarah Merriams,
daughter of Rufus and Sarah (Hotchkiss) Merriams of
Prospect, Conn. She died Oct. 18, 1867. He has always
been a farmer, residing at Cheshire, Prospect, Huntington, and now (1883), in Trumbull, Conn., with his
daughter Mrs. Baldwin.

143　　VI. Susan Salina Hall, born in Cheshire, Oct. 13,　379
1817. She married, Oct. 12, 1839, Henry Livingston of
Brunswick, Ohio, son of Henry G. Livingston, Jr., who
served in the War of 1812, and grandson of Henry G.
Livingston, a major in the Continental Army during the
Revolution. His maternal grandfather was Nathan Swift,
who also served in the Continental Army, and fought in

the battle of Bunker Hill. Mr. Livingston was born in Schodack, Rensselaer County, N. Y., Sept. 18, 1818; at the age of 16 removed to Ohio with his father and settled in Brunswick, where he now resides, engaged in farming. Mrs. Livingston died May 5, 1885.

144   VII. **Henrietta Elizabeth Hall,** born April 30,   **384**
1821. She married Edward Terrell of Waterbury, died Feb. 5, 1870, and is buried in Riverside cemetery. He was born in Waterbury, Jan. 16, 1820. By trade he is a designer and tool-maker, and has been in the employ of the Scoville Manufacturing Company for forty years, having charge of the button-chasing department. He is a member of the Baptist Church, its treasurer, and member of the church committee.

CHILDREN OF DANIEL AND POLLY (BONTECOU) BENE-   **43**
DICT.

145   I. **George Rice Benedict,** born in St. Albans, Vt.,   **385**
July 8, 1802. When a lad of 14 he emigrated to Genesee County, N. Y.; in 1824 removed to Niagara County and settled in the town of Royalton, of which place he continued a resident until his death. He married, Sept. 17, 1827, Laurinda, daughter of Elias Safford of Royalton. She was born Dec. 24, 1808, and in 1882 was still living. Mr. Benedict was one of the earliest settlers of South Royalton, having followed the Indian trail there. In 1837 he united with the Methodist Episcopal Church, and was always one of its strong friends and supporters. For twenty years he held the office of assessor in Royalton. He died Dec. 31, 1872.

146   II. **Julius Hoyt Benedict,** born in St. Albans, Vt.,   **391**
Aug. 5, 1804, where he lived until about twenty years of age, when he removed with his parents to Niagara County, N. Y. He purchased land in Royalton, and owned and

cleared several farms. He married, June 12, 1831, Olive
Crego, daughter of Ruluf D. and Elsie (Strenihen) Crego
of Clarence, Erie County, N. Y. She was born Jan. 9,
1810. In 1839 he left New York State for Michigan,
and after temporarily stopping at Brest, Monroe County,
and Franklin, Oakland County, he settled in Lenawee
County, and engaged in farming about four miles north of
Adrian. In the spring of 1845 he moved into the village, and engaged in the grocery trade. He was an
active, energetic man, and one of the first to engage
in the fur trade, doing a large business with the hunters
and trappers of his region, and journeying as far northwest as St. Paul, mingling with the Indians, and purchasing of them at one time $20,000 worth of furs. He
was a man of sterling integrity and probity, and until
old age and feeble health came upon him, his time was
spent in active business pursuits. He died in Adrian,
April 19, 1876. His wife died Feb. 1, 1871.

147   III. Nancy Rice Benedict, born in St. Albans, Vt.,   396
Oct. 14, 1810. She married, Oct. 16, 1827, George Haynor Utley of Connecticut. He died Dec. 23, 1880. She
was living in 1882, at Rapids, Niagara County, N. Y.

148   IV. Amanda Benedict, born in St. Albans, Vt.,   405
Oct. 17, 1812. She married, Feb. 10, 1830, George Clin-
ton Crego of Clarence, N. Y., and died in Adrian, Mich.,
Nov. 11, 1871. Mr. Crego resides (1882) in Adrian.

CHILDREN OF THADDEUS AND NANCY (BONTECOU) RICE.   44

149   I. Alvin Bontecou Rice, born in St. Albans, Vt.,   414
in 1803. He married Cornelia Smith, daughter of Samuel M. and Theodosia (Waterman) Smith of Vermont,
who was born in 1799. He removed to Erie County,
N. Y., in 1834, and in 1857 to Grand Rapids Township,

Mich., where he died, January, 1862. He was a farmer.
Mrs. Rice died there. Sept. 18, 1872.

150   II. **Charles Benham Rice,** born in St. Albans, Vt.,   **419**
in 1805, and was baptized in Trinity Church, New Haven,
Conn., July 5, 1812. Somewhere between 1835 and 1840
he removed to Buffalo, N. Y. He married Mrs. Alma
Augusta Brooker of Buffalo (born in 1800), widow of
Phipps Waldo Brooker. Her maiden name was Williams.
Mr. Rice served as clerk and steward on Lake steamers.
He died at his home on Delaware Avenue (present number
867), July 26, 1863. Mrs. Rice died in Buffalo, April 23,
1879, aged 79.

CHILDREN OF JAMES AND CLARISSA (BONTECOU) DOU-   **45**
GREY.

151   I. **Hannah Dougrey,** born Dec. 13, 1806. She mar-   **420**
ried, Oct. 5, 1831, James Nichols. He was a native of
England; came to America when a young man, and established himself in the grocery business in Lansingburg,
N. Y. He died suddenly, Sept. 26, 1851. She died July
30, 1872.

152   II. **James Dougrey, Jr.,** born July 13, 1808. He   **424**
married, Oct. 4, 1831, Frances Elizabeth Moulton, daughter of Howard and Elizabeth (Turner) Moulton of Troy,
N. Y. Mr. Dougrey has always resided in Lansingburg
(with the exception of a short time in New York when
a young man), in the same house for seventy-five years;
has been actively engaged in mercantile business; and
has held various positions of trust in his native town, as
assessor, supervisor, justice of the peace, etc. He and
his wife are both living.

153   III. **Clarissa Ann Dougrey,** born Nov. 16, 1809.   **430**
She married, May 6, 1834, Charles Dikeman Smith of
13

Lansingburg. Mr. Smith pursued various lines of business there. He removed to Michigan at an early day in its history, purchased a large tract of land on which the city of Marshall now stands, and built the first frame house there. He held many positions of public trust: county clerk, postmaster, justice of the peace, etc. He afterwards removed to Chicago, and died there, May 3, 1870. Mrs. Smith died at Turner Junction, near Chicago, Aug. 6, 1853.

154   IV. **John Dougrey**, born Oct. 26, 1811; died Nov. 14, 1825.

155   V. **Mary Elizabeth Dougrey**, born May 23, 1818. **435**
She married, May 9, 1839, James Norman Barker, a druggist of Lansingburg. She died in Chicago, Ill., Jan. 24, 1880. He resides (1883) in Lansingburg.

156   VI. **Julia Dougrey**, born March 1, 1821. She married, Dec. 24, 1845, William Brownell Cory of Lansing- **439** burg, a native of Cambridge, N. Y. He was the proprietor of a line of omnibuses running between Lansingburg and Troy, and was at one time in the hotel business. He died Oct. 10, 1854.

CHILDREN OF ANTHONY AND JULIA (BONTECOU)   **47**
BRISTOL.

157   I. **Julia Ann Bristol**, born Dec. 7, 1811. She married, Nov. 30, 1830, Andrew Winton French. He was **441** born in Milford, Conn., Nov. 11, 1811, where he lived until 1867, when, after two years spent in Florida, he settled in Athens, Pa., where he now (1883) resides. He learned the shoemaker's trade, but has been chiefly engaged in clerical duties. His wife died in Milford, June 5, 1868.

158   II. **Henrietta Eliza Bristol**, born Aug. 28, 1813. **445**
She married, Aug. 21, 1842, John Sanford, a merchant of

Milford, Conn. He was a descendant of one of the early settlers of the town; was born there in 1811, and died there, April 2. 1862. Mrs. Sanford died there, Jan. 19, 1885.

159   **III. William Bonteeou Bristoll** (so he spelled his   **448** name) was born in Milford, Conn., April 3, 1815. He learned the coach-trimming and harness-making trade, and remained in the vicinity of Milford and New Haven until 1837, when he removed to Charleston. S. C., and engaged in the shoe trade. He married, Oct. 11, 1838, Sarah A. Merrick, daughter of Harvey Josiah and Melitta (Downs) Merrick of Seymour, Conn. Mr. Bristoll remained at Charleston until the firing upon Fort Sumter, at the beginning of the war, when he returned to Milford, where he died June 28, 1883. He was greatly interested in this genealogical work, and to his energy and enterprise the compiler is indebted for much relating to the Bristol line.

160   **IV. Timothy Mason Bristol,** born Dec. 15, 1816.   **454** He married, Aug. 15, 1844, Jane Matilda McDonough, daughter of Cornelius and Sarah (De Vere) McDonough. She died in New York City, Feb. 24, 1883. Mr. Bristol is engaged in the shoe business at 250 King Street, Charleston, S. C., but the family home is at 165 West 22d Street, New York.

161   **V. Mary Hanford Bristol,** born Nov. 12, 1818.   **461** She married, Aug. 13, 1837, Charles G. Newton, who was born in New Haven in 1816. He removed to Missouri with his father when six years old, but returned to New Haven at the age of 18, and there served an apprenticeship to the carriage-making trade. After his marriage he removed with his wife to the Indian Territory, settling in Tahlequah, the capital of the Cherokee Nation, and

engaged in trade with the Indians. In 1847 they crossed
the border into Washington County, Ark., remaining but
a short time, however, before removing to near Dallas,
Texas. In 1849 or 1850 they removed to Austin, where
she died March 5, 1852. After her death he moved back
to Dallas, and again married. He improved a farm and
lived on it two years, and then moved into the city and
took up his trade. He was a member of the reserve
corps of the Confederate Army during the Civil War, and
detailed to operate machinery in the government shops
in Dallas, receiving no pay for his services. In civil life
he held the office of justice of the peace. Mr. Newton
was originally a Presbyterian, but after his second marriage removed his relations to the Methodist Episcopal
Church. He died in Dallas, Jan. 9, 1872.

162   VI. Nancy Bontecou Bristol, born Jan. 3, 1821. 468
She married, June 23, 1850, Stephen Sears of New Haven,
as his second wife. He was born in Monroe, Conn., Sept.
5, 1815. He engaged in the blacksmith's trade, but after
pursuing it a year or two, met with a severe accident
which deprived him of his left hand, and incapacitated
him from further following the business. He then learned
the coach-painting trade, which he still follows. He resides at 24 Prince Street, New Haven. Mrs. Sears died
in New Haven, Aug. 31, 1885.

163   VII. Thomas Bristol, born in Milford, Conn., Dec. 470
15, 1822. In 1838 he joined his brothers William and
Thomas in Charleston, and remained in their employ
about three years. He then returned to the North, and
commenced the shoe business for himself (William having an interest in it), at 55 Catharine Street, New York.
He married, Aug. 29, 1850, Sarah Brooks, daughter of
Alexander and Sarah (Holgate) Brooks of Factoryville,
Tioga County, N. Y. Their present address is 359 Sixth

Avenue. Mr. Bristol has been a deacon in the Allen Street Presbyterian Church, but both he and his wife are now connected with the Fourth Avenue Presbyterian Church.

164   VIII. A daughter, born and died June 4, 1825.

165   IX. John Dougrey Bristoll, born July 17, 1826. He commenced his business life in his brother Timothy's shoe store in Charleston, but returned North and finally settled in Athens, Pa., where he now (1883) resides. He is not actively engaged in business, and is unmarried.

166   X. James Anthony Bristoll, born March 2, 1829.   472 He married, June 20, 1860, Ellen Martha Page, daughter of Thomas and Anne (West) Page of Athens, Pa. He was employed when a young man by his brother William, in Charleston. From there he removed to Athens, and engaged in the grocery and general store business with his brother-in-law F. N. Page. He is at present in the iron trade, and was employed in the erection of one of the elevated railroads in New York. His home is at Athens.

167   XI. Jane Augusta Bristol, born Dec. 25, 1830. She married, May 3, 1881, Anon Clark of Milford, Conn., as his second wife. Mr. Clark was born in Milford, Feb. 14, 1808. He was a merchant in that town, and always resided there; represented it in the State Legislature in 1846, 1869, and 1870; and died there, Sept. 21, 1884. He was a member of the Baptist Church.

168   XII. Charles Edward Bristol, born April 22, 1834.   478 He married, May 15, 1858, Grace Ann Stowe, daughter of Capt. Elisha Hopkins and Susan (Davidson) Stowe of Milford. He was originally employed by his brothers in the shoe business in Charleston, S. C., but is now a hat maker, and resides in Danbury, Conn.

169   I. Mary Ann Hanford, born Oct. 22, 1814. She   **486**
married, May 19, 1834, Francis Wright Jesup, and died
Oct. 31. 1863. He died Nov. 22, 1876. Their place of
residence was Westport, Conn.

170   II. Richard Bontecou Hanford, born Feb. 24,
1816; died May 9, 1851, unmarried. He was employed
as a clerk in his father's business.

171   III. Julia Bristol Hanford, born Oct. 23, 1819.   **491**
She married, April 25, 1839, Horace White Day. He is
a native of Saratoga County, N. Y., and in early life settled in Lansingburg, and commenced his business career
as a clerk in the dry-goods business; became a merchant,
and is still in business with his son Hanford. For many
years he was connected with the bank of Lansingburg,
as director, vice-president, and president. He is one of
the wardens of Trinity Church. Mrs. Day died in April,
1885.

172   IV. Harriet Pynchon Hanford, born Nov. 16, 1830.   **493**
She married, April 28, 1851, George Abbott Lally, a suc-
cessful merchant of Lansingburg. He died June 27, 1881.
Mrs. Lally resides in Lansingburg.

173   V. Levi Cooley Hanford, born in Lansingburg, July   **496**
5, 1833. He married, Oct. 11, 1861, Margaret Good-
man, daughter of Thomas and Elizabeth (Wool) Goodman of Lansingburg, born Nov. 22, 1837. They reside
at Norwalk, Conn., where he is superintendent of the Gas
Light Company.

CHILDREN OF ANSON AND HENRIETTA (BONTECOU) **50**
SMITH.

174   **I. Richard Hanford Smith,** born July 11, 1823; died in 1846, at Saltillo, Mexico, where he was in the service of his country as a soldier.

175   **II. James Dougrey Smith,** born Aug. 17, 1825; drowned Oct. 6, 1834.

176   **III. Francis Smith,** born in New Haven, Nov. 19, **500** 1827. He married, April 10, 1851, Mary Jane Prindle, from whom he was afterwards divorced. She was the daughter of Isaac and Mary R. (Riggs) Prindle of Simsbury, Conn. Mr. Smith is a mason by trade, and a life-·long resident of New Haven. For several years he filled the office of lieutenant of police. He enlisted in the 12th Regiment, Connecticut Volunteers, and was mustered in as a sergeant in Company F, Nov. 19, 1861. Sept. 20, 1862, he was promoted to the second-lieutenancy of the same company, and Dec. 9, 1863, was appointed first lieutenant of Company H, of which he became captain Dec. 2, 1864. He was wounded in the thigh at the battle of Cedar Creek, Va., Oct. 19, 1864. He married (2d), Feb. 26, 1875, Mrs. Julia Maria Allen of New Haven, widow of Charles Allen, and daughter of Benjamin Tyler and Julia Ann (Baldwin) Henry. Her father was the inventor of the Henry rifle. There are no children by the second marriage.

177   **IV. Clarissa Ann Smith,** born Sept. 12, 1829; died Aug. 29, 1830.

178   **V. Clarissa Ann Smith,** born March 3, 1831. She **502** married, May 19, 1851, Charles Edwin Stannard, and died in Brooklyn, N. Y., Nov. 16, 1864. Mr. Stannard was born in Guilford, Conn., Jan. 24, 1828. He learned

the bookbinder's trade in New Haven, and remained in that city until 1851, when he removed to New York, and two years later to Brooklyn, E. D., where he now resides at 168 Lee Avenue. He married (2d), May 1, 1879, Miss Sarah Jane Viele.

179   VI. **George Smith**, born Sept. 30, 1832; died July 30, 1851.

180   VII. **Mary Jesup Smith**, born March 19, 1834.   504
She married, Oct. 8, 1855, Charles William Strong of Milford, Conn., a shoemaker. He died Oct. 18, 1857. She resides in Milford.

181·   VIII. **Hannah Eliza Smith**, born Dec. 19, 1836.   505
She married, Nov. 30, 1854, George R. Munson, who was born in Milford, Conn., Nov. 27, 1831. They reside in Cincinnati, Ohio. He is a merchant.

CHILD OF WILLIAM B. AND NANCY (BONTECOU) THOMAS.   53

182   I. **Julia Ann Thomas**, born Jan. 7, 1824; died Feb. 12, 1832.

CHILDREN OF MENEMON AND HARRIET (BONTECOU)   57
SANFORD.

183   I. **Thomas Bontecou Sanford**, born in New Haven, Oct. 25, 1816. He married, June 3, 1846, Elizabeth Prentice Taylor, daughter of Abner and Anna (Hammond) Taylor of Bangor, Me. She was born in Bangor, Sept. 18, 1819, and died Sept. 5, 1876. Mr. Sanford was engaged in steamboating, first as clerk and afterward as master. After his marriage he settled in Bangor. He died March 4, 1858. They had no children.

184   II. **Susan Bontecou Sanford**, born in New Haven, Sept. 5, 1818; died July 13, 1875, unmarried.

185   III.   Asa Menemon Sanford, born in New Haven,   507
March 19, 1821. He married, April 10, 1842, Lucinda
Kidder, daughter of Samuel and Harriet Kidder of New
York. He commenced steamboating as clerk, and became
master at the age of 21. He resided in New York until
the spring of 1849, when he removed his residence to
Chelsea, Mass. On the 9th of September of the same
year he died in Bangor, Me. Mrs. Sanford is living
(1883).

186   IV.   Edward Huntington Sanford, born in New   510
Haven, June 1, 1823. He married, Dec. 19, 1846, Mary
Foster, daughter of John and Nancy (Dillaway) Foster
of Boston. She was born Nov. 5, 1827. He became
master of a steamboat when about twenty-one years old,
having previously served as clerk. After his marriage
he settled in Boston. He died in St. Catharines, Ont.,
Sept. 27, 1865. Mrs. Sanford died in October, 1862.

187   V.   William Higby Bontecou Sanford, born in New
Haven, July 11, 1825. Like his brothers he entered the
steamboat service, and became master at the age of 21.
He resided in New York. June 10, 1864, he sailed
as passenger in the ship " Blenheim," bound on a voyage
to the Pacific. The ship was spoken June 20, but was
never heard from subsequently. He had previously made
voyages to California in 1849, Europe in 1858, and China
in 1859 and 1862. He was unmarried.

188   VI.   Charles Benjamin Sanford, born in New   511
Haven, May 23, 1828. He married, June 23, 1850,
Frances Pomeroy Taylor, daughter of Abner and Anna
(Hammond) Taylor of Bangor, and sister of his brother
Thomas's wife. She was born April 18, 1829, and died
July 20, 1858. He married (2d), Nov. 28, 1860, Marie
Taylor French, daughter of George Smith and Anna

14

Sophia (Taylor) French. She was born Aug. 18, 1836, and died in Brooklyn, N. Y., June 15, 1874. There were no children by this marriage. Charles B. Sanford commenced as a steamboat clerk, and became master in 1850, continuing as such until 1876, when he retired. After his first marriage he settled in Bangor, Me., but in 1852 removed to Brooklyn, N. Y. In 1859 he returned to Bangor, remaining until 1857, when he removed to Fort Point, Me., where he now resides.

189   VII. **Maria Huntington Sanford,** born in New Haven, Aug. 2, 1830; died in New York, Oct. 8, 1857, unmarried.

190   VIII. **Harriet Ann Sanford,** born in New Haven, Oct. 23, 1832; resides (1883) at Oakland, Cal.

191   IX. **James Thompson Sanford,** born in Hartford, Conn., June 10, 1835. He resided in New York for many years, as manager of Sanford's lines of steamers, between Boston and Bangor, and New York and Philadelphia. Some years ago he removed to California, where he was interested in coal-mining operations, and died May 2, 1885, in San Francisco. He was unmarried. To him the compiler is indebted for most of the data relating to this branch.

192   X. **George Washington Sanford,** born in Hartford, Jan. 9, 1839; died at Flushing Bay, L. I., Aug. 11, 1870. He never married, and was never engaged in active business.

193   XI. **Josephine Leonora Sanford,** born in New York, Feb. 13, 1841; resides (1883) at Oakland, Cal.

194   XII. **David Stebins Sanford,** born in New York, July 8, 1843; died Oct. 19, 1845.

CHILDREN OF ZACHEUS AND ELIZABETH (HOOD) MAPLES.   62

195   I. Elizabeth Hood Maples, born Feb. 12, 1821 ; died Feb. 27, 1821, in New Haven, Conn.

196   II. Sarah Elizabeth Maples, born Dec. 17, 1822 ; died Sept. 22, 1846, in New Haven, unmarried.

197   III. Adaline Sale Maples, born Feb. 14, 1824. She has never married.

198   IV. Maria Louise Maples, born Nov. 23, 1827 ; died Jan. 24, 1869, in Brooklyn, N. Y., unmarried.

199   V. James Bixby Maples, born May 22, 1829 ; died in Kingston, N. C., Aug. 3, 1855. He was a carriage trimmer.

200   VI. Charles Reese Maples, born April 1, 1832. He learned the trade of machinist at the Secor Iron Works, New York. In 1862 he entered the United States Navy, and was attached to the gunboat "Gertrude" as chief engineer; served about a year, and then resigned and accepted a position as manager of the Columbia Iron Works, at Columbia, Pa., where he remained for twelve or thirteen years. He married, in Columbia, Mrs. Ann Mack. They had no children. His present place of residence is unknown.

201   VII. Edward William Maples, born June 25, 1836.   513 He married, Oct. 21, 1858, Ellen Agnes Gillen, daughter of Hugh and Ann Gillen of Brooklyn, N. Y. Mr. Maples partly learned the machinist's trade, but abandoned it, and became a salesman in the window-shade line, in which he still continues. In June, 1863, he entered the United States Navy, and was attached to the United States gunboat "Iuka" as third assistant engineer: participated in the battle of Mobile Bay, and resigned on

account of ill health. in February, 1864. He resides at 162 Adelphi Street, Brooklyn, N. Y.

CHILD OF ROSWELL AND ABBY MEEKER (BEACH) HOOD.   67

202   I. James Bontecou Hood, born Feb. 5, 1840. He married, May 21, 1864, Harriet Searles, daughter of Julius P. and Mary (Wright) Searles of New Haven. She died Dec. 31, 1865. He married (2d), May 22, 1871, Mrs. Maria Kingsbury Scranton, widow of John H. Scranton, and daughter of Chancelor and Lucy (Rowe) Kingsbury of Fair Haven, Conn. No children by either marriage. Mr. Hood is not actively engaged in business. His home is at 77 William Street, New Haven.

CHILD OF CHARLES HUBBARD AND SARAH (KEELER)   68
BONTECOU.

203   I. Margaret Pynchon Bontecou, born March 14, 1827; resides in Lansingburg, N. Y.

CHILDREN OF EBEN NORTON AND SARAH PARMALEE   80
(MERRIMAN) THOMSON.

204   I. Sarah Cornelia Thomson, born Oct. 8, 1818. 516 She married, Oct. 8, 1838, George Rice of New Haven, a dry-goods merchant. She resides at 40 Elm Street.

205   II. Juliet Mayer Thomson, born April 10, 1821. 520 She married, July, 1843, William North, a lawyer of Elmira, N. Y. He was born in Goshen, Conn., in 1816; removed to Elmira with his parents in early life. He died Sept. 21, 1844. She married (2d). June 2, 1850, Horatio Nelson Lyman of New Haven, as his second wife. He is the son of Erastus Lyman, and was born in Goshen, Conn., May 2, 1804. He was a merchant there for many years. but subsequently removed to Waterbury, Conn.. and finally to New Haven, where they now reside, at 209 Orange Street.

206   III.   **William Sparks Thomson,** born March 22, **523**
1823.   He married, Jan. 8, 1850. Jane Lewis, daughter
of Henry and Martha (Nash) Lewis of Farmington,
Conn.   They reside in London, England.

207   IV.   **Mary Nicholson Thomson,** born Aug. 19, 1825;
died in New Orleans, Sept. 11, 1847.

208   V.   **Charles Thomson,** born June 18, 1827; died Jan.
10, 1828.

209   VI.   **Eliza Lyman Thomson,** born April 21, 1831.   **526**
She married, June 8, 1858, William Nettleton of Stock-
bridge, Mass.   He was educated at Williams College, but
left before graduation on account of ill health.   He is
engaged in the manufacture of corsets.   They reside in
Bridgeport, Conn.

210   VII.   **Charles Henry Thomson,** born in New Haven,   **530**
Dec. 5, 1836.   He married, Nov. 23, 1858. Cecile Lewis,
daughter of Henry and Martha (Nash) Lewis of Farmington, Conn.   She died Dec. 4, 1860.   Mr. Thomson was
brought up to the dry-goods trade.   At the age of eighteen went into business with his brother William, and continued in the partnership, both in America and Europe,
until 1868, at which time he retired from mercantile
business.   Mr. Thomson has been an extensive traveler,
and for many years resided in England, France, and Ger-
many.   His home is now in New Haven, at 40 Elm Street.

CHILDREN OF GEORGE AND POLLY (STORER) MILES.   85

211   I.   **George Washington Miles,** born Nov. 24, 1807;
died at Erie, Pa., Feb. 27, 1826.

212   II.   **Mary Augusta Miles,** born July 16, 1809.   She   **531**
married at Erie, June 10, 1831. Thomas McConkey.   He
was deputy United States collector of the port of Erie,

and was drowned May 14, 1834, by the upsetting of a sail-
boat, by which seven out of nine were lost; his brother-
in-law, Thomas II. Miles, being one of the saved. Mrs.
McConkey died in Erie, June 4, 1872.

Extract from Miss L. Sanford's *History of Erie County,
Pa.:* — "The morning of the 14th of May, 1834, was
very bright and balmy, and it bade fair to be a day
unusually pleasant. The steamer 'New York,' commanded by Capt. Miles (father-in-law of young Mr.
McConkey) anchored at the outer pier. The yacht
belonging to the collector of customs was immediately
put in readiness. Previous to this, Capt. James Maurice,
a very intimate friend of Mr. McConkey, said to him
(perhaps at the breakfast table), 'Don't be afraid, Tom,
of drowning: a man born to be hung will never be
drowned.' Just before he started, a woman came to see
him, and said she wanted to go aboard the boat and take
some clothing to her husband, who was one of the crew of
the 'New York'; but he refused, and she then said, 'If
it is safe for you to go, it is safe for me.' This woman
accompanied Mr. McConkey; and the yacht started with
eleven on board. There was a gentle breeze from the
west. This was between eight and nine o'clock. When
she had proceeded about half-way, the sky became suddenly dark, and there arose one of the most terrific
storms known on the lake. The waves lashed in relent-
less fury, the boat capsized, and all but two found a
watery grave. The *snow* came down in sheets, as it were;
and a gentleman informed the writer that when he heard
of the accident he hurried to the bank: the storm was
raging furiously, and by the time he got there, there were
six inches of snow on the ground. Thomas (son of
Capt. Miles) was saved by clinging to the boat, and when
rescued, life was nearly extinct. The body of Thomas
McConkey was not recovered for eleven days afterward.

Capt. James Maurice was appointed deputy in his place, and while proceeding in his official capacity discovered an elbow out of the water, and immediately recognized the body as that of Capt. McConkey."

213   III. John William Miles, born in October, 1811. 532
He married, Oct. 21, 1834, Catharine Donnell, daughter of John and Frances Donnell of Buffalo, N. Y. Mr. Miles was for many years an engineer on lake steamers running between Buffalo and Chicago. His residence was at Erie, Pa. He died very suddenly, of cholera, at Buffalo, Aug. 18, 1850, being perfectly well at six o'clock, and dead before midnight. He was engineer of the steamer " Louisiana " at this time. His widow is living (1883) at 17 Second Street, Erie, Pa.

214   IV. Thomas Henry Miles, born Feb. 14, 1815, in 539
New Haven, in the midst of the rejoicing over the news that peace with England had been declared. When he was two years old his parents removed to Pennsylvania, but he remained with his grandfather in New Haven until the death of the latter, when he was 12. At the age of 16 he repaired to Buffalo, N. Y. (from Erie, Pa., where his parents lived), and spent two years learning the watchmaking business. He then tried a sailor's life on the Lakes for two seasons, and in May, 1834, was nearly drowned in Erie Bay. In November of that year he sailed from New York on board the ship " Panama," for a voyage to China. He writes : " Coasting in the China Sea forty-eight years ago was not as pleasant as it might have been, having to look out for the Ladrone pirates on one hand and typhoons on the other." He reached New York again in 1836, and after a period spent in coasting out of New York and New Haven, returned again to the Lakes, and from 1837 to 1850 was engaged in steamboating. The latter year he retired from the business; and on

Jan. 3, 1856, was married to Henrietta Miner Brown, daughter of Jacob and Henrietta (Miles) Brown, and settled down to a farmer's life. They reside at New Richmond, Pa.

215   V. **Susan Storer Miles**, born in New Richmond, Pa.,   541 May 4, 1818. She married, Oct. 25, 1840, Elias Handy Halliday. He was born in Canastota, Madison County, N. Y., Sept. 2, 1815; removed to Erie, Pa., in 1836, and lived there, and at Cleveland and Massillon, Ohio, engaged in mercantile business, until the fall of 1843, when he removed to Lafayette, Ind., and after ten years spent in mercantile business there, engaged with others in a contract to build a portion of the Toledo and Wabash Railway. During the progress of this work he died, Nov. 20, 1857. His widow died in Cleveland, Ohio, May 12, 1876.

216   VI. **Harriet Elizabeth Miles**, born in New Richmond, Pa., Oct. 9, 1821. She married, July 18, 1861, Rev. Nathaniel Peck Charlot. He was born in Morristown, N. J., in 1810, from which place he removed with his parents to Pennsylvania, and when he was about eleven years old, to the eastern part of Ohio. He graduated from Franklin College, Ohio, in 1835, and in 1837 was ordained to the ministry of the Presbyterian Church, and was settled at Sharon, Ohio. In 1847 he went as a missionary to Texas, and labored at different points for about five years, when he left the Presbyterian and united with the Protestant Episcopal Church. After his ordination in this, he became rector of St. Paul's Church, Cold Springs, Texas, and afterwards of St. Matthew's, at Richmond in the same State, where he was laboring when the War of the Rebellion broke out, and he was obliged to seek safety at the North, which he accomplished with no little difficulty. In a few months after reaching the

State of Indiana, he was appointed chaplain of the 22d Regiment of Volunteer Infantry, and served with them through the war. At its close he became rector of St. Paul's Church, Collamer, Ohio, and later of St. Matthew's, East Plymouth, Ohio; from which, in 1877, he removed to Preëmption, Ill., and accepted the rectorship of St. John's Church. In July, 1882, they removed back to Collamer. They have had no children.

217   VII. George Washington Miles, born in Erie,   549 Pa., Aug. 10, 1829. He married, Oct. 10, 1856, Maria Louise Kendrick, daughter of Stewart Brown and Maria (Houghtaling) Kendrick of Glens Falls, N. Y. They resided at Logansport, Ind., where he was engaged in the banking business. He died there, Aug. 11, 1861. Mrs. Miles resides (1883) at Saratoga, N. Y.

CHILDREN OF PETER AND HANNAH ELIZA (WOODRUFF)   86 STORER.

218   I. Nathaniel Storer, born April 11, 1814; drowned in crossing the Sacramento River, Cal., July 8, 1850. He was unmarried.

219   II. John Peter Storer, born June 4, 1817; died Sept. 20, 1827.

220   III. Timothy Storer, born May 25, 1818; married Augusta A. Hyde of Baltimore, Md. At one time he was United States collector at the port of Benicia, Cal. He now (1883) resides at Virginia City, Nevada.

221   IV. Susan Storer, born Feb. 2, 1820. She married,   551 Oct. 21, 1840, Frederick Boric Hedge of Chatham, Conn., who was born Nov. 2, 1817. He is a ship-carpenter. They reside in Brookhaven, L. I.

CHILDREN OF CHAUNCEY AND HANNAH AUGUSTA   88
(STORER) IVES.

222   I.   Elizabeth Mary Ives, born Nov. 5, 1821. She resides at 146 Livingston Street, Brooklyn, N. Y.

223   I.   James Merritt Ives, born March 5, 1824. He   557 married, June 24, 1846, Caroline Clark, daughter of Dr. Nathan Satterlee and Beulah (Sterns) Clark of Clinton-ville, N. Y. Mr. Ives is a publisher of popular pictures, at 115 Nassau Street, New York. He held a captain's commission in Company F, 23d Regiment, New York State National Guard; served a brief period in Pennsylvania at the time of Lee's invasion of that State during the Rebellion; was on the march to Gettysburg when Lee commenced his retreat, and followed his forces to Falling Waters, where he crossed to Virginia. He resides in Rye, Westchester County, N. Y.

224   III.   John Henry Ives, born April 20, 1826; died in infancy.

225   IV.   George Henry Ives, born in New York, May 2,   564 1830. He married, Jan. 24, 1851, in New York, Margaret Gibbens, daughter of John and Margaret (Ryan) Gibbens of Waterford, Ireland. Mr. Ives removed to Philadelphia when quite a young man, and established himself in the stationery business, in which he continued until his death, which occurred March 1, 1871. His widow resides at 2127 Aubrey Place, Philadelphia.

226   V.   Augustus Chauncey Ives, born April 29, 1835; died in infancy.

CHILDREN OF GROVE AND LYDIA (STORER) SMITH.   89

227   I.   George Miles Smith, born Jan. 12, 1824; died March 13, 1845.

228   II.   Henry Wilson Smith, born Aug. 20, 1826; died June 2, 1831.

229   III.   Edward Grove Smith, born June 16, 1827; died Aug. 30, 1848.

230   IV.   Mary Augusta Smith, born Dec. 25, 1829. She resides at 146 Livingston Street, Brooklyn, N. Y.

CHILDREN OF CHARLES PARSONS AND JANE (BONTECOU)   91
BISHOP.

231   I.   James Bontecou Bishop, born in New Haven, July 17, 1834.   He married, Nov. 16, 1875, at Long Branch, N. J., Marie Baldwin DeKlyn, daughter of John B. and Rhoda (Little) DeKlyn. They reside at No. 11 Fair Street, New Haven, Conn. He is a jeweler. They have no children.

232   II.   Grace Caroline Bishop, born in New Haven,   575
Sept. 11, 1837. She married, May 7, 1867, Dr. Edward Bulkeley, son of Edward and Lucy (Mansfield) Bulkeley of New Haven, where he was born May 15, 1833. Dr. Bulkeley graduated from the medical department of Yale College in 1856, and practiced his profession in New Haven until 1861, when he received the appointment of assistant surgeon in the 6th Regiment Connecticut Volunteers. After three years' service he was appointed volunteer·acting assistant surgeon in the United States Army, and assigned to duty on the hospital transport " Cosmopolitan," from Charleston to New York. Remaining in this service six months, he was then assigned to hospital duty at Harewood General Hospital, Washington, with Dr. R. B. Bontecou, where he served nearly a year. He then returned to New Haven and resumed the practice of medicine. He died there Nov. 5, 1880. Mrs. Bulkeley resides in New Haven.

116   BONTECOU FAMILY.

CHILDREN OF ELISHA AND GRACE (BONTECOU) PECK.   92

233   I. Evelina Peck, born in New Haven, Oct. 5, 1834.   580
She married, Nov. 19, 1857, Capt. William Whittemore
Low of the United States Navy. He was the son of
Henry Somes and Mary Ann Low, and was born in Boston, Mass., April 15, 1825. He entered the navy as a midshipman in 1841, and spent thirty-six years in the service,
twenty-one of them at sea. He was actively engaged
during the Civil War, principally in the operations against
the city of Mobile, in command of the gunboat "Octo-
rara"; the fire from this vessel caused the evacuation
of Forts Huger and Tracy. In all Capt. Low's naval
career, no one act secured for him so much commendation
as his destruction of the piratical steamer "Forward," on
the coast of Mexico, in the year 1870. While in command of the United States gunboat "Mohican," in going
from San Francisco down the coast of Mexico, Capt.
Low learned that the "Forward" had sacked the town
of Guaymas and taken captive an American citizen, and
was on its way down the coast to plunder other cities, and
it was reported also to capture, if possible, the Panama
steamer, then heavily laden with treasure. Having made
international law a study, he decided that according to the
law of nations the "Forward" was a pirate; and acting
on his own responsibility, pursued, captured, and destroyed
her. Capt. Low was in command of the United States
ship "Tennessee," on the coast of China, when he contracted the disease which eventually resulted in his death.
He returned to the United States on sick leave in July,
1876, and died at Frankford Arsenal, Philadelphia, June
24, 1877. Mrs. Low resides at 129 Wooster Street, New
Haven.

234   II. Joanna Bontecou Peck, born in New Haven,   584
March 1, 1837. She married, June 24, 1863, Captain

James Madison Whittemore of the United States Army.
He is the son of Dr. James M. Whittemore, and was
born in Brighton, Mass., March 4, 1836. He entered the
United States Military Academy at West Point in June,
1855, and graduated in July, 1860. He served through
the War of the Rebellion, at first as lieutenant of artillery, but was transferred to the ordnance department,
Sept. 27, 1861. He was stationed at Fort Pickens, Fla.,
from Feb. 7 to Oct. 25, 1861, being engaged in repelling
the Confederate night attack on Santa Rosa Island,
Oct. 9. From thence he was transferred to Washington
Arsenal as assistant ordnance officer, Oct. 28, remaining
in that position until Jan. 27, 1862. From the latter
date till April 18 he assisted in covering the defenses of
Washington, and then was at Frankford Arsenal, Philadelphia, till Aug. 29. He was then assigned to duty at
the Military Academy at West Point, as assistant professor of mathematics, and May 3, 1863, received his
commission as captain of ordnance. He remained at
West Point until Jan. 27, 1864, when he was appointed
to the command of the Indianapolis Arsenal, remaining
in that position till Sept. 15, 1866. From there he was
transferred to the Watervliet Arsenal at West Troy, N. Y.,
which place he left in November, 1868, for the Watertown
(Mass.) Arsenal, leaving there in 1869 to take command
of the Kennebec Arsenal at Augusta, Me. June 23, 1874,
he received his commission as major. In 1876 he was
transferred from Augusta to the Frankford Arsenal at
Philadelphia. Aug. 2, 1879, he was commissioned lieutenant-colonel, and in 1880 was assigned to duty in the
office of the chief of ordnance at Washington, where at
this time (1883) he still remains.

235   III.   **Henry Lewis Peck,** born in New Haven, Jan.
4, 1839. He enlisted in 1861 in Company G, 7th Regiment Connecticut Volunteers, and took part in the cap-

ture of Fort Pulaski, the battle of Pocotaligo, the operations on Morris Island resulting in its capture and the
destruction of Fort Sumter, and the battle of Olustee,
Fla. In the spring of 1864 the regiment joined the
Army of the James and engaged in the battle of Drury's
Bluff, and the battles and skirmishes of that summer on
the Bermuda Hundred front, north of the James River,
and before Petersburg. His term of service in the army
having expired, he entered the navy as captain's clerk,
and was on blockade duty in Mobile Bay till the close of
the war. After the war he engaged in various pursuits,
being five years in the navy, mostly in Asiatic waters,
on board the United States flag-ship "Tennessee," Capt.
William W. Low (his brother-in-law), and making the
tour of the world. He has never married, and resides
(1883) at 129 Wooster Street, New Haven.

CHILDREN OF WILLIAM AND REBECCA (TROWBRIDGE)   94
TOWNSEND.

236   I. Henry Alonzo Townsend, born Oct. 17, 1833;
died March 1, 1841.

237   II. Charles Timothy Townsend, born Oct. 17,   585
1833, in New Haven. He married, Oct. 25, 1855, Elizabeth Augusta Ford, daughter of Harvey and Bessey
(Coutes) Ford of Hamden, Conn. She died, April 17,
1861, aged 27, without children. He married (2d), May
20, 1863, Adella Josephine Barnes, daughter of Zerah
and Abigail S. (Donns) Barnes of New Haven. Mr.
Townsend served an apprenticeship to the carriage-making trade, and at the age of 22 engaged in business
for himself, in which he has since successfully continued.
His factory is on Charles Street, and his residence at 246
Dixwell Avenue, New Haven.

238   III.   James Edwin Townsend, born Dec. 10, 1835;
died Feb. 18, 1853.

239   IV.   Emily Rebecca Townsend, born Oct. 20, 1837 ;
died Feb. 5, 1844.

CHILDREN OF JAMES AND CHARITY (CANNON) TROW-   95
BRIDGE.

240   I.   Marcus Henry Trowbridge, born in New Haven,   586
March 27, 1827. He married, May 7, 1854, Harriet Gunn,
daughter of Medad Hunt and Anne (Decker) Gunn of
Windham, N. Y.   Mr. Trowbridge removed to Catskill,
N. Y., with his father, and learned the printer's trade.
In 1845, when only eighteen years of age, he took up the
publication of the *Catskill Examiner*, and still continues
it. He is a prominent man in his community, and has
frequently been solicited to accept public office, but has
always declined, preferring to devote his time to the publication of his paper.

241   II.   Sarah Rebecca Trowbridge, born May 19, 1829.
Resides in Catskill.

242   III.   Imogene Trowbridge, born Jan. 3, 1835. Resides in Catskill.

CHILDREN OF CHARLES AND EMILY (SCOTT) TROW-   97
BRIDGE.

243   I.   Sarah Malinda Trowbridge, born Sept. 23, 1831;
died Aug. 10, 1856.

244   II.   Emily Trowbridge, born June 15, 1834. Resides in Catskill, N. Y.

245   III.   Hobart Trowbridge, born in Catskill, Sept.   588
1, 1837. He married, April 5, 1868, Katharine V. W.

Miller, daughter of Cornelius and Mary (Van Wagenen) Miller of Hudson, N. Y. He died at Hudson, Nov. 9, 1869. He held clerical positions in various lines of business at Catskill and Albany, and had established himself in the general grocery trade at Hudson a short time before his death.

246 **IV. Charles Trowbridge, Jr.,** born in Catskill, 589 Sept. 24, 1840. He married, Nov. 19, 1873, Mary Joesbury, daughter of Joseph and Eliza (West) Joesbury of Birmingham, England. He learned the business of watchmaking, but never practiced it. He was for a short time established in the grocery trade at Catskill, but abandoned it and entered the employ of his father in the chandlery business, and at his father's death became his successor in the business.

247 **V. Caroline Louisa Trowbridge,** born March 8, 1845. Resides in Catskill.

248 **VI. Harriet Augusta Trowbridge,** born April 3, 1847. Resides in Catskill.

CHILD OF PETER AND SEMANTHA (BROCKWAY) BON- 99 TECOU.

249 **I. Reed Brockway Bontecou,** born in Troy, N. Y., $\left\{ \begin{array}{l} 590 \\ 630 \end{array} \right.$ April 22, 1824. He married, July 18, 1849, Susan Northrup, daughter of Moses and Susanna (Bontecou, 101) Northrup. She was born Jan. 11, 1828. "He received his education in the public schools of Troy, Rensselaer Polytechnic Institute (Troy), and Poultney, Vt., Academy; attended the medical department of the University of New York; graduated from the Castleton, Vt., Medical College, in May, 1847, and at once entered into practice with Dr. Brinsmade of Troy, with whom he had at one time studied his profession. He has always resided in his

native city. In 1846 he made a voyage up the Amazon River, passing the whole of that year exploring that region in the interests of natural science. He is a member of the Rensselaer County Medical Society, the New York Medical Society, and the American Medical Association. For several years he held the offices of coroner and examining surgeon for pensions; also acting assistant United States surgeon at Watervliet Arsenal, in West Troy. Dr. Bontecou held the office of surgeon of the Second Regiment New York Volunteers, from its organization in April until September, 1861, when he was commissioned surgeon of volunteers, and given charge of the Hygiene United States Army General Hospital at Fortress Monroe, Va., where he remained until its destruction in September, 1862. He was then ordered to the Army of the Potomac and placed on duty in the Surgeon-General's office for a short time, after which he was given charge of one of the hospitals at Beaufort, S. C., and subsequently appointed chief medical officer of all the hospitals there. He afterwards had charge of the hospital steamer 'Cosmopolitan,' lying off Charleston during the siege of that city. In October, 1863, he was ordered to Washington, D. C., to take charge of the Harewood United States Army General Hospital, where he continued on duty until its discontinuance in May, 1866; and in June of the same year he was mustered out of the service. He was brevetted colonel of volunteers, March 13, 1865, for faithful and meritorious services during the war. Dr. Bontecou was one of the largest contributors to the *Surgical History of the War*, and to the army medical museum."

CHILDREN OF PETER AND SOPHIA (THOMPSON) BON-   **99**
TECOU.

250   I. James Bontecou, born July 19, 1829. He removed to the far West in 1852, and after various vicis-
16

situdes found himself in Gibbonsville, Idaho Territory, where he remained until his death, which occurred Oct. 31, 1882. He was a bright, companionable man; a fine linguist, being proficient in the use of four or five languages. He was unmarried.

251   II. **Semantha Brockway Bontecou**, born in Troy, 595
N. Y., Aug. 21, 1831. She married there, Jan. 9, 1854, James Keeler Selleck, born in Troy, Aug. 21, 1831. He was engaged in mercantile business in his native city until 1861, when he removed to Hudson County, N. J., and engaged in the purchase, improvement, and sale of real estate. In 1873-4 he represented the Eighth District of Hudson County in the State Legislature. His wife died at Homestead, N. J., Dec. 5, 1873. Mr. Selleck subsequently married Miss Kate Curtis, daughter of Stiles Curtis of Norwalk, Conn. They reside in New York, where he is engaged in the interests of silver mining in California.

252   III. **David Bontecou**, born July 7, 1833, died Dec. 17, 1836.

253   IV. **Julia Bontecou**, born in Troy, Sept. 17, 1835. 605
She married, June 23, 1856, Wilbur F. Goss, son of a Methodist clergyman. He died in Troy, in May, 1869. She died there, Dec. 13, 1877.

254   V. **George Bontecou**, born Dec. 14, 1837; died June 23, 1841.

255   VI. **David Bontecou**, born Oct. 5, 1839; died Oct. 3, 1872, unmarried.

256   VII. **Elizabeth Bontecou**, born in Troy, Nov. 2, 609
1841. She married, June 18, 1863, John William Alfred Cluett, born in Wolverhampton, England, June 10, 1834.

His father was a book dealer in Wolverhampton and Birmingham, and in 1850 emigrated with his family to America, and established himself in the same business in Troy. In 1858, Mr. Cluett, who had for some years been employed as clerk in a linen-collar manufactory, became a partner in his father's business; but in 1863 both father and son gave up the book business, and were admitted into the collar business with George B. Cluett, a brother of John. The business has been very successful, and their present factory is one of the largest in the trade. J. W. A. Cluett is the inventor of several valuable and well-known improvements in the manufacture of shirts, collars, and cuffs. He is a hard student, and his time away from his business is devoted to books and music. He has composed and published a number of hymns, anthems, and popular songs. For several years he conducted the music of the Methodist Episcopal Church in Troy, of which he was a member for twenty years, and for many years a trustee. In 1877 he severed his connection with the Methodist Church, and became a member of Christ (Episcopal) Church, of which he is now a vestryman.

257   VIII.   **Charles Sherman Bontecou,** born Feb. 4, 1844; died Dec. 3, 1848.

258   IX.   **Susan Bontecou,** born Aug. 1, 1846; died July 12, 1848.

CHILDREN OF MOSES AND SUSANNAH (BONTECOU) NOR-   **101**
THRUP.

259   I.   **John Northrup,** born in New Baltimore, N. Y.,   **616** July 16, 1821. He married, Sept. 25, 1844, Louisa Abigail Gregory, daughter of John and Abigail (Huntington) Gregory of Ithaca, N. Y. She was born Sept. 21, 1822.

They reside at Ithaca. He was a harness-maker and carriage-trimmer until 1865, since which time he has carried on the spring-bed, mattress, and sewing-machine business. He was for twenty-seven years a trustee of the Baptist Church. Town and county offices have repeatedly sought him. but he has accepted only one, that of overseer of the poor.

260   II.   James Northrup, born in New Baltimore, N. Y., 621
March 3, 1823.   He married, March 21, 1844, Mary Gillett, daughter of Horatio and Marilla Gillett, who was born in Scott, N. Y., Aug. 4, 1826. She died Dec. 18, 1844. He married (2d). April 29, 1847, Elsina S. Bennett, daughter of Cephas and Stella (Kneeland) Bennett of Utica, N. Y. She resides at Homer, N. Y. He was a carriage-trimmer and patent-rights agent, and died Aug. 6, 1884.

261   III.   Elizabeth Northrup, born Feb. 26, 1825 ; died Feb. 10, 1834.

262   IV.   Charles Northrup, born Jan. 7, 1827 ; died March 14, 1827.

263   V.   Susan Northrup, born Jan. 11, 1828.   She mar- ⎱ 590
ried, July 18, 1849, her cousin, Dr. Reed B. Bontecou ⎰ 630
(249) of Troy, N. Y.

CHILDREN OF JAMES CLARK AND ABBY (CONNABLE)   102
BONTECOU.

264   I.   Joseph Connable Bontecou, born in Bristol, R. I., 635
Nov. 5, 1838, and removed with his parents to Ohio in 1840.   At the breaking out of the War of the Rebellion, he was an undergraduate of the Ohio Wesleyan University, but enlisted under the President's first call for troops in the 2d Kentucky Infantry, which, being disowned by

the State on the ground of the State's neutrality, were accepted by the general government as three-years troops, and sent into West Virginia in June, 1861. He took part in all the operations of that campaign, being promoted to a lieutenancy and assigned to staff duty. The following winter he joined with his command the Army of the Cumberland, and accompanied it on the forced march it made to support Grant on the Tennessee. On the second day of the battle of Pittsburg Landing, Lieut. Bontecou commanded his company, losing more than half his men in killed and wounded. In the advance on Corinth, he led the forlorn hope which charged the log bridge and causeway on Tishemingo Creek, and in this bloody conflict lost the greater part of his small command. After the fall of Corinth, he was sent with Nelson's division to occupy Murfreesboro; and while guarding a railroad bridge south of Nashville, was captured by Gen. N. B. Forrest. For many months afterward he endured the miseries of a prisoner of war. While confined at Macon, Ga., he was engaged in several unsuccessful attempts to escape. With health broken, he was transferred to Salisbury, and at last into Libby Prison, where he was finally paroled as being effectually spoiled for further service against the Confederacy. He rejoined his command in 1863, but shortly afterward resigned his commission and returned home. His health being in a measure re-established, he enlisted in the 10th Ohio Independent Battery, and joined his new command at Vicksburg in December; was promoted to corporal, sergeant, quartermaster-sergeant, and lieutenant during the following six months, and accompanied Sherman in the Atlanta campaign, taking part in all the battles from Resaca to Peach Tree Creek. On the fall of Atlanta, the Battery was sent with Thomas to defend Nashville, and after the crushing defeat of Hood before that city, was stationed

in East Tennessee. In August, 1865, he was mustered
out of the service at Camp Dennison, Ohio. After the
war he prepared for the bar; but abandoning the profession, engaged in business, traveling for a number of
years, and afterwards becoming interested in manufacturing enterprises. Since 1876 he has been active in the
temperance work in the West, particularly in Michigan,
where, as chairman of the State central committee of the
various temperance organizations, and the general agent
of the State Alliance, he has been prominently identified
with the movement for the constitutional prohibition of
the liquor traffic. In the spring of 1883, having purchased the *Petosky Herald*, he removed to that town, and
devotes his time to the conduct of his paper. He married in Macon, Mich., June 1, 1870, Maria Priscilla Oven,
daughter of John and Margaret (Eckley) Oven of Shob-
den, Herefordshire, England. Her parents removed to
Detroit, Mich., in 1850, and settled in Macon in 1856.

265　　II. **Sarah Celestia Bontecou,** born in Circleville,
Ohio, Dec. 29, 1842. Resides at Xenia, Ohio.

266　　III. **Abby C. Bontecou,** born in Athens, Ohio, May
20, 1846; died in Xenia, July 8, 1846.

CHILDREN OF GILBERT DEAN AND SARAH (BONTECOU)　　103
GOLDEN.

267　　I. **Elizabeth Golden,** born in Troy, N. Y., Jan. 6,
1835. She married, Jan. 11, 1872, Sidney Tuttle Cary,
son of Wolsey Cary. He was born in Coeymans, N. Y.,
Nov. 18, 1838, and is a salesman. They reside at 84
Fifth Street, Troy. They have no children.

268　　II. **Maria Frances Golden,** born Jan. 26, 1837;
died Dec. 31, 1837.

269   III.   Sarah Bontecou Golden, born in Troy, Sept.   636
26, 1839. She married, Sept. 15, 1863, George Bywater
Cluett, whose brother, J. W. A. Cluett, married Elizabeth
Bontecou (256), her cousin. He is the son of William
Cluett, and was born in England in 1838; is a manu-
facturer of collars, etc., at Troy.   Mrs. Cluett died in
Troy, Aug. 1, 1864.

270   IV.   Gilbert Golden, born Sept. 19, 1841; died April
5, 1842.

271   V.   James Golden, born Dec. 27, 1842; died April
1, 1874, unmarried.

272   VI.   Mary Anna Golden, born Feb. 17, 1845; died
Jan. 11, 1852.

CHILDREN OF GEORGE AND LYDIA ANN (WHIPPLE)   106
BONTECOU.

273   I.   Mary Hannah Bontecou, born in Troy, N. Y.,   637
Aug. 19, 1839. She married there, May 8, 1862, Rev. Ira
Glazier Bidwell. He was born in Willington, Conn., Feb.
22, 1835, and died in Syracuse, N. Y., Dec. 25, 1878.
Mrs. Bidwell resides at No. 5 Allen Street, Buffalo, N. Y.

From the *Northern Christian Advocate*, Syracuse, Jan.
2, 1879 : — "The home of his childhood was blessed with
the influence of parental piety. From his birth he was
consecrated to the Lord, and to the fulfillment of the
vows of that consecration he attributed the most salu-
tary molding influences of his early life. His time during
his youth, when he was not in school, was divided between
employment in a factory and work on a farm. At the
age of 16 he entered the Seminary at Wilbraham, Mass.
Having finished there his preparation for college, he
entered the Wesleyan University [Middletown, Conn.],
where he remained one year. He afterwards went to

Union College, Schenectady, N. Y., where he was graduated in 1859. He stood high in his classes as a student,
and during his college course was noted for his manly and
Christian character. . . . The history of his ministry
cannot be written. It may be briefly characterized as a
series of remarkably successful — in some cases almost
marvelously successful — pastorates. He possessed many
of the characteristics of genius. He seemed to achieve
success without effort. His spirit seemed to be that of
restful activity. Though abundant in labor, he never
appeared to be anxious, confused, or in haste. His self-
possession was Christ-like. His courage, though manifest,
was without noise or bluster. He met emergencies with
a promptness and ease which often made great difficulties
seem like trifles. Hence he was readily accepted and
trusted as a leader. When duty was presented he acted
without hesitancy, and with such quiet firmness as to
put an end to all controversy. These qualities, connected
with great modesty, with entire absence of self-seeking,
with gentleness of manner, with quick, warm sympathy,
and with uniform cheerfulness, gave him great personal
influence over all who enjoyed his acquaintance. As a
preacher he was simple, earnest, convincing, always in-
structive, and often eloquent. His hearers never tired
while listening to him, and few men preach sermons so
easily remembered as his. His rhetoric was of a high
order, and always honest; the tricks of sensationalism
he utterly despised. Few preachers were less open to
criticism, but few probably ever made less effort to be
faultless: he was simply *himself*. As a student he was
diligent and accurate; as a thinker he was broad and
charitable; as a Christian he was sincere and devout."

Mr. Bidwell filled, during his ministry, the following
pastorates: Portland, Conn., one or two years; State
Street Church, Troy, N. Y., two years; Lansingburg,

N. Y., two years; Hudson Avenue Church, Albany, three years; Chestnut Street Church, Providence, R. I., two years; (then taught a year in Auburndale, Mass.;) Harvard Street Church, Cambridgeport, Mass., two years; Trinity Church, Worcester, Mass., two years; Bromfield Street Church, Boston, one year; (he then went abroad for six months for the benefit of his health;) Delaware Avenue Church, Buffalo, N. Y., three years; First Church, Syracuse, N. Y., where, after a pastorate of three months, he died at the close of a brief illness.

A friend said of him: "Born on the birthday of the Father of his Country, and dying on the birthday of the Saviour of the World, there was much in him to remind us of the two characters so prominent in history."

274   II.   William Whipple Bontecou, born Aug. 17, 1841; died Oct. 14, 1842.

275   III.   Susan Bontecou, born in Troy, May 29, 1843.   639 She married, Jan. 22, 1863, Frederick Webster Pickering of that city. He was born in Beckingham, England, April 15, 1841, the son of George Smith and Ann Pickering. The family emigrated to America in 1846 and settled in Troy, on a farm near which his early life was spent. Soon after his marriage he went South, and. for a while was employed as sutler's clerk in the army; was subsequently in the employment of the Freedmen's Bureau, and given charge of farms in the vicinity of Norfolk, Va. In the spring of 1865 he left the employ of the Bureau and rented the farm upon which his family had been living, and in the summer of 1866 purchased a farm near Portsmouth, Va., and engaged in raising fruit and vegetables for the market. In 1867 he was appointed a justice of the peace, and served over two years, when he was elected by the people for a further term of two years. In 1868 Mrs. Pickering's health began to fail, and she went North

17

for change of scene, but died at her father's home in Vineland, N. J., May 20, 1869. In November, 1872, he married Virginia C. Stoakes of Portsmouth, Va., and now resides in Troy, N. Y.

276   **IV.   William Wright Whipple Bontecou** was born   **642** in Troy, June 19, 1845, and passed his early life in that vicinity.   Aug. 30, 1862, he enlisted as a private in Company G, 169th Regiment New York State Volunteers, and did duty in and near Washington, D. C., until April, 1863, when his regiment was ordered to Suffolk, Va., and on the 21st engaged in their first fight, on the Edenton road. A portion of June and July was passed on the "Peninsula," raiding and destroying railroads and bridges and some of the enemy's supplies.   The regiment was then transported to Folly Island, S. C., and took part in the capture of Fort Wagner and the reduction of Fort Sumter.   In September Mr. Bontecou (now corporal) was ordered on detached service on the hospital steamer "Cosmopolitan," remaining there until March, 1864, when he rejoined his regiment at West Point, Va., taking part with it in the battle of Cold Harbor and various other fights before Petersburg and Richmond.   In December the regiment was ordered to South Carolina, arriving on Christmas Day, just in time to take part in the capture of Fort Fisher, at the mouth of the Cape Fear River.   Remaining there until the middle of the following February, they then advanced on Wilmington, N. C., capturing the city, and shortly afterward marched to Raleigh, where they were mustered out of the service, July 10, 1865, and Mr. Bontecou returned to Troy.   The following year he went to Vineland, N. J., whither his father had removed, and assisted him on the farm.   He married there, Dec. 23, 1868, Florence C. Neale, daughter of James and Mary Ann (Lake) Neale of Vineland, born Feb. 22, 1850.

In 1870 they removed to Minnesota, and in April, 1871, settled in Spring Valley, where they now reside, and where he is employed in charge of a lumber business.

277   V.   **Elijah Whipple Bontecou,** born in Troy, June   646
27, 1847. He married, Oct. 20, 1873, Clara Holland, daughter of Dr. Charles and Sophronia Brown (Cobb) Holland of Chicago, Ill. She was born in Springfield, Mass., Aug. 22, 1850. He is employed as a salesman in the wholesale millinery business. Their residence is at 334 Center Street, Chicago.

278   VI.   **George Henry Bontecou,** born in Troy, May   648
17, 1849. After some business employment in that city, part of the time as errand boy in his Uncle Peter's shoe store, he obtained a situation on a steam-tug plying on the Hudson River. In 1856 he attempted fruit culture at Vineland, N. J.; but this did not suit his roving disposition, and the following year he began railroading, serving as a locomotive fireman on the Hudson River Railroad. In August, 1868, he started out to seek his fortune at the West, having, after purchasing his ticket, a capital of just thirty-seven cents. He reached La Crosse, Wis., and secured employment with the Southern Minnesota Railroad as telegraph operator at Houston; was shortly afterward appointed station agent at Lanesborough, and a year later was transferred to Fountain Station. He married, April 27, 1870, at Sing Sing, N. Y., Anna Nevins, daughter of Morgan and Ellen (Nelson) Nevins of Sing Sing. She was born Jan. 24, 1852, and died April 2, 1872. After the death of his wife Mr. Bontecou returned to the East, and was appointed telegraph operator in Sing Sing prison. In August, 1872, he received the appointment of terminal agent for the Newburg, Dutchess & Connecticut Railroad at Dutchess Junction, N. Y.; and in August, 1880, in conjunction with his other duties, became station agent of

the New York Central & Hudson River Railroad. He is
also agent of the American Express Company, and in
1880 was appointed United States postmaster at Dutchess
Junction. In all of these positions he has been found
honest, trusty, and capable, filling them to the entire satisfaction of all concerned. March 24, 1875, he married
(2d) Emma Masc, daughter of Sylvester Howell and Al-
mira (Cornwell) Masc of Matteawan, N. Y. She was born
Jan. 22, 1855. Mr. Bontecou enlisted as a bugler, January, 1865, in the 21st regiment New York State Cavalry,
and with a detachment of recruits joined the regiment near
Washington, but could not "pass muster," and shortly
afterward returned home. He is a member of the Methodist Church at Matteawan, and served for two years as
vice-president of the Young Men's Christian Association.
He is also a member of the order of Freemasons.

279   VII.   Philip Dorlon Bontecou, born in Troy, Jan.   651
23, 1853. His early life was spent chiefly in Troy, and
on his father's farm in Vineland, N. J. In the fall of
1869 he passed a short time in the employ of his uncle
Francis, in the lumber business, in New York City; but
the following year went West "to seek his fortune," and
shortly after entered the employ of his brother William,
who had charge of a lumber business in Spring Valley,
Fillmore County, Minn. June 15, 1876, he married Ada
Florence Ewing, daughter of William R. and Achsah Eliza
(White) Ewing of Spring Valley. She was born in Hamlet, Chautauqua County, N. Y., Feb. 17, 1858. In February,
1878, he removed to Armstrong, Minn., and engaged in the
lumber business, holding at the same time the position of
agent of the Southern Minnesota Railroad. July 1, 1881,
he removed to Ortonville, and purchased a half interest in
the Lake House, a new hotel just opened; but not satisfied,
he sold out and went back to the railroad, being located

first at Dexter and then at Brownsdale, remaining but a short time, when he was obliged to resign on account of ill health. He returned to Ortonville, purchased an interest in the livery business, and continued in this pursuit until the health of his wife compelled removal to Colorado, where he obtained the position of station agent for the Denver and Rio Grande Railroad at Mears, Chaffee County, and was also appointed United States postmaster there. He has recently removed to Percy, Carbon County, Wyoming Territory.

280   VIII. Abby Whipple Bontecou, born April 12, 1856; resides in Buffalo, N. Y., with her sister, Mrs. Bidwell.

281   IX. Reed Bontecou, born Dec. 26, 1858. He entered the railroad service at 19, and in 1878 was appointed baggage-master on the Freehold & New York Railroad, and shortly afterward conductor. July 19, 1879, while in the performance of his duty, he was killed near Marlborough, N. J. He was a consistent member of the Methodist Church, and respected by all his associates as an honest, upright young man. His pastor said of him: " He was a young man of rare mental ability; his conduct spoke well of his early training; he proved to be a most excellent young man, and was fast growing in the esteem of all with whom he became acquainted."

282   X. Francis Bontecou, twin with Reed; died July 24, 1859.

CHILDREN OF GEORGE AND MARGARET (DUSTIN) BON- 106
TECOU.

283   I. Lydia Ann Bontecou, born April 5, 1870.

284   II. John Bontecou, born Feb. 20, 1876; died April 4, 1879.

CHILDREN OF EDWARD AND CORNELIA (KEIFER) **107**
BONTECOU.

285   **I. Sarah Maria Bontecou,** born in Cocymans, N. Y., **654**
June 17, 1843. She married, June 7, 1876, James Covil
Archibald, son of Thomas Archibald of Troy, born there,
May 28, 1845. In 1871 he obtained a clerkship with E.
A. Burrows, in the wholesale house-furnishing business,
and a year later became his partner. In February, 1884,
he sold his interest in this business, and became a partner
in the house of Fellows & Co., manufacturers of collars
and cuffs, and the oldest establishment in this line in
Troy. He is a prominent member of the State Street
Methodist Episcopal Church in Troy.

286   **II. Helen Maria Bontecou,** born in 1845; died in
1850.

287   **III. David Francis Bontecou,** born in Cocymans
Hollow, N. Y., Dec. 11, 1852. In 1869 he entered the
jewelry trade in New York City, and in 1878 became
cashier and head salesman for Jacques & Marcus, Union
Square. Feb. 1, 1880, he became a member of the firm
of E. A. Burrows & Co., 209 River Street, Troy. He is
unmarried.

CHILDREN OF FRANCIS AND CLARISSA MARIA (LANDON) **108**
BONTECOU.

288   **I. Alvin Francis Bontecou,** born in Troy, N. Y.,
Dec. 30, 1846. He married, Dec. 14, 1870, Lucy Wood
Bowker, daughter of Gustavus G. and Henrietta (Saun-
ders) Bowker. He served in the 37th and 71st Regi-
ments New York State Militia for nearly eight years,
doing post duty with the former, during the war, at the
fortifications at the entrance to New York Harbor. He
has been engaged in the dry-goods, provision, and lumber

trades during the past fifteen years, mainly in the latter, and at present conducts a box-making business at 87 Walker Street. They have no children

289 II. **Gardner Landon Bontecou,** born in Troy, $\begin{cases} 657 \\ 998 \end{cases}$ March 25, 1849. He married, Oct. 10, 1872, Mary Elizabeth Northrup (617), daughter of John (259) and Louisa A. (Gregory) Northrup of Ithaca, N. Y. He was formerly engaged with his father in the lumber business in New York, and removed with him to Toronto, Kan., and engaged in stock-raising, in 1878. In the spring of 1883 he removed to Emporia, Kan., and engaged again in the lumber trade, and later moved to Eureka, Greenwood County, in the same State.

290 III. **Mary Kate Bontecou,** born in New York, Feb. **658** 10, 1852. She married, Dec. 26, 1877, Ambrose Ryder Adams, who was born in Putnam County, N. Y., Oct. 9, 1851. In 1861 his parents removed to New York City, and in 1865 he commenced his business life in the hosiery commission house of Kibbe, Chaffee, Shreve & Co., 71 and 73 Worth Street, and has ever since remained in their employ.

291 IV. **Helen Estelle Bontecou,** born in New York, July 29, 1859; resides with her parents in Toronto, Kan.

292 V. **Fannie Louise Bontecou,** born in New York, Nov. 2, 1861. She resides in Toronto, Kan.

CHILDREN OF JOHN PECK AND CAROLINE STARR **110** (RAYNER) BURRITT.

293 I. **Cornelia Eliza Burritt,** born March 20, 1828; died Sept. 7, 1828.

294 II. **Joseph Burritt,** born June 21, 1829; died Jan. 24, 1833.

295   III. Mary Jane Burritt, born Jan. 9, 1831. She married, Oct. 31, 1867, Lucius Bonaparte Allyn, son of Nathan Allyn of Hartford, Conn., and former husband of her aunt, Mary Martha Rayner (117). He died in Washington, D. C., Aug. 7, 1876. She resides at 610 M Street, N. W., in that city. She has no children.

296   IV. Charlotte Caroline Burritt, born Sept. 26,   660
1832. She married, March 3, 1852, Gilman Fay. They reside in Westborough, Mass.

297   V. Miriam Rayner Burritt, born Jan. 11, 1835; died April 27, 1844.

298   VI. Frances Cornelia Burritt, born July 7, 1836; died April 20, 1837.

299   VII. John Menzies Burritt, born June 21, 1837.   663
From 1855 to 1860 he was engaged with his brother Frank in the grocery business in New York City. In the latter year he removed to Wisconsin. He married March 6, 1859, Harriet Muir Knapp, daughter of David and Ellen (Boyce) Knapp of New York. They were afterwards divorced, and he married (2d), October, 1867, Kate Morrison of Stoughton, Wis. They reside at Clear Lake, Minn.

300   VIII. Frank Duffie Burritt, born in Newtown,   665
Conn., Sept. 23, 1840. He married, Dec. 3, 1867, Harriet Muir Burritt. When he was two years old his father died, and the family removed to New York. In 1855, when he was only 15, he went into the grocery business with his brother John, at 171 Second Street, and in 1857 they opened another store at 49 Avenue C. They continued together in the business until 1860, when they sold out the business and removed to Stoughton, Wis., where he has ever since resided, engaged in farming.

CHILD OF BENJAMIN LESTER AND NANCY (MERRILL)   **112**
RAYNER.

301   I. **Benjamin Stuart Rayner,** born in Troy, N. Y.,   **667**
March 31, 1836. He removed with his parents, when an
infant, to New York, in which city he has ever since
resided. He graduated from the College of the City of
New York in 1853, taking the second place in his class.
He entered the Tradesmen's Bank in 1853, and has
served in various capacities, having been paying teller
since 1867. He married, June 4, 1857, Julia Maria
Harden, daughter of John W. and Jane Maria (Smith)
Harden of New York. She died Sept. 24, 1881. Mr.
Rayner is connected with the South Unitarian Church of
New York, and has filled the positions of trustee, treas-
urer, and Sunday-school superintendent.

CHILDREN OF DANIEL OLCOTT AND FRANCES (CASE)   **114**
RAYNER.

302   I. **James Chauncey Rayner,** born Sept. 1, 1836;
died March 20, 1844.

303   II. **Carrie Francis Rayner,** born Aug. 26, 1849.
She married, Feb. 6, 1871, Charles Vincent. They reside
at Sioux Falls, Dakota, where he is engaged in the hardware business. They have no children.

CHILDREN OF MENZIES AND ANN ELIZABETH (STEVENS)   **116**
RAYNER.

304   I. **Ann Elizabeth Rayner,** born in Portland, Me.,
Oct. 18, 1834; died in Trenton, N. J., Aug. 7, 1855, unmarried.

305   II. **Caroline Ellen Rayner,** born in New York, Feb.
19, 1840; died Sept. 1, 1855.

18

306   III.   Peter Cooper Rayner, born in New York, Oct. 20, 1841; died March 26, 1842.

307   IV.   Mary Margaret Rayner, born in New York, Oct. 18, 1843; died Dec. 24, 1843.

CHILDREN OF MENZIES AND SUSAN (NODINE) RAYNER.   116

308   I.   Sarah Emma Rayner, born in New York, June 9,   670
1845. She married, June 9, 1864, William Henry Long, who was born in Mercer County, N. J., Jan. 1, 1843. Mr. Long served an apprenticeship to the machinist trade in Trenton, N. J., and followed the business of machinist and engineer, in that city and in Bordentown, N. J., remaining in the latter place about six years; next in Janesville, Appleton, and Kaukauna, in Wisconsin; then in Burlington, N. J., remaining five years; then again in Trenton, but returning to Burlington in February, 1880, he took charge of the engine of the National Bureau of Engraving and Manufacturing Company. He is a deacon in the Presbyterian Church.

309   II.   Susan Rebecca Rayner, born in Trenton, N. J.,   674
July 22, 1848. She married, Dec. 24, 1868, William Henry Carrick. He was preparing for college when the war broke out, but enlisted in the 23d Regiment Pennsylvania Volunteers, for three months, and afterwards in the 46th Regiment Pennsylvania Volunteers; was then transferred to the 214th Regiment as sergeant-major; was advanced to first lieutenant, and acting assistant adjutant-general on the staff of Brig.-Gen. David B. McKibbin. His service was with the armies of the Potomac and the Shenandoah. He is now (1883) engaged with his father in the manufacturing baking business, at 118 and 120 North 22d Street, Philadelphia. He resides at 112 North 21st Street.

310   III. Menzies Bontecou Rayner, born in Trenton, N. J., Sept. 23, 1856; died in Janesville, Wis., Jan. 11, 1873.

CHILDREN OF GEORGE GILMAN AND JANE ELIZABETH   118
BARRY (RAYNER) WARNER.

311   1. William Rayner Warner, born in Walpole, N. H.,   677
May 6, 1842. In April, 1861, he enlisted in Company K, 13th Regiment Massachusetts Volunteers; was promoted to second lieutenant May 1, 1863, and to first lieutenant March 10, 1864; participated in the battles of Fredericksburg, Chancellorsville, Gettysburg, the Wilderness, and Petersburg. He was mustered out of service July 16, 1864, and married, May 1, 1865, Ellen Maria Henry, daughter of Dr. Samuel G. and Nancy D. (French) Henry of Westborough, Mass. After his return from the war, he engaged in the grocery and general merchandise business, in Westborough, until 1867; afterwards in Boston and Hyde Park, Mass., and in October, 1875, removed to Fall River, Mass., where they now reside.

312   II. Elizabeth Gilman Warner, born in Walpole,   679
N. H., July 1, 1844; she married, in Westborough, Mass., July 6, 1865, William Augustus Prickitt, who was born in Monmouth County, N. J., March 20, 1839. Mr. Prickitt enlisted, Aug. 9, 1862, as a private in Company G, 14th Regiment New Jersey Volunteers; was promoted to corporal in September, and in August, 1863, to sergeant. Participated in the battle of Locust Grove at Mine Run, Va., Nov. 29, 1863, where one-fourth of his company were killed or wounded. In January, 1864, he passed examination before Corey's examining board and was promoted to captain, and attached to Company G, 25th Regiment United States colored troops, passing the greater part of the time at Fort Barrancas, Fla., until mustered out of ser-

vice in December, 1865. In 1868 he engaged in insurance
and banking at Trenton, N. J., in 1872 purchased a
membership in the New York Stock Exchange, which he
sold in 1876 and removed to Farmingdale, N. J., where
they still reside. He is engaged in farming.

CHILDREN OF WELLS AND CATHARINE RHODES (BON-   **120**
TECOU) LATHROP.

313   I. **Elizabeth Lathrop,** born April 28, 1821. She   684
married, Aug. 23, 1842, George Bliss Morris, son of Hon.
Oliver B. and Caroline (Bliss) Morris of Springfield,
Mass. He was born Nov. 12, 1818; graduated from
Amherst College in 1837, and later from the Cambridge
Law School. "He was admitted to the Hampden County
Bar in 1840; appointed clerk of the courts of Hampden
County in 1853. In 1856 the office was made an elective
one, and he was chosen by the people to fill it, and was
thrice re-elected to terms of five years each. He died
July 7, 1872, when about one year of his last term of
office had expired. His courtesy and efficiency in the
transaction of the business of his office made him popular
with the people and the bar." His widow resides in New
York City.

314   II. **James Lathrop,** born Aug. 7, 1823. He mar-   687
ried, Aug. 23, 1848, Harriet Angeline Day, daughter of
Almon and Betsey (Ashley) Day of South Hadley Falls,
Mass. She was born Oct. 25, 1827. He was educated as
a civil engineer, but served the greater part of his business
life as a book-keeper in Boston and New York. During
the Fourth Avenue improvements in the latter city he occupied the position of confidential clerk to the contractor,
Sidney Dillon. Mr. Lathrop suffered much from ill health
during the later years of his life, and died in Brooklyn,
N. Y., Sept. 29, 1884.

315   **III.   Catharine Bontecou Lathrop,** born Dec. 23,   **689**
1826.   She married. Oct. 22, 1863, Oliver Ellsworth
Wood, son of Hon. Joseph and Fanny (Ellsworth) Wood,
whose first wife, Martha Potter Bontecou (123), was her
aunt.   Mr. Wood died in Westport, Conn., Dec. 18, 1883.
She resides in New York.

316   **IV.   Daniel Bontecou Lathrop,** born June 16, 1829.
He was of a restless, adventurous temperament.   He was
one of the California "forty-niners," and one of "Fili-
buster Walker's" men, in his raid upon Sonora and afterwards in the Nicaragua campaign.   He returned from the
Isthmus in the summer of 1857, much broken in health,
and remained quietly at his father's house in South Hadley, Mass.   Aug. 16, 1858, he crossed the river to Holyoke
in a row-boat, and when about to return was assaulted
without cause by a ruffian, horribly beaten about the head
with a club, and on attempting to escape in his boat,
forced into the water by the scoundrel's companions who
had collected, and drowned.

CHILDREN OF OLIVER ELLSWORTH AND MARTHA POTTER   **123**
(BONTECOU) WOOD.

317   **I.   Frances Ellsworth Wood,** born June 24, 1838;
died April 9, 1842.

318   **II.   Catharine Bontecou Wood,** born April 20, 1843.
She is a resident of New York City, and engaged in literary work.

CHILDREN OF RICHARD DARIUS AND SYBIL PEASE   **124**
(BONTECOU) MORRIS.

319   **I.   Richard Bontecou Morris,** born in Springfield,   **690**
Mass., Aug. 3, 1833.   He was educated to the profes-
sion of civil engineer, and first pursued this business in

142 BONTECOU FAMILY.

Ohio; was subsequently engaged in railroad construction in Connecticut, New York, Massachusetts, Mississippi, Illinois, and Missouri. He married, June 20, 1859, Mary Ripley, daughter of John B. and Mary (Durant) Ripley of Adrian, Mich. In 1866 they removed to Kansas, and now reside at Atchison. He is a Democrat in his political affiliations, and for many years served as a member of the State central committee; also as delegate to the national conventions of 1872, 1876, and 1880. In 1883, he was appointed by the Governor to the office of Superintendent of Insurance of the State of Kansas, which office he now holds. He is a vestryman in Trinity Church, Atchison.

320   II. **Edward Morris,** born and died in February, 1837.

321   III. **Harriet Bontecou Morris,** born in Springfield,   694
May 19, 1840. She married, Dec. 25, 1862, Ransom Williams Dunham. He was born in Savoy, Mass., March 21, 1838; was educated at the common school, and the high school in Springfield; was employed in a clerical capacity in the office of the Massachusetts Mutual Life Insurance Company from 1855 to 1860, and in August of that year removed to Chicago, and became a grain and provision commission merchant. Has been president of the Board of Trade of Chicago. In 1882 he was elected to Congress as Representative from the first district of Illinois, and has since been re-elected.

322   IV. **Catharine Sybil Morris,** born in Springfield,   695
Nov. 8, 1851. She married, Feb. 24, 1870, Frank Reed, son of Edwin W. Reed of Springfield. He was born in 1848, and is a merchant; they reside in Chicago.

CHILD OF HENRY AND HARRIET (BONTECOU) MORRIS.   127

323   I. **John Emery Morris,** born in Springfield, Mass., 698
Nov. 30, 1843. He married, May 15, 1867, in Hartford.

Conn., Mary Pamelia Felt, daughter of Festus C. and Sarah King (Lincoln) Felt of New York, who was born in New York City, Jan. 1, 1848. They reside in Hartford. His business life was begun in 1860 in the Charter Oak Bank of Hartford. In 1864 he obtained a clerical position in the Travelers Insurance Company, then just commencing business, of which company he has been assistant secretary since May, 1874. Sept. 20, 1862, he enlisted in Company B, 22d Regiment Connecticut Volunteers, and served as corporal until mustered out, July 7, 1863.

CHILDREN OF WILLIAM ELY AND CAROLINE CODDING- **128**
TON (THAYER) BONTECOU.

324   I. **Daniel Bontecou**, born in Springfield, Mass., Sept. 14, 1851. Graduated from the College of the City of New York in 1871. He married, Oct. 7, 1885, at Falmouth, Mass., Nathalie Holdrege, who was born Oct. 8, 1857. He is a civil engineer by profession, and for a number of years was engaged on the public works of New York City. He now resides in Kansas City, Mo., and is chief engineer of the Kansas City Belt Railway Company.

325   II. **Frederick Thayer Bontecou**, born in Springfield, Oct. 29, 1856 ; died Nov. 17, 1856.

326   III. **Nathaniel Frederick Thayer Bontecou**, born in Brooklyn, N. Y., March 1, 1860. Resides in New York City. He is a stock broker.

SEVENTH GENERATION.

327   I. Harriet Elizabeth Bontecou, born Jan. 6, 1828.   701
She married, Jan. 28, 1849, James Hook, who was born
in New York City, Oct. 31, 1815.   In 1836 Mr. Hook
removed to Mobile, Ala., and pursued his business as a
mason; he also had charge of the fire department of that
city. In 1840 he returned North, and settled in Newburg. N. Y., removing to Dunkirk in 1852, where he still
resides, and where his wife died, Feb. 20, 1878. He is
the proprietor of a steam bakery.

328   II. Mary Louisa Bontecou, born March 1, 1831;
died June 27, 1841.

329   III. Josephine Bontecou, born in Newburg, N. Y.,   705
Sept. 24. 1833. She married, Oct. 15, 1853, Eugene Oscar Warring, who was born Sept. 25, 1831. He was a
railroad bridge builder. She died Jan. 20, 1858. He is
said to have died in Illinois about 1869.

330   IV. Walter Henry Bontecou, born in Newburg,   706
Oct. 12, 1836. He was a baker. He married, July 1,
1862, Mary Mosher, who was born Sept. 5, 1841. He
died Aug. 7, 1868, in Newburg. His widow married, April
24, 1869, George Bell, and resides (1883) at 13 Mill
Street, Newburg.

CHILD OF GEORGE WASHINGTON AND MARY (BONTE- **131**
COU) BRADLEY.

331   I. **Lois Bradley**, born in East Haven, Conn., Aug. 2,
1826; died there, May 7, 1882, unmarried.

CHILDREN OF JAMES AND HARRIET (BONTECOU) HAM- **132**
ILTON.

332   I. **Robert John Hamilton**, born in Newburg, N. Y., **709**
March 11, 1837. He learned the machinist's trade in
New York; but being of an adventurous disposition, joined
in 1856 the forces commanded by William Walker, and
engaged with them in the noted filibustering expedition
against Nicaragua. On his return he was employed for
a time in his father's store in Newburg, and in 1858
removed to New York. He married, Jan. 25, 1858, Ellen
Jane Sullivan, daughter of James and Margaret (Sullivan) Sullivan of Brooklyn, N. Y. He enlisted, May 16,
1861, in Company B, 36th Regiment New York Volunteers,
and participated in every fight that the Army of the
Potomac was engaged in during his two-years' term of
service, including of course the battles of Fredericksburg,
Fair Oaks, Seven Pines, the seven-days' fight at Malvern
Hill, South Mountain, Antietam, and Chancellorsville.
On his return from the war he obtained employment at
the Washington Iron Works, in Newburg, and on Oct. 3,
1863, was very severely injured by the explosion of the
boiler of the United States gunboat "Lenape," which was
being tested; his left arm was broken, and the bones never
united, rendering the member nearly useless. He afterwards learned the painter's trade, and became foreman of
painters at the iron works. In 1872 the Washington
works suffered failure and were closed, and Mr. Hamilton
removed to Astoria, L. I., where he still resides, following
his trade of painter.
19

333   II. Agnes Jane Hamilton, born in Newburg, Jan.   719
18, 1839. She married, Oct. 15, 1861, Charles Frederick
Chapman, who was born in Newburg, Aug. 5, 1835. He
has been engaged in the grocery business, but now (1883)
is clerk in a bakery establishment. They reside at 169
Lander Street.

334   III. Elias Pitts Hamilton, born March 2, 1841;
died Aug. 22, 1841.

335   IV. Margaret Anna Hamilton, born in Newburg,
Oct. 22, 1843. She married, Oct. 8, 1862, Charles William Brooks, born in Glenham, Dutchess County, N. Y.,
Sept. 9, 1837. He removed to Newburg when quite young,
and remained there, engaged in the grocery business,
until his death, which occurred in March, 1871. Mrs.
Brooks died Aug. 19, 1863. They had no children.

336   V. Mary Louisa Hamilton, born in Newburg, Feb.   721
10, 1845. She married, Sept. 6, 1864, Arthur Wilson,
a native of Matteawan, Dutchess County, N. Y., who
was born Sept. 4, 1842. His early childhood was passed
in Poughkeepsie, but since 1848 he has resided in Newburg. He is the cashier of the Highland National Bank.
They reside on Grand Street.

337   VI. James Ranwick Hamilton, born March 18,
1847. He was a printer in Newburg. He died at War-
wick, N. Y., Dec. 2, 1878, to which place he had removed
three years before.

338   VII. William Henry Hamilton, born Sept. 1, 1849;
was drowned at Newburg, July 4, 1859.

339   VIII. Samuel Hamilton, born June 18, 1854; died
at Newburg, March 10, 1872.

CHILDREN OF NORMAN AND JULIA ELIZABETH (BEN- **133**
HAM) HAYDEN.

340   I. Charles Benham Hayden, born March 17, 1815;
died Feb. 29, 1816.

341   II. Charles Benham Hayden, born in New Haven, **723**
Conn., Jan. 21, 1817. When he was eight years old his
widowed mother removed to Smithfield, Isle of Wight
County,Va. He was thrice married: (1st,) Aug. 12, 1840,
to Louisiana Susan Cocke, daughter of Lieutenant William H. Cocke, United States Navy, and Eliza Woddrap
Johnson of Smithfield. She died at Abington, Va., July
18, 1843. (2d,) To Mary Elizabeth Kilby, Aug. 21, 1844,
daughter of John Thompson and Ann Newton (Jones)
Kilby. She was born May 19, 1819, and died Dec. 27,
1861. (3d,) To Mrs. Julia Ann Wilson, Nov. 11, 1867,
who was the widow of James Wilson, and daughter of
George and Ann Matilda Banks (Hening) Cabaniss. She
is living in Smithfield. Mr. Hayden entered William and
Mary College in 1834, and took his academic degree in
1836. He attended one session at the University of Virginia and graduated in several of its schools, intending
to return and complete the law course, but was persuaded
by Prof. William B. Rogers to engage with him in the
geological survey of the State of Virginia, which occupied
four years. From 1840 to 1843 he engaged in teaching
in Smithfield and Abington, Va. Having at the same
time prepared himself in the law, he was admitted to the
bar, Nov. 25, 1843, and attained distinction in the courts
in which he practiced. For many years he was attorney
for the Commonwealth. He died in Smithfield, Jan. 28,
1883. The following extract is taken from the published
Resolutions of the Isle of Wight County Bar:

    "Superbly learned in law, profoundly skilled in science,
thoroughly read in literature, widely and extensively ex-

perienced in business, with a judgment and common-sense as conspicuous and luminous as his talents, he daily surprised those with whom he came into contact with the great extent, the vast variety, and surprising minuteness of his knowledge, and made it difficult if not impossible for them to say in what department of knowledge or of life he most excelled.

"Coming into the bar when law was a science and not a trade, he brought to its practice a profound and varied knowledge, and delighted his judge with his respectful deference and his brethren at the bar with a ready and exquisite courtesy.

"Falling in our midst, we cannot fail to feel and to lament the loss of his guidance, his companionship, his talents, his influence, and his example."

342   **III. Norman Edward Brockling Hayden,** born July 8, 1819; died Jan. 27, 1820.

CHILD OF SAMPSON AND JULIA ELIZABETH (HAYDEN)   133
WHITE.

343   **I. Julia Augusta Todd White,** born May 20, 1834; died Aug. 30, 1844.

CHILDREN OF CLEVELAND JARMAN AND SUSAN C.   134
(BENHAM) SALTER.

344   **I. Julia Rebecca Salter,** born in New Haven,   732
Conn., Feb. 24, 1819. She married, June 12, 1843, William Homes of St. Louis, Mo., son of Henry and Isabella (Porter) Homes of Boston, Mass., and grand-nephew of Hon. Rufus King. He died Jan. 19, 1869. Mrs. Homes resides in Waverly, Ill.

345   **II. Mary Louisa Salter,** born in New Haven, Feb.   739
24, 1819 (twin with Julia R.). She married, July 8,

1841. Charles Roger Welles of Springfield, Ill., son of Hon. Martin Welles of Wethersfield, Conn. He graduated from Yale College in 1834; died July 23, 1854. He was a lawyer. Mrs. Welles resides in Elwyn, Pa.

CHILDREN OF ELISHA MANDEVILLE AND ABBY (KIM-BERLY) BENHAM. **135**

346 I. **Susan Benham,** born Jan. 22, 1823. She married, Aug. 28, 1848, Washington Holmes Bardwell of Whately, Mass. They removed to New Haven, Conn., then to Springfield, Mass., and now reside in Monsonville, N. H. He is a chair-maker. **745**

347 II. **Louisa Waters Benham,** born Jan. 27, 1825. She married, April 16, 1844, Ralph Childs, a native of Deerfield, Mass. He served as a private in the 2d Battery, 8th Massachusetts Artillery; enlisted Sept. 6, 1864, and was discharged at Vicksburg, Miss., June 11, 1865, being at the time sick in hospital. He never regained his usual health, and died in Whately, Mass., Dec. 12, 1867. He was a carriage-maker. She resides in Providence, R. I. **748**

348 III. **Francis Kimberly Benham,** born in Orange, Conn., Sept. 13, 1827. He learned the trade of carriage blacksmith, and worked at that and gun-making until about 1870. He married, Nov. 30, 1848, in Hamden, Conn., Emily Jane Leek, daughter of Henry and Martha (Beecher) Leek of New Haven. He is now engaged in the grocery business, and is a member of the firm of Smith & Co., 7 Broadway, New Haven. They reside at 324 George Street. **756**

349 IV. **Robert Alexander Benham,** born June 10, 1831, in Orange. When sixteen years of age he removed to New Haven, and learned the carriage-trimming busi- **762**

ness, continuing in it until 1867. He married, July 25, 1852, Delia Delight Leek, sister of his brother Francis's wife. In 1867 he opened a boot and shoe store, in which business he still continues, at 814 Chapel Street, New Haven. His residence is at 93 Lyon Street.

CHILDREN OF FRANCIS W. AND LOUISA WALTER (BEN-   136
HAM) BUSHNELL.

350   I. **William Edward Bushnell**, born Dec. 27, 1821.   763
He married, Dec. 22, 1857, Rose Linda Clark, daughter of Silas and Hannah Atwell (Tenant) Clark of Chicago, Ill. He went to sea at an early age, but finally settled in California, and is now in the employ of the Central Pacific Railroad Company, in command of one of their steamers plying between San Francisco and Oakland. His home is at 14 Turk Street, San Francisco.

351   II. **Douglas Ritchie Bushnell**, born in Norwich,   764
Conn., June 17, 1824. He received a thorough education, and adopted the profession of civil engineer. He married, Sept. 16, 1849, at Highgate, Vt., Emily Juanna Catharine Edson, daughter of Captain John and Emily Perlee (Clement) Edson of Highgate. In 1850 they removed to Illinois, and settled at Sterling. He was prominently connected there with several railway lines, among them what is now the Chicago & Northwestern, of which he was chief engineer. In the spring of 1861, when the call was made for troops to defend the Union, he was one of the first to respond, and was elected captain of Company B, 13th Illinois Infantry. The early part of his campaign was passed in Missouri and Arkansas; but in December, 1862, the regiment was ordered to Vicksburg, Miss., and engaged in the fights of the 28th and 29th of that month. Here he was promoted to be major, and highly distinguished himself by his coolness and courage. On the

10th and 11th of January, 1863. he displayed the same heroic devotion at the assault and capture of Arkansas Post. In Sherman's operations against Johnston after the fall of Vicksburg, Major Bushnell acted as lieutenant-colonel until the return to quarters in August. He passed safely through the fierce contests of Lookout Mountain and Missionary Ridge, on the 24th and 25th of November. On the morning of the 27th, in the advance of his regiment over an open field, before Ringgold, Ga., in the face of a hot fire from the enemy, he was killed. "Death found him where it might have found him at any moment of his career as a soldier, — at his post." His body was sent home under military escort, and was impressively buried, with Masonic ceremonies, in the presence of a large number of sympathizing friends and citizens.

In 1864 Mrs. Bushnell was appointed postmistress of Sterling, and held the office for seven years. She married, Oct. 12. 1871, Hon. Miles S. Henry, lawyer, railroad president, major and paymaster during the war, and at the time of his death, which occurred Nov. 26, 1878, mayor of the city. Mrs. Henry is still living in Sterling.

352   **III. Francis Hayden Bushnell,** born in Norwich,   768 June 10, 1827. He graduated from Trinity College, Hartford, in 1850, and from Berkeley Divinity School, Middletown, in 1853. He was ordained to the Diaconate, Dec. 19, 1852, by Right Rev. T. C. Brownell, D. D. In 1853 he became assistant minister of Christ Church, Louisville, Ky., and in April, 1854, was ordained to the priesthood by Right Rev. B. B. Smith, D. D. In 1855 he became rector of Grace Church in that city. He married, Aug. 2, 1858, Mary Virginia Breeden, daughter of John N. and Jane (Keller) Breeden of Louisville. She died there, May 28, 1860. He again married, Feb. 2. 1863, Theodosia Coxe Cumming, daughter of Samuel T. and Theodosia H. (Coxe) Cumming of Hunterdon County,

N. J.   In 1866 he removed to Philadelphia and became rector of St. David's Church; but resigned his pastorate in 1875, to take the position of general agent of the Board of Missions of the Diocese of Pennsylvania.   In 1877 he resigned this position and became rector of the Church of the Messiah in Philadelphia, where he now remains.

353   IV.   Henry Harrington Bushnell, born May 18, 1828; died Dec. 29, 1850.

354   V.   Richard Wells Bushnell, born in Norwich, 769 Aug. 10, 1830.   He married, Sept. 19, 1853, Mary B. Turner of Norwich.   She died in Chicago in 1863.   He married (2d), May 5, 1869, Mary Sophia Thomas, daughter of Ozro and Mary (Hurd) Thomas of New Hampshire.   He is master mechanic of the Burlington, Cedar Rapids & Northern Railroad, and resides in Cedar Rapids, Iowa.

CHILDREN OF WILLIAM AND ELIZA ANN (HALL) 138
PRITCHARD.

355   I.   Caroline Uretta Pritchard, born March 28, 1826. 776 She married, Sept. 16, 1845, in Ohio, Anson Munson Durand, who was born in Canandaigua, N. Y., July 6, 1822. He followed the life of a farmer in New York, Ohio, Wisconsin, and Iowa; and in 1870 removed with his family to Missouri and settled in Carthage, where he engaged in the sale of agricultural implements.   He enlisted in a Wisconsin regiment during the Civil War, but failed to pass the medical examination on account of impaired health caused by a sun-stroke, from the effect of which he never fully recovered.   He was a member of the Congregational Church, and a justice of the peace.   He died in St. Joseph, Mo., Jan. 21, 1881.   Mrs. Durand resides in Des Moines, Iowa.

356   II.   William Wicks Pritchard, born in Waterbury,   785
Conn., Oct. 28, 1827.   He removed with his parents to
Brunswick, Medina County, Ohio, when about five years
old.   He married, Oct. 28, 1851, Mary Clarinda Stebbins,
daughter of Hervey and Julia (Robinson) Stebbins of
Brunswick, who was born March 31, 1832, and died Nov.
10, 1882.   Mr. Pritchard died March 7, 1873.   He was a
printer by trade, and held the office of deacon in the
Congregational Church.

357   III.   Charles Frederick Pritchard, born Oct. 31,   789
1829.   He married, March 29, 1856, Mary Susan Westcott, daughter of Jesse and Lucy (Mason) Westcott of
Buffalo, N. Y.   She was born in Buffalo, May 4, 1836,
and died Feb. 9, 1882.   Mr. Pritchard is a farmer, and
resides at Blue Mills, Jackson County, Mo.

358   IV.   George Anson Pritchard, born in Liverpool,   795
Ohio, May 5, 1832.   He left school at the age of eleven
years, and was employed by his father in the business of
buying and selling cattle.   During the first year of his
work in this line, he personally superintended the trans-
fer of a drove of 260 head from Madison County, Ohio, to
Cleveland.   He continued in his father's employ until he
became of age, when he engaged in the same business on
his own account, and has ever since followed it.   He married, Oct. 10, 1854, Jane Elizabeth Freese, daughter of
¹Abram and Jane (Deming) Freese of Des Moines, Iowa.
She was born April 14, 1832, and died August 8, 1878.
He married (2d), March 1, 1880, Mrs. Florence Agnes

¹ Abram Freese came from Lee, Mass., in 1813, and settled in the
Western Reserve district of Ohio.   He bore the commission of sur-
veyor to the new Connecticut colony, and arrived in the first *sail*-boat
that crossed Lake Erie,— a rude barge fitted with canvas and called
" The Little Mayflower."   The greater part of the surveying of this
new country was done under his supervision.

20

Maulsby Duncan, daughter of Rev. John and Mary C.
(Kimmerle) Maulsby of Indiana.   Mr. Pritchard removed to Des Moines, Iowa, in 1862, and to Denver, Col.,
in 1883.

359   V. Henry Harrison Pritchard, born May 31, 1835.   797
He married, Oct. 16, 1870, Cornelia Harrison, daughter
of Lawson Nourse and Mary Jane (Gilman) Harrison of
Des Moines.   They reside in Des Moines, Iowa.   He is
engaged in the cattle business.   He and his brother
George were the first to ship cattle from the Rocky
Mountains, East, and were also the first to ship hogs by
rail from Iowa to San Francisco.

360   VI. Elizabeth Adelaide Pritchard, born in Madi- 802
son, Ohio, May 24, 1837.   She married, Oct. 4, 1863,
John Franklin Rollins, son of Richard Rollins, who was
born in Lebanon, Me., Oct. 4, 1838.   He removed to Des
Moines in 1856, and has ever since resided there except
during the year 1870, which he passed in Pittsburg, Pa.
He was engaged for a few years in the drug business, but
is now a wholesale paper merchant.

361   VII. Susan Henrietta Pritchard, born June 20,   806
1840.   She married, Oct. 20, 1869, Oscar Cornelius Rose,
who was born in Canandaigua, N. Y., Sept. 1, 1841.   He
removed when thirteen years of age to Dane County,
Wis., with his parents, and remained there on a farm till
1864, when he enlisted in the 43d Wisconsin Volunteers,
became a corporal in Company I. and served one year.
During this time his health became impaired, and on his
discharge from the army, removed to Iowa.   After his
marriage they lived, until 1879, in Sciola, Montgomery
County, and now reside in Carbon, Adams County.   He
is a coal dealer; also president of the school board of
Carbon.

362   VIII.   Eliza Frances Pritchard, born April 1, 1843;
died at Des Moines. March 21, 1871.   Unmarried.

363   IX.   Mary Ellen Pritchard, born Nov. 15. 1845:
died at Brunswick, Ohio, Sept. 16, 1847.

CHILDREN OF CHARLES AND AMY (MOSS) HALL.   139

364   I.   Celia Eliza Hall, born in Cheshire. Conn., Sept.
12. 1831: died Aug. 13, 1835.

365   II.   Willis Charles Hall, born in Cheshire, March   808
16. 1833.   When he was five years old his parents removed to Ohio, but returned to Cheshire in 1843.   In
1848 he entered the grocery trade as a clerk, in Cheshire,
subsequently removing to Waterbury. and in 1882 sold
his interest in the business to his partner, and retired
from trade.   He married, May 26. 1857, Elizabeth Heatly.
daughter of William Heatly of England, whose ancestor
served under William of Orange at the battle of the
Boyne.   She was born near Dublin, Ireland, in January
1833. and died in Waterbury, Conn., Nov. 20, 1873.   He
married (2d), June 13. 1876, Orinda Daniels, daughter
of Joseph B. and Eleanor (Miller) Daniels of Waterbury.
She was born in Poughkeepsie, N. Y., May 29, 1843.

366   III.   Ellen Mary Hall, born in Cheshire, Jan. 12,   812
1835.   She married, May 23, 1858, Seth Eliada Frost,
who was born in Wolcott, Conn., Feb. 24, 1832.   His father
was Sylvester Higby Frost, and his mother Philinda Tuttle. both of Wolcott.   In 1844 he removed to Southington.
Conn., and since 1861 has been engaged in farming.   He
is a member of the Baptist Church, and has three times
been elected justice of the peace.

367   IV.   Emma Celia Hall, born in Cheshire, Aug. 11,   815
1837.   She was married. Dec. 25, 1860. by Rev. John S.

C. Abbott, to Elmer William Hitchcock, son of Benjamin Truman and Julia (Frisbie) Hitchcock of Waterbury. They reside in the western part of Cheshire, where he is engaged in farming.

368   **V. Gardner Moss Hall,** born in Brunswick, Ohio, **816** Jan. 11, 1841. When three years old his parents removed to Connecticut. He commenced his business life as a peddler of ice in Waterbury, and gradually built up a large business. He became a member of the firm of Upson & Hall of Waterbury, and was also president of the Naugatuck Valley Ice Company of Bridgeport. He married, May 10, 1870, Georgiana Elizabeth Mullings, daughter of John and Elizabeth (Brooks) Mullings. He died in Waterbury, Oct. 13, 1880. The local paper said of him: "The deceased was highly esteemed and had a large circle of friends. He was of a retiring disposition, but was a business man of strict integrity and applied himself closely to the interests of the firm and Company he was identified with." His widow resides in Waterbury.

369   **VI. Franklin Amos Hall,** born in Brunswick, Ohio, **818** Aug. 1, 1843; removed in infancy to Cheshire, Conn., where his boyhood was spent on his father's farm. When 19 years of age he enlisted in Company H, 20th regiment, Connecticut volunteers, and at the battle of Chancellorsville, Va., May 3d, 1863, was captured and confined for a time in Libby Prison, Richmond. After his return from the war he traveled for several years in the grocery trade, and then removed to Holyoke, Mass. where he opened a hotel, remaining there about two years. He then became the proprietor of the Earl House, Waterbury, Conn., which he kept until his death. He married, Oct. 9, 1867, Adelaide Ulissa Munger, daughter of Daniel Tuttle, and

Eliza Ann (Russell) Munger of Waterbury. He died in Waterbury, Feb. 20, 1879. "He was greatly beloved by his comrades and friends, and endured, with cheerful patience the years of suffering occasioned by the disease which ended his life."— *Waterbury paper.*

370 VII. **Denison Asahel Hall**, born in Cheshire. Conn., Jan. 18, 1847. He was a book-agent, and traveled through Maine and the British Provinces. He died, Dec. 2, 1875; unmarried.

371 VIII. **Adelaide Eliza Hall**, born in Cheshire, Sept. 819 17, 1849. She married, June 14, 1871, George Britain Lawton of Waterbury, son of Richard Carlisle and Elizabeth (Hibbin) Lawton. He is a die sinker at the Scoville Manufacturing Company, Waterbury.

372 IX. **Warren Leander Hall**, born in Cheshire, May 821b. 21, 1856. He married, Dec. 14, 1881, Etta Louisa Andrews, daughter of Samuel M. and Amelia (Thompson) Andrews of Naugatuck, Conn. They reside in Naugatuck. He is an importer and dealer in foreign and domestic fruits at 258 Washington Street, New York.

CHILD OF HIRAM AND NANCY (HALL) BRADLEY. 140

373 I. **Orilla Elizabeth Bradley**, born January, 1834; died June 9, 1834.

CHILDREN OF AMOS, JR., AND ARPATIA (DOOLITTLE) 141
HALL.

374 I. **Louisa Elizabeth Hall**, born Sept. 10, 1835. She 822 married, June 7, 1869, Almer B. Hitchcock, son of Gains and Betsey (Brown) Hitchcock of Waterbury. He was born in Waterbury, March 23, 1835. By trade he is a clock-maker, and is employed in a clock factory at Waterbury as a "pinion turner."

375   II.   Leander Wilson Hall, born March 15, 1837 ; died in Brunswick, Ohio, Sept. 21, 1840.

376   III.   Nancy Orilla Hall, born June 26, 1842. She **823** married, Oct. 30, 1872, George Hauxhurst. They reside in Southington, Conn. He is a harness-maker.

CHILDREN OF GEORGE ANSON AND SARAH (MER- **142** RIAMS) HALL.

377   I.   Sarah Jane Hall, born April 7, 1840. She married, Jan. 9, 1872, Joseph Scott. He was a baker. They lived in Waterbury, where he died. Jan. 29, 1877. She married (2d). Sept. 4. 1877. Joseph Baldwin. They reside in Trumbull, Conn. He is a farmer. She has no children.

378   II.   Nancy Orilla Hall, born June 5. 1841. She **824** married, Nov. 21. 1871. John David Benham of Middlebury, Conn. She died in Westville, Conn., Nov. 20. 1872. Mr. Benham is a stage-driver and proprietor of the stage route between Middlebury and Southbury, Conn.

CHILDREN OF HENRY AND SUSAN SALINA (HALL) **143** LIVINGSTON.

379   I.   Emma Eliza Livingston, born Oct. 10, 1841 ; **825** married, Feb. 28. 1862. William Peebles, who was born in Hinckley, Ohio, Nov. 22, 1840, and died April 28, 1872. Mr. Peebles was a farmer, a resident of Hinckley, and enlisted in 1862 as a minute-man for the defense of Cincinnati, at the time it was menaced by the Confederate forces during the War of the Rebellion. She married (2d), July 27, 1881. Horace Carpenter, who was born in Strongsville, Cuyahoga County, Ohio, Nov. 20, 1830. He has resided in Brunswick, Ohio, since 1855, engaged as farmer and cattle broker, and has held a number of town offices.

380   II. Amos Livingston, born Dec. 27, 1843. He **827**
married, May 6, 1869, Carrie Retteg. They reside in
Weymouth, Medina County, Ohio, where he is engaged in
the dry-goods business.

381   III. Mary Elbertine Livingston, born Sept. 24,
1848; married, June 14, 1864, William Gay, who was
born in East Bloomfield, Ontario County, N. Y., April 18,
1833. He removed to Hinckley, Medina County, Ohio, in
1836, and is a farmer and fruit-grower. They have no
children.

382   IV. Frederick Charles Livingston, born Feb. 14,
1852. He married, May 13, 1878, Ida Bell Moody,
daughter of Asahel Wright and Paulina (Culver) Moody
of Brunswick, Ohio. They reside in Brunswick, where
he is a farmer. No children.

383   V. Hiram Edward Livingston, born March 24, **829**
1855; married, May 12, 1881, Hattie Curtis Ellis,
daughter of George Otis and Clarissa R. (Dunbar) Ellis,
of Middlebury, Conn. He is engaged in the grocery
business in Waterbury, Conn.

CHILD OF EDWARD AND HENRIETTA ELIZABETH (HALL) **144**
TERRELL.

384   I. Mary Elizabeth Terrell, born Dec. 2, 1852. She **830**
married, Oct. 17, 1878, Isaiah Alexander Uffendale, who
was born in Williamsburg (Brooklyn, E. D.), N. Y., June
15, 1854. In 1870 he removed to Waterbury, where he
now resides. He has charge of the soldering department
at Holmes, Booth & Hayden's brass goods manufactory.

CHILDREN OF GEORGE RICE AND LAURINDA (SAFFORD) **145**
BENEDICT.

385   I. **George Thaddeus Benedict,** born Aug. 19, 1828;
died Oct. 25, 1828.

386   II. **Charles Laurens Benedict,** born in Niagara   **832**
County, N. Y., Dec. 30, 1829. He married, Dec. 30,
1856, Julia Adelaide Lusk, daughter of Alfred and
Martha (Parker) Lusk of Edwardsville, Ill., who was
born Jan. 24, 1839. Mr. Benedict was a miller by trade,
but from 1866 to 1869 was engaged in merchandising,
at which time he resided in Gillespie, Ill. He then
removed to Edwardsville, Ill., and engaged in railroading
until his death, which occurred Dec. 22, 1875.

387   III. **George Rice Benedict, Jr.,** born at South   **835**
Royalton, Niagara County, N. Y., June 17, 1832. He
remained at home on the farm until twenty-four years of
age, when he entered upon the profession of a teacher, and
followed it until 1862, having lived during this time at
several places in the West, his last residence being in Nemaha County, Kan. He enlisted as a private in Company
1, 13th Regiment Kansas Volunteers, serving until November, 1863, when he was detached from that regiment and
assigned to the 2d Kansas Colored Volunteers as sergeant-
major. In January, 1864, he was promoted to be second
lieutenant, and in April, at the battle of Jenkins Ferry,
Saline River, Ark., received a bullet wound in the left arm
which retired him to hospital at Little Rock, and from
the effects of which he did not recover for a year,
although he rejoined his regiment in July. He was discharged from the service Dec. 23, 1864, having participated in the battles of Kane's Hill, Ark., Nov. 27, 1862;
Prairie Grove, Dec. 7, 1862; Van Buren, Dec. 28, 1862;
and Jenkins Ferry, April 30, 1864, besides many skir-

mishes and reconnoissances. During the years 1864 and 1865 he made a number of trips by wagon across the plains to the Rocky Mountains, a distance of 650 miles. In the winter of 1866-7 he taught school at Granada, Kan., and the following spring commenced breaking prairie for a farm. He married, March 12, 1868, Sarah Isabel Hart, daughter of William Jewett and Mary E. (Collings) Hart of Granada, who was born in Putnam County, Ind., July 16, 1849. Mr. Benedict continued as a farmer until January, 1873, when, having been elected to the office of clerk of the District Court for Nemaha County, he entered upon its duties, and served in this capacity until 1880. He is now a real-estate and loan agent; is and always has been a total abstainer from the use of spirituous liquors, and an advocate of prohibition. He is justly proud of his adopted State, her soil, climate, schools, churches, laws, and her undeveloped resources.

388   IV. **Henry Linnæus Benedict**, born Aug. 18, 1834; resides at Royalton, N. Y., unmarried.

389   V. **Emily Safford Benedict**, born April 4, 1837. She married, June 17, 1866, Charles L. Fisk. They reside in Royalton, N. Y., and have no children.

390   VI. **Edward C. Delavan Benedict**, born March 25, 1842; died Jan. 28, 1843.

CHILDREN OF JULIUS HOYT AND OLIVE (CREGO) BENE   146
DICT.

391   I. **Daniel Benedict**, born in Rutland, N. Y., April   838
2, 1832. He removed to Michigan with his parents in 1839, and followed all the business pursuits in which his father was engaged. With his brothers he built a large stone-front store on Maumee Street, Adrian, in which he now continues in the clothing business. He served four

21

years as deputy sheriff, and one term as alderman from the fourth ward of Adrian. He married, Dec. 26, 1872, Margaret Elizabeth Thompson, daughter of Charles and Sarah Adaline (Van Fosson) Thompson of Ypsilanti, Mich. She was born in Conway, Shiawassee County, Mich., Oct. 19, 1846.

392   II.   **Julius Benedict,** born in Royalton, N. Y., June   839
30, 1834. He settled with his father in Adrian, Mich., and for many years has been a successful merchant there. He married, Aug. 17, 1859, Harriet Munger, daughter of Algernon S. and Adeline (Crego) Munger of Bay City, Mich., born Oct. 1, 1842.

393   III.   **Oscar Benedict,** born March 9, 1837; married, April 26, 1877, Mattie Mirick, daughter of Hiram T. and Rowena (Gardner) Mirick of Lyons, Wayne County, N. Y. She was born in Lyons, Nov. 17, 1853. They have no children. Mr. Benedict is a merchant in Adrian.

394   IV.   **Mortimer Benedict,** born May 16, 1842; died March 25, 1843.

395   V.   **George Benedict,** born June 2, 1851; died Aug. 2, 1851.

CHILDREN OF GEORGE HAYNOR AND NANCY RICE   147
(BENEDICT) UTLEY.

396   I.   **Laurinda Utley,** born July 20, 1828; died young.

397   II.   **Daniel Palmer Utley,** born June 11, 1830. He   841
married, July 25, 1871, Eunice Elderkin, daughter of Jedediah and Emily (Andres) Elderkin of Pendleton, N. Y. He is a farmer, and resides in Flint, Mich.

398   III.   **Julia Ann Utley,** born Oct. 25, 1832. She married, Feb. 6, 1856, Horace Browning, son of Rev.

Crawford Browning of Royalton, N. Y. They reside in Wolcottville, N. Y., and have no children. He is a farmer.

399   IV. Emily Eliza Utley, born in Royalton, N. Y.,   842
May 26, 1835; married, Nov. 1, 1854, George Washington Van Valkenburgh, son of William A. and Rosanna (Worden) Van Valkenburgh of Lockport, N. Y. He was born in Lockport in 1842; was brought up to the harness-making trade, but became a farmer, and in 1858 purchased a farm at Davison Center, Genesee County, Mich. He enlisted in 1861 in the 23d Regiment Michigan Volunteers, and was appointed corporal in Company H. At the battle of Resaca, Ga., he was the color-bearer of his regiment, and was killed in that action, May 14, 1864. He is buried in the National Cemetery at Chattanooga, Tenn. She married (2d), July 5, 1877, Lafayette Riddle, a native of Elba, Genesee County, N. Y., as his second wife. At the age of 16 Mr. Riddle settled in Niagara County, N. Y., and has ever since resided there, his present home being in Rapids. He is a farmer.

400   V. Oscar Enoch Utley, born Sept. 8, 1837. He married, Oct. 12, 1866, Cordelia Elderkin, daughter of Jedediah and Emily (Andres) Elderkin of Pendleton, N. Y. They reside in Franklinmouth, Mich. He is a farmer. They have no children.

401   VI. Timothy Franklin Utley, born April 19, 1840. He married, April 30, 1863, Maria Freelove Van Valkenburgh, daughter of William A. and Rosanna (Worden) Van Valkenburgh of Lockport, N. Y. He is a merchant in Lockport. They have no children.

402   VII. Morris Eugene Utley, born May 14, 1845.   844
He married, March 31, 1866, Desdemona Stimson, daughter of Walter and Amanda M. (Walters) Stimson of Pen-

dleton, N. Y. He is a farmer, and resides in Clarence Hollow, N. Y.

403   VIII. Alma Augusta Utley, born Nov. 18, 1848;   846
married, Sept. 30, 1872, Almer W. Mitchell, son of Horace
W. and Dollie (Crego) Mitchell of Royalton, N. Y. They
reside in Rapids, N. Y. He is a merchant.

404   IX. George Benedict Utley, born June 29, 1853;   847
married, Feb. 28, 1877, Emma Jane Laraway, daughter
of Joseph and Cordelia (Cummings) Laraway of Clarence,
N. Y. He is a farmer at Rapids, N. Y.

*CHILDREN OF GEORGE CLINTON AND AMANDA (BENE-   148
DICT) CREGO.

405   I. Julius Francelo Crego, born March 28, 1831.   850
He married, February, 1853, Amy Gallup, daughter of
Hiram and Eliza (Striclen) Gallup of Erie County, N. Y.
She died in May, 1859. He married (2d), Nov. 18, 1862,
Caroline M. Chandler, daughter of William A. and Fannie
M. (Green) Chandler of Lenawee County, Mich. They
reside near Traverse City, Mich. He is a farmer.

406   II. Martha Ann Crego, born May 2, 1840. She   853
married, June 29, 1862, Harrison Ostrander. They
reside in Adrian, Mich. He is a cattle dealer.

407   III. Nancy Laurinda Crego, born Dec. 24, 1842.
She married, Dec. 10, 1868, William Martin Duryee, who
was born Dec. 31, 1845, in Livingston County, N. Y.
Mrs. Duryee died in Adrian, April 12, 1870. She had
no children. Mr. Duryee again married, and resides in
Michigan Center. He is a market gardener.

408   IV. George Clinton Crego, born in 1844; mar-   855
ried, May 30, 1868, Mary Eleanor Lawrence, daughter of

---

* These are probably not arranged in order of age.

Hiram and Hannah (McCaulay) Lawrence of Rome, Lenawee County, Mich. He was a cattle dealer, and died in Adrian, June 13, 1876. His widow married, Oct. 24, 1882, Isaac Mortimer Dean, and resides in Adrian.

409   V.   James Henry Crego, born in Clarence, Niagara   857 County, N. Y., June 8, 1850. He married, June 22, 1870, Anna Scott, daughter of Giles and Anna Scott of Rome, Mich., who died in September, 1874. He is a stock-drover, and resides in Adrian.

410   VI.   Nancy Jane Crego, died at the age of seven years.

411   VII.   Thaddeus Crego, died in infancy.

412   VIII.   Polly Lavinia Crego, died when twenty years old.

413   IX.   Sherman Crego, died at eleven years of age.

CHILDREN OF ALVIN BONTECOU AND CORNELIA (SMITH)   149 RICE.

414   I.   Nancy Elizabeth Rice, born March 25, 1830.   859 She married, Aug. 14, 1849, James Noah Finch, son of Noah Finch of Athol, N. Y., where he was born May 27, 1824. They removed to Michigan in 1855, and now reside in Solon Township, Kent County. He is a lumberman and farmer.

415   II.   Charles Benham Rice, born Nov. 6, 1832. He   864 removed from New York State to Michigan in 1854, and later to Illinois, where he now resides in Limestone, Kankakee County. He married, June 3, 1863, Mrs. Lois Mariette Shear, widow of DeWitt Clinton Shear of Putnam, Washington County, N. Y., and daughter of James Lawson and Sallie A. (Beckwith) Smith of Orwell, Vt. Mr. Rice is a farmer.

416   III. Eben Smith Rice, born Nov. 19, 1834. He   867
removed to Michigan from New York State in 1855.
He married, Oct. 15, 1857, Cinderella Burt, daughter of
Justus and Betsey (Hill) Burt of Ada, Kent County,
Mich. He died at Ada, March 30, 1863. Mrs. Rice is
living in Ada.

417   IV. Theodosia Phebe Rice, born April 18, 1836.   869
She married, March 12, 1863, John Conley of Ada, Mich.,
a farmer. She died in Grand Rapids, April 24, 1875.
Mr. Conley's place of residence is unknown.

418   V. Thaddeus Rice, died in infancy in Erie County,
N. Y.

CHILD OF CHARLES BENHAM AND ALMA AUGUSTA   150
(BROOKER) RICE.

419   I. Alma Augusta, born in 1841; died October, 1843,
at Buffalo, N. Y.

CHILDREN OF JAMES AND HANNAH (DOUGREY) NICHOLS.   151

420   I. Jane Nichols, born Sept. 8, 1832. Resides in
Lansingburg, N. Y.

421   II. Anna Nichols, born April 21, 1834. Resides in
Lansingburg.

422   III. John Dougrey Nichols, born Dec. 30, 1837.   872
Married, March 20, 1859, Elizabeth Van Zandt, daughter
of Barent V. and Maria (Houghtaling) Van Zandt of New
Scotland, Albany County, N. Y. He is engaged in the
wholesale drug business in Albany. His residence is at
Lansingburg.

423   IV. Thomas Marris Nichols, born Dec. 7, 1840;
died Aug. 1, 1866.

CHILDREN OF JAMES, JR., AND FRANCES ELIZABETH **152**
(MOULTON) DOUGREY.

424   I. **John Dougrey,** born Aug. 9, 1832. He married, **875**
May 8, 1858, Isabel Mary Montgomery, daughter of John
and Mary (Hallowell) Montgomery of Stockport, Columbia County, N. Y. She was born in Stockport, March
10, 1840. They reside in Lansingburg. He conducts a
local express business between Lansingburg, Troy, and
Albany.

425   II. **James Dougrey (3d),** born Oct. 23, 1834. He **879**
married, July 15, 1859, Jane Amanda Jones, daughter of
Nahum P. and Sarah Ann (Alexander) Jones of Lansingburg. She was born March 21, 1840. James Dougrey,
in early life, opened a livery establishment in Saratoga
Springs, N. Y., and afterwards conducted a similar establishment at Troy. He built and occupied the *Park House,*
on Whipple Avenue, between Lansingburg and Troy. In
1875 he was appointed by the State to the office of section superintendent on the Champlain Canal, and held it
for four years. He now resides in Stillwater, Saratoga
County, where he owns a fine farm, and makes a specialty
of blooded stock.

426   III. **Elizabeth Moulton Dougrey,** born Feb. 1,
1837; died Jan. 9, 1872, unmarried.

427   IV. **Howard Moulton Dougrey,** born Sept. 1, 1839.
Resides in Troy, unmarried. He holds a responsible position in the office of the National Express Company.

428   V. **George Moulton Dougrey,** born Oct. 12, 1841;
died Feb. 17, 1842.

429   VI. **Clarissa Bontecou Dougrey,** born June 1, 1834. **882**
She married, Dec. 22, 1869, Chandler Hezekiah Loomis of
Syracuse, N. Y. He was born in Pompey, N. Y., Jan.

28, 1836. Since 1858 he has been engaged in contracting in New York, Pennsylvania, and Canada, and is now superintendent of the Union Dredging Company of New York. They reside at 432 West 20th Street.

CHILDREN OF CHARLES DIKEMAN AND CLARISSA ANN 153 (DOUGREY) SMITH.

430   I. **David Reeves Smith**, born in Marshall, Mich.,   884 April 26, 1835. He is a civil and mechanical engineer. In his professional capacity he has conducted operations in many States of this Republic, and in South and Central Americas; his residence in different parts of Spanish America aggregating eighteen years. He married, April 23, 1861, in Copiapo, Chile, S. A., Juana Carrasco, daughter of Tadeo and Martina (Guerra) Carrasco of Santiago. Their present place of residence is in Cohoes, N. Y., where he fills the position of secretary to the Folded Filter Manufacturing Company. Mr. Smith is the author of a work entitled *Ownership and Sovereignty*, published in Cohoes, 1883.

431   II. **James Dougrey Smith**, born in Marshall, Mich., Nov. 6, 1837. He married, April 15, 1868, Ellen Livingston, daughter of James and Christina (McDougal) Livingston of Chicago, Ill. Mr. Smith graduated from Monmouth College, Ill., in 1866, and from the United Presbyterian Theological Seminary of the Northwest, Monmouth, in March, 1870. He entered upon the work of the ministry in the Presbyterian communion, as pastor of the church in Hanover, Jo Daviess County, Ill., in May of the same year, and was installed Oct. 17. He remained in charge of this church until Nov. 9, 1878, when failing health compelled rest for a few months. In August, 1879, he recommenced preaching, at Red Oak, Iowa; then labored from Oct. 1, 1879, to the end of 1880, at various places

in Western Pennsylvania, under appointment of the General Assembly. He resides at present at Lodi, Columbia County, Wis., having entered this field Jan. 1, 1881. They have no children.

432   III. Anna Mary Smith, born in Marshall, Mich.,   895
March 31, 1840. She married, in Pulaski, Ill., Dec. 21, 1859, Albert Jacob Mitchell of Du Quoin, Ill. He is a native of Manchester, N. H., and at one time resided in Grand Rapids, Mich., where he was a music dealer. He is now agent of the C., R. I. & P. R. R., at Englewood, near Chicago, Ill.

433   IV. Day Kellogg Smith, born in Chicago, Ill., Jan.   899
16, 1845. He married, Jan. 4, 1867, at Topeka, Kan., Mary Elizabeth Torry, daughter of John and Elizabeth (Jacobs) Torry of Lockport, Ill. She died at Peoria, Ill., Oct. 20, 1868. He married (2d), at Peoria, Sept. 19, 1870, Margaret Virginia Donlevy, daughter of Owen and Clarissa (King) Donlevy of Peoria. Mr. Smith commenced his business life in 1858, as a telegraph operator, and remained in this employment until 1865, during a portion of the time in the military telegraph service in Tennessee. In the fall of 1865 he removed to Peoria, and became train dispatcher and superintendent of telegraph for the T., P. & W. R. R., and in 1868 was appointed superintendent of the road. In 1876 he went to Cheyenne, Wyoming Territory, as chief dispatcher of the Union Pacific Railroad; then to Port Huron, Mich., as a general ticket agent; next to Paris, Ill., as superintendent of the Illinois Midland Railway; to St. Paul in 1880, and to Crookston, Minn., in 1882, as division superintendent of the St. Paul, Minneapolis & Manitoba Railroad; and later to Como, Col., as division superintendent of the Missouri Pacific Railroad. July 1, 1885, he was appointed superintendent of the Kansas City Belt Railroad Company,

22

and removed to that city, where he resides at 2102 Woodland Avenue.

434   **V. Clara Frances Smith,** born July 29, 1850. She   **904** married, in Cheyenne, Wyoming Territory, in March, 1877, Edgar W. Nye, better known as " Bill Nye," the humorist. He was born in Shirley, Me., Aug. 25, 1850. His father was Franklin Nye, a direct descendant of the French *Neys*, a family to which Marshal Ney belonged. His mother was Eliza Mitchell Loring, a descendant of the famous brothers of France, whose names were given to the Province of Lorraine. At the age of three years he removed to the West with his parents, and has ever since lived in that section, and is a thoroughly Western American. In politics he is a strong Republican. By profession he is a lawyer, but by practice has become known to the world as the "king bee of humorists." For a number of years he was the editor of the *Laramie Boomerang*, and clippings from that paper could be found in every sheet published in this country. Mr. Nye was an office-holder in Wyoming Territory for seven years. "He had a narrow escape from being elected a member of the Wyoming Legislature in 1877, and only eluded his pursuers by a lucky stratagem." At one time he won fame as postmaster at Laramie City, and his letter of acceptance of the appointment (a copy of which is here given) to Second Assistant Postmaster-General Hatton, was copied by the press throughout the land, and editorially commented on by the *London News*, in a grave way:

THE DAILY BOOMERANG,   )
LARAMIE CITY, WY., Aug. 9, 1882.)

My Dear General: — I have received the news by telegraph of my nomination and confirmation as postmaster at Laramie, and wish to extend my thanks for the same. I have ordered an entirely new set of boxes and post-office

outfit, including new corrugated cuspidors for the lady
clerks. I look upon the appointment myself as a triumph
of eternal truth over error and wrong. It is one of the
epochs, as I may say, in the Nation's onward march toward political purity and perfection. I don't know when
I have noticed any stride in the affairs of state which so
thoroughly impressed me with its wisdom. Now that we
are co-workers in the same department, I trust that you
will not feel shy or backward in consulting me at any
time relative to matters concerning post-office affairs. Be
perfectly frank with me, and feel perfectly free to just
bring anything of that kind right to me. Do not feel re-
luctant because I may appear cold and reserved. Perhaps
you think I do not know the difference between a general
delivery window and a three-m quad, but that is a mistake.
My general information is far beyond those of my years.

With profoundest regard,

I remain sincerely yours,

BILL NYE, P. M.

Mr. Nye is the author of several books, prominent
among them being *Bill Nye and Boomerang*, and *The
Forty Liars*. In the winter of 1882–3 he suffered from
a severe illness. His recovery was very slow and tedious,
and he gave up literary work for a time; he also left
Laramie, and removed to Hudson, Wis., where he now
resides. As a fair specimen of his vein of humor, the
following letter to the *Boston Globe* is subjoined:

HUDSON, WIS., March 10, 1885.

To the Editor of The Globe: — Referring to the matter
of life insurance and its benefits, I can hardly give the
Globe a very extended experience so far as I am individu-
ally concerned.

I carry an insurance of $7,000 only; and though that
may look small to you, Mr. Taylor, I am sure that if you

could see me and converse with me you would say it was
plenty large enough. If I were to die suddenly to-morrow,
I should be almost ashamed to claim the full amount of
the policy. 1 am trying now to lead such a life that by
next fall I would have no hesitation in asking the companies to raise my insurance to $10,000.

I look upon life insurance as a great comfort, not only
to the beneficiary, but to the insured, who very rarely
lives to realize anything pecuniarily from his venture.
Twice I have almost raised my wife to affluence and cast
a gloom over the community in which I lived; but something happened to the physician for a few days so that he
could not attend to me, and I recovered. For nearly two
years I was under the doctor's care. He had his finger
on my pulse or in my pocket all that time. He was a
young Western physician, who attended me on Tuesdays
and Fridays. The rest of the week he devoted his medical
skill to horses that were mentally and physically broken
down. He said he attended me largely for my society.
I felt flattered to know that he enjoyed my society, after
having been thrown all the week among horses that had
had much greater advantages than I.

My wife at first objected seriously to an insurance on
my life, and said she would never, never touch a dollar
of the money if I were to die; but after I had been sick
nearly two years, and my disposition had suffered a good
deal, she said that I need not delay the obsequies on that
account. But the life insurance slipped through my fin-
gers somehow, and I recovered.

I have built up two life-insurance companies and placed
them on their feet since that. I hope they will not forget
it when I come to call on them for a favor. One of them
is an "old-liner" and the other is an assessment company.
I took a policy in the assessment company because I had
been in politics some, and when I went out I missed my

assessment sadly. I had become a slave to the assessment habit, and so had to do something in order to supply its place. I now feel first-rate. When I get my assessment notice I imagine that I am an office-holder and that it is a billet-doux from the central committee, so it is like old times almost.

Life insurance is a good thing. I would not be without it. My health is greatly improved since I got my new policy. Formerly I used to have a seal-brown taste in my mouth when I arose in the morning, but that has disappeared entirely. I am more hopeful and happy, and my hair is getting thicker on top. I would not try to keep house without life insurance. Last September I was caught in one of the most destructive cyclones that ever visited a republican form of government. A great deal of property was destroyed and many lives were lost, but I was spared. People who had no insurance were mowed down on every hand, but aside from a broken leg I was entirely unharmed.

Since insuring my life I sleep better nights, and my neighbors are getting more reckless about leaving their watermelons and clothes-lines out over night. If I had a voice that could be heard on the other side of the Soudan it would still be for good, solid life insurance. In these days of dynamite and roller rinks and the gory meat-axe of a new administration, we ought to make some provision for the future.

BILL NYE.

CHILDREN OF JAMES NORMAN AND MARY ELIZABETH 155
(DOUGREY) BARKER.

435 I. Calvin John Barker, born March 18, 1840. He 906 married, June 3, 1863, Celia Frances Curran, daughter of Thomas and Hannah (Burbank) Curran of Lansingburg. He is a brushmaker. They reside in Lansingburg.

174   BONTECOU FAMILY.

436   II.   Irene Hawley Barker, born Feb. 22,1842.

437   III.   Agnes Burton Barker, born Oct. 9, 1843.

438   IV.   Clara Dougrey Barker, born Dec. 16, 1844; died Sept. 1, 1846.

CHILDREN OF WILLIAM BROWNELL AND JULIA (DOU-   **156** GREY) CORY.

439   I.   William Julius Cory, born in Lansingburg, July 31, 1848. He is unmarried. He has long held the position of shipping clerk in a large bakery establishment in Lansingburg; is one of the village trustees, and a strong temperance advocate.

440   II.   Alice Magdalene Cory, born Sept. 21, 1850. She **910** married, Feb. 15, 1881, James Albert Whittaker, a native of Fall River, Mass. They reside in Lansingburg. He is a tinsmith.

CHILDREN OF ANDREW WINTON AND JULIA ANN   **157** (BRISTOL) FRENCH.

441   I.   Martha Sackett French, born Sept. 22, 1831; died in 1870, unmarried.

442   II.   Maria Dickinson French, born Nov. 17, 1834.   **911** She married, Aug. 30, 1854, Frederick North Page, who was born in Athens, Bradford County, Pa., Dec. 5, 1832. At about the age of 20 Mr. Page engaged in mercantile business in Athens, continuing fifteen years. In 1867 he removed to Williamsport, Pa., and with the exception of a year or two in Philadelphia has ever since lived there, engaged in the manufacture of furniture. While in Athens he was a vestryman in Trinity (Episcopal) Church, and has held the same office both in Christ and Trinity Churches, Williamsport. Mrs. Page died in Wil-

liamsport, Oct. 21, 1875, and he again married, June 5,
1877, Martha White of that city.

443 III. **Mary Glenney French**, born Aug. 1, 1838. **921**
She married, Oct. 12, 1857, John M. Ackerman of Milford, Conn., a tinsmith and plumber. He died in 1878.
She married (2d), Aug. 1, 1881, Sidney Buckingham of
Sterling, Ill. He formerly lived in Milford, and was
brought up to the shoemaking business; but went West,
and made a fortune in mining operations. They removed
to Creston, Iowa, in 1882, and later to Oakland, Cal.

444 IV. **Julia Cassandana French**, born Jan. 8, 1846. **923**
She married, July 5, 1866, Fountain Thomas Page, who
was born in Athens, Pa., Jan. 1, 1842. He is the son of
Thomas and Anna Page. In 1862 he commenced a mercantile career in Athens, and by untiring energy, strict
integrity, and honorable dealing has won the confidence
of the entire community. He still continues as a merchant, and is also express agent. He has served several
terms as a councilman, and twice filled the office of
burgess.

CHILDREN OF JOHN AND HENRIETTA ELIZA (BRISTOL) **158**
SANFORD.

445 I. **John Ferdinand Sanford,** born in Milford, Conn., **927**
Oct. 8, 1843. At the age of 16 he went to New York
as clerk in his uncle Thomas Bristol's shoe store. In the
spring of 1862 he enlisted for three months' service in
the 71st Regiment New York State Militia; soon after
the expiration of this term he enlisted in the 27th Regiment Connecticut Volunteers, and with it participated
in the battles of Fredericksburg, Chancellorsville, and
Gettysburg. His term of service having expired, he
again enlisted, this time in the First Connecticut Heavy
Artillery; but having received a commission as second

lieutenant in the 30th Connecticut (colored) Volunteers,
he did not join the former body. He was afterwards
transferred to the 31st United States colored troops, and
served with them in the Armies of the Potomac and the
James until the close of the war, being promoted in the
mean time to a first-lieutenancy. He was sent to Texas
in the summer of 1865, and was mustered out of the
service in October of the same year at Brownsville.
Shortly after this he went to Charleston, S. C., and entered
the employ of his uncle Timothy M. Bristol, in the shoe
trade. From there he removed to Marshall, Mich., and
entered the grocery business; then to Topeka, Kan., in
the grocery and drygoods business; and shortly afterwards assumed a position as salesman in the wholesale
shoe trade at 122 Duane Street, New York. At present
he is employed as salesman in the umbrella and parasol
trade, at 299 Broadway. He married, Dec. 25, 1867,
Sarah Buckingham, daughter of John and Sarah Ann
(Clark) Buckingham of Milford. They reside at 432
Van Buren Street, Brooklyn, N. Y.

446   II. Julia Isabella Sanford, born March 9, 1845.
Resides in Milford, Conn.

447   III. Helen Sanford, born Sept. 22, 1849. She
resides in Milford.

CHILDREN OF WILLIAM BONTECOU AND SARAH A. (MER-   159
RICK) BRISTOLL.

448   I. William Merrick Bristoll, born in Milford,
Conn., Sept. 3, 1839. The greater part of his childhood
until 1851 was passed in Charleston, S. C. In that year
he was sent North to his native place, and the next few
years were spent in preparation for college; and in 1860
he graduated from Yale. He entered upon the profession
of a teacher, and the breaking out of the Civil War found

him located at Charleston. On attempting to escape to the North with such portion of his father's property as he could transport, he was arrested and the property confiscated. He finally gained the North by a circuitous route through Georgia, Tennessee, and Kentucky, after a hard journey of three weeks, much of it on foot, some of the time prisoner of guerrillas, and later under arrest as a spy in the Federal lines. He resumed his occupation as teacher, and in January, 1862, became principal of a public school in Milwaukee. In July, 1863, he enlisted in the 13th Wisconsin Battery, of which he became junior second lieutenant Jan. 5, 1864, senior second lieutenant Oct. 22, 1864, and junior first lieutenant Jan. 30, 1865. The battery was stationed at Baton Rouge, La., in January, 1864, and Lieut. Bristoll was detailed on general court-martial; on Board to examine commissioned officers; on Board of Survey; also as member of a military commission. He was detailed as depot ordnance officer at Baton Rouge, Sept. 29, 1864, and served until the close of February, 1865. He was appointed depot ordnance officer at New Orleans, March 24, 1865; and at the time of his discharge from the service, Jan. 14, 1866, was assistant chief of ordnance of the military division of the Gulf. In September, 1866, he entered the Andover, Mass., Theological Seminary, and remained two years of the course, intending to finish in the Chicago Seminary; but in 1868 was called to be professor of Latin in Ripon College, Wis. He served five years, and resigned to take the same chair in Atlanta University, Atlanta, Ga. He married, Dec. 1, 1870, Rosa Olds, daughter of Leavitt Ira and Rhoda Ann (Randall) Olds of Afton, Washington County, Minn. They have had no children. Mrs. Bristoll was a graduate from Ripon College in 1870, with the highest honors of her class. During his stay in Ripon, Mr. Bristoll was deacon of the Congregational Church.

23

In Atlanta he was librarian of Graves Library and
treasurer of the University, in addition to his professor-
ship, and Mrs. Bristoll was secretary of the Faculty.
Owing to Mrs. Bristoll's failing health they were obliged
to leave the South, and removed to Yankton, Dak., where
he became principal of Yankton Academy, his wife also
being a teacher. This institution became merged in the
public-school system of Yankton in 1875, and Mr. Bristoll was elected secretary of the Board of Education, and
ex officio Superintendent of Schools. He resigned this
position Aug. 31, 1882, and accepted that of professor of
Latin and principal of the preparatory department in
Yankton College. Subsequently he gave up these positions, and after a few months spent in Minneapolis,
entered upon educational work in connection with the
freedmen's interest in Charleston, S. C., where he now
is. During his residence in Yankton he was organist of
the First Congregational Church; always connected with
Sunday-school work, and the latter part of the time
deacon in the church.

449   II. **Julia Bristoll,** born Dec. 12, 1844; died the
same day.

450   III. **Julia Alice Bristoll,** born Sept. 5, 1846. She   929
married, Sept. 5, 1873, Lucien White Stilwell, who was
born in Manlius, Onondaga County, N. Y., March 24,
1844. He is the son of Lorson and Mary K. Stilwell.
In 1846 his parents removed to Wisconsin, settling near
Ripon. He obtained his education in the district school
and Ripon College, and at the age of 19 removed to Cairo,
Ill., where he obtained a clerkship in the post-office, which
was then actively engaged in handling mail for the army.
Finding this occupation too confining, he leased a stall in
the market-house and dealt in produce, and subsequently
formed a partnership in the grocery business, in which he

continued with increasing success for ten years. In 1874 he sold his interest to his partner and embarked in the commission flour and grain trade, which owing to the stringency of the times proved a failure. From this time for a number of years he was sometimes employed as a traveling salesman, and at others as book-keeper. In 1878 he removed his family from Cairo on account of the yellow-fever scourge then prevailing, and after a short residence in St. Louis, Chicago, and Elgin, Ill., settled, in June, 1879, in Deadwood, Dak., where he became book-keeper in the First National Bank, a position he still holds. Mr. Stilwell is a member of the Methodist Church, and has filled most of its lay offices, being particularly active in Sunday-school work.

451   IV.   Edward James Bristoll, born March 20, 1851. Resides in Milford, Conn. Unmarried.

452   V.   Charles Bristoll, born Nov. 10, 1855; died Oct. 18, 1869.

453   VI.   Mary Hanford Bristoll, born May 29, 1857; **932** married, March 15, 1879, Arthur Henry Davidson, a shoe manufacturer of Milford.

CHILDREN OF TIMOTHY MASON AND JANE MATILDA **160** (McDONOUGH) BRISTOL.

454   I.   Ella Bristol, born May 18, 1845. She married, **933** March 31, 1869, Henry Dunham of Abington, Mass., an inventor of leather machinery. He died Sept. 22, 1884.

From the *Abington Herald:*—" In the death of Henry Dunham, which occurred Monday morning at his home on Center Avenue, of inflammation of the bowels, the town of Abington loses one of its most prominent, widely known, and esteemed citizens. Mr. Dunham was one of twelve children. His father was Gen. Henry Dunham, son of Ezra, whose grand-father was Cornelius Dunham, born in Plymouth in 1724. The name is among the oldest and most distinguished of the Old Colony names. The mother of the deceased, still living at the age of eighty-one, was Mary Cushing, daughter of Col. Brackley Cushing — another old and honored Old Colony family name. Mr. Dunham began business life as a shoe manufacturer in the large factory on Lake Street that bears his name. He retired in 1873, and turned his attention to shoe machinery, and has given to the world some very important inventions and improvements in this direction. The three most important are the Dunham riveting machine, the toe nail machine, and the Dunham quilting machine; a detailed description of all these appeared in the *Herald* of Sept. 5. Mr. Dunham made the first quilting nail ever produced, and is believed to be the originator of the idea of inserting nails into the sole while off the boot. The funeral took place at his late residence Thursday afternoon, Rev. Messrs. Pettee and Warren officiating, with music by the new church choir. The esteem in which the deceased was held was attested not only by a profusion of flowers, but also by the presence of many prominent citizens of this and other towns. Mr. Dunham leaves a wife and three children, two boys and a girl."

455   II.   **Julia Bristol,** born Sept. 30, 1846; died Nov. 10, 1846.

456   III.   **Ida Bristol,** born Aug. 21, 1848; married, Oct.   937
4. 1871, Hugh Bradford Jackson. He died April 7, 1874. Mrs. Jackson resides in New York City.

457   IV.   **Frank Jessup Bristol,** born Aug. 16, 1850. Resides in Charleston, S. C., and is engaged with his father in the shoe business. He is unmarried.

458   V.   Arthur LeRoy Bristol, born Sept. 25, 1853. He is with his father in the shoe business, in Charleston, and is unmarried.

459   VI.   Henry Herbert Bristol, born Feb. 2, 1859.

460   VII.   Florence Marie Bristol, born March 1, 1865.

CHILDREN OF CHARLES G. AND MARY HANFORD (BRIS-   161 TOL) NEWTON.

461   1.   Charles Samuel Newton, born in Tahlequah,   938 Cherokee Nation, Aug. 11, 1838. In 1847 he removed with his father to Texas, and lived chiefly in Dallas until 1872, when he settled in Valley View, Cooke County, where he now resides. He married, April 22, 1866, Kentucky Ann Thomas, daughter of Isham and Adah (Hart) Thomas of Dallas. She died Nov. 12, 1869. He married (2d), Aug. 9, 1871, Mary Elizabeth Jones, daughter of Robert Deggs and Martha Eliza (King) Jones of Dallas. Mr. Newton is a wheelwright by trade, but for many years past has been engaged in milling, being one of the proprietors of "Newton's cotton elevator"; he is also occupied in farming and stock-raising. Mr. Newton served in the Confederate Army through the Civil War, as a private in Douglas's Texas Battery: was engaged in the battle of Pea Ridge, Mo., and in nearly all the engagements of the Army of the Tennessee; was with Kirby Smith at Richmond, Ky., his battery opening the fight, and closing it by a charge through the streets of Richmond; took part in the battles of Chickamauga, Missionary Ridge, Murfreesborough, the retreat through Georgia, Resaca, New Hope, Kenesaw, and other places; was in Hood's charge on Peach Tree Creek, July 22. 1864, and at several other points around Atlanta. His battery opened the fight at Jonesborough, and then took up the march for Tennessee; forced the passage of the Tennessee at Florence,

Ala.; went in advance to Franklin; was in the front line opposite the cotton gin, where a very large number of the Texas troops fell; was in the line around Nashville, and in the engagement there the battery was taken. After the Confederate forces fell back to Mississippi, Mr. Newton received his first furlough, Feb. 28, 1865, of ninety days, and walked from Columbus, Miss., to Dallas, Texas, a distance of six hundred miles. On the expiration of his furlough he started to join his company at Mobile, Ala., but was ordered back from Natchitoches, La., to await further orders, which up to the present time have not been received. During this long and arduous war service he did not receive a scratch. Mr. Newton holds the office of ruling elder in the Presbyterian Church, and is school trustee of Valley View.

462   II. **Mary Alice Newton,** born March 21, 1841. She married, Jan. 29, 1862, Armenius Wright, of Sulphur Springs, Johnston County, Texas. He was the son of a Methodist clergyman, and was born Dec. 23, 1838. He entered the Confederate Army in the spring of 1862, and served until his death, which occurred Nov. 30 of the same year. She married (2d), July 17, 1864, John Clark Becker. who was born in Davidson County, N. C., Nov. 3, 1828. Mr. Becker was brought up on a farm, but left it when a young man, and engaged in a variety of occupations, residing in different places until the fall of 1859, when he located in Texas and established himself as a miller. He enlisted in Parsons's Regiment of Texas Cavalry, and became quartermaster-sergeant, but owing to impaired health was employed chiefly on detached duty. After the war he carried on the mill and grocery business, but is at present engaged in gardening. There have been no children.

463   III. **William Frederick Newton,** born Dec. 11,   945 1842, at Cone Hill, Ark. He followed the fortunes of

his father's family, residing in Dallas, Texas, and other places, until 1872, when he settled in Valley View with his brother Charles, and engaged in milling, farming, and stock-raising. He is the inventor and one of the proprietors of "Newton's cotton elevator." By trade he is a carriage-maker; in the order of Freemasons he holds the office of Master, and is a deacon in the Presbyterian Church. He enlisted during the war in Company A, 31st Texas Regiment, but was employed on detached service most of the time, the last eighteen months in the engineers' department, and engaged principally in the woodwork department of the government shops at Shreveport, La. He married, April 6, 1869, Reulina Elfire King, daughter of Rev. Finus and Sarah Angeline (Weir) King of Orilla, Ellis County, Texas. She died March 2, 1871. He married (2d), June 10, 1877, Nancy Elizabeth Kendal, daughter of William Adison and Mary Catherine (Daily) Kendal of Pilot Point, Denton County, Texas.

464   IV.   George Ella Newton, born Dec. 23, 1845; died Oct. 27, 1847.

465   V.   Jane Eliza Newton, born at Dallas, Texas, April   947 9, 1849.   She married, Dec. 29, 1869, Edward Alexander Bullock, who was born in Pike County, Miss., Sept. 22, 1845.   When sixteen years of age he joined the 33d Mississippi Regiment, and served in Company H.   In March, 1862, at the battle of Corinth, was wounded in the hip by a minie ball.   He was engaged in the fight near Vicksburg; at Champion Hill, in the rear of Vicksburg, during the siege; next at Jackson, Miss.; then at the battle of Resaca, Ga., and from there back to Atlanta, fighting at different points on the way; was in the engagement at Peach Tree Creek, and wounded in the lower part of the abdomen by a minie ball while charging the Federal works, and was unable to rejoin his regiment until the

night of the battle of Franklin, Tenn.; was with the army on the retreat from Tennessee, and engaged in the several fights. At one time he served for three months as courier for Gen. Featherstone. Mr. Bullock removed to Texas in 1866, and at present resides in Valley View. He is a practical engineer by profession, a member of the Methodist Episcopal Church, and holds the rank of Master in the order of Freemasons. Mrs. Bullock died April 9, 1880.

466   **VI. Julia Augusta Newton,** born Dec. 25, 1851; died in April, 1852.

467   **VII. Julius Augustus Newton,** born Dec. 25, 1851; died in August, 1852.

CHILDREN OF STEPHEN AND NANCY BONTECOU (BRIS-   162
TOL) SEARS.

468   **I. George Edward Sears,** born Jan. 7, 1852; died Dec. 2, 1856.

469   **II. James William Sears,** born April 19, 1857. He was for seven or eight years a clerk in the drug business in New Haven, and in the fall of 1882 entered the medical department of Yale College. He graduated June 24, 1885, with the degree of M. D., and resides in New Haven, at 24 Prince Street.

CHILDREN OF THOMAS AND SARAH (BROOKS) BRISTOL.   163

470   **I. Walter Brooks Bristol,** born Dec. 10, 1859; died July 8, 1860.

471   **II. Thomas Levering Bristol,** born Aug. 31, 1863.

CHILDREN OF JAMES ANTHONY AND ELLEN MARTHA   166
(PAGE) BRISTOLL.

472   **I. Clara Bristoll,** born Dec. 16, 1861.

473   II.   **Anna Page Bristoll,** born Sept. 26, 1863; died Sept. 15, 1866.

474   III.   **Elizabeth Bristoll,** born Aug. 3, 1865.

475   IV.   **Ellen May Bristoll,** born May 12, 1868.

476   V.   **Thomas Page Bristoll,** born Jan. 29, 1871.

477   VI.   **Julia Bontecou Bristoll,** born April 6, 1876.

CHILDREN OF CHARLES EDWARD AND GRACE ANN **168**
(STOWE) BRISTOL.

478   I.   **Wallace Spear Bristol,** born April 25, 1859; died April 8, 1860.

479   II.   **William Reed Bristol,** born Sept. 27, 1860. He is a silversmith, and resides at Beaufort, S. C. He married there, July 14, 1885, Grace Whitman.

480   III.   **John Seymour Bristol,** born Oct. 23, 1862.

481   IV.   **Susan Stowe Bristol,** born June 5, 1867.

482   V.   **Henry Bontecou Bristol,** born Nov. 13, 1869.

483   VI.   **Walter Hopkins Bristol,** born Feb. 5, 1873; died June 27, 1876.

484   VII.   **Lena Augusta Bristol,** born Aug. 5, 1874; died March 19, 1876.

485   VIII.   **Charles Marcus Bristol,** born Sept. 2, 1876.

CHILDREN OF FRANCIS WRIGHT AND MARY ANN (HAN- **169**
FORD) JESUP.

486   I.   **Louisa Hanford Jesup,** born May 24, 1835; died Dec. 12, 1839.

24

487   II. **Emma Jesup,** born Jan. 24, 1837. She married,   951
June 7, 1866, William Gay Sheldon of Memphis, Tenn.
He died Sept. 12, 1868. He was engaged in the carriage
business. Mrs. Gay resides at 414 Macon Street, Brooklyn, N. Y.

488   III. **Ebenezer Jesup,** born June 15, 1839; died Jan.
20, 1840.   .

489   IV. **Louisa Hanford Jesup,** born Oct. 10, 1841;   952
married, June 12, 1865, Edward Henry Cuddy, wholesale
dry-goods merchant in New York. He died Feb. 20,
1876. She resides in Brooklyn.

490   V. **Francis Wright Jesup, Jr.,** born Jan. 14, 1844.   953
He married, June 4, 1879, Effie Crook, daughter of Rufus
and Mira (Hibbard) Crook of Brooklyn. He is engaged
in the iron business, and resides in Brooklyn.

CHILDREN OF HORACE WHITE AND JULIA BRISTOL   171
(HANFORD) DAY.

491   I. **Hanford Day,** born Dec. 16, 1839. He married,   954
June 20, 1866, Annie Maria Tator, daughter of Henry
and Elizabeth S. (Disbrow) Tator of Troy, N. Y. She
was born May 26, 1843. They reside in Lansingburg,
N. Y., where he is a dry-goods merchant.

492   II. **Horace Day,** born Dec. 16, 1839; died in infancy.

CHILDREN OF GEORGE ABBOTT AND HARRIET PYNCHON   172
(HANFORD) LALLY.

493   I. **George Hanford Lally,** born March 4, 1852; resides in Chicago, Ill., unmarried.

494   II. **Frederick Lally,** born Nov. 13, 1855. Resides
in Lansingburg, N. Y., unmarried.

495   III. Fannie Lally, born Dec. 27, 1857; died Feb. 27, 1860.

CHILDREN OF LEVI COOLEY AND MARGARET (GOOD-   173
MAN) HANFORD.

496   I. Robert Goodman Hanford, born Jan. 1, 1863.

497   II. Mary Ann Hanford, born Aug. 14, 1865; died June 3, 1879.

498   III. Horace Day Hanford, born Oct. 22, 1867.

499   IV. Harry Norman Hanford, born April 23, 1870.

CHILDREN OF FRANCIS AND MARY JANE (PRINDLE)   176
SMITH.

500   I. Emma Martha Smith, born Dec. 21, 1851.

501   II. Lillia Frances Smith, born June 17, 1853. She   955
married, April 3, 1880, Charles Gustavus Wilson of New Haven, Conn.

CHILDREN OF CHARLES EDWIN AND CLARISSA ANN   178
(SMITH) STANNARD.

502   I. Ella Mary Stannard, born Feb. 25, 1853, in New York City. She resides in Brooklyn, E. D.

503   II. Julia Henrietta Stannard, born Dec. 23, 1858, in Brooklyn, N. Y. Resides with her father in Brooklyn.

CHILD OF CHARLES WILLIAM AND MARY JESUP (SMITH)   180
STRONG.

504   I. Martha Henrietta Strong, born Aug. 29, 1856;   956
married, Oct. 27, 1880, Charles Henry Fowler, who was born March 18, 1852. They reside in Milford, Conn. He is employed in a straw-goods manufactory.

CHILDREN OF GEORGE R. AND HANNAH ELIZA (SMITH)   181
MUNSON.

505   I. **George Francis Munson**, born Jan. 19, 1857. He   957
married, April 16, 1879. Clara M. Matthews, daughter
of William Thomas and Clarissa (Corson) Matthews of
Cincinnati, Ohio. They reside in Cincinnati. He is a
salesman.

506   II. **William Lewis Munson**, born Aug. 5, 1859.

CHILDREN OF ASA MENEMON AND LUCINDA (KIDDER)   185
SANFORD.

507   I. **Susan Harriet Sanford**, died in infancy.

508   II. **Maria Elizabeth Sanford**, born May 4, 1845.   958
She married, Oct. 23, 1867, Touro Robertson of New
York, a vice-president of the American Bank Note Com-
pany. They reside at 13 East Fifty-sixth Street.

509   III. **Asa Menemon Sanford, Jr.**, born October,
1847.

CHILD OF EDWARD HUNTINGTON AND MARY (FOSTER)   186
SANFORD.

510   I. **John Edward Menemon Sanford**, born Nov. 15,   961
1847. He married, June 3, 1869, Martha Clark Taylor,
daughter of Thomas Augustus and Nancy (Clark) Taylor
of Bangor, Me. She was born in Bangor, March 20, 1851.
They reside at 29 Shepard Street, Cambridge, Mass. He
is connected, editorially, with the *Boston Evening Star.*

CHILDREN OF CHARLES BENJAMIN AND FRANCES POM-   188
EROY (TAYLOR) SANFORD.

511   I. **Charles Edward Sanford**, born in Bangor, Me.,   963
April 16, 1851. He married, Jan. 23, 1873, Kate Laim-

beer, daughter of Richard Harper and Katharine (Rad-cliff) Laimbeer of Brooklyn, N. Y. She was born March 13. 1849. He is in the commission flour business in New York. and is the inventor of " Sanford's improved watch-man's register." They reside at 7 First Place, Brooklyn.

512 II. Kittie Sanford, born in Brooklyn, Jan. 24, 1854; died Oct. 19, 1855.

CHILDREN OF EDWARD WILLIAM AND ELLEN AGNES **201**
(GILLEN) MAPLES.

513 I. Edward William Maples, Jr., born Aug. 30, 1859; died Aug. 30, 1859.

514 II. Benjamin Hood Maples, born Aug. 17, 1860. He is a clerk in the brokerage business in New York.

515 III. Lillieus Adela, born April 8, 1866; died May 4, 1868.

CHILDREN OF GEORGE AND SARAH CORNELIA (THOM- **204**
SON) RICE.

516 I. George Rice, born March 2, 1840; died Nov. 10, 1840.

517 II. William Forbes Rice, born Feb. 6, 1843; died in St. Louis, Mo., May 8, 1866.

518 III. Mary Hutton Rice, born Dec. 4, 1846. She **964** married, Oct. 25, 1871, Sherman F. Foote, who was born in New Haven, Conn., Nov. 27, 1841. He has always resided in that city, and was engaged in the boot and shoe trade until 1870. He is now secretary and treasurer of the Seamless Rubber Company.

519 IV. Lillie Cornelia Rice, born May 2, 1855.

190   BONTECOU FAMILY.

CHILDREN OF HORATIO NELSON AND JULIET MAYER **205**
(NORTH) LYMAN.

520 I. **William Thomson Lyman,** born March 5, 1851;
died Feb. 15, 1853.

521 II. **George Nelson Lyman,** born Aug. 29, 1852;
died in Goshen, Conn., Feb. 19, 1853.

522 III. **Edward Norman Lyman,** born July 1, 1855;
died in Waterbury, Conn., Oct. 29, 1855.

CHILDREN OF WILLIAM SPARKS AND JANE (LEWIS) **206**
THOMSON.

523 I. **William Thomson,** born Jan. 14, 1855.

524 II. **Annie Lewis Thomson,** born July 28, 1857.

525 III. **Charles Ernest Thomson,** born Dec. 2, 1861.

CHILDREN OF WILLIAM AND ELIZA LYMAN (THOMSON) **209**
NETTLETON.

526 I. **Mary Eliza Nettleton,** born Aug. 28, 1859; died
Jan. 10, 1879.

527 II. **Walter Eben Nettleton,** born June 19, 1861.

528 III. **Anne Thomson Nettleton,** born June 16, 1865.

529 IV. **Grace Langdon Nettleton,** born Nov. 9, 1871.

CHILD OF CHARLES HENRY AND CECILE (LEWIS) THOM- **210**
SON.

530 I. **Arthur Cecil Thomson,** born March 19, 1860.

CHILD OF THOMAS AND MARY AUGUSTA (MILES) McCON- **212**
KEY.

531 I. **Thomas McConkey, Jr.,** born Aug. 9, 1834. He **966**
married, May 20, 1861, Mary Alasebia Bennett, daughter

of Gates Abiatha and Caroline (Starr) Bennett of Erie, Pa. He removed from Erie to Toledo, Ohio, where he now resides at 109 Locust Street. He is a book-keeper.

CHILDREN OF JOHN WILLIAM AND CATHARINE (DON- **213** NELL) MILES.

532   I.   John Leonard Miles, born July 17, 1835; died Jan. 6, 1881. He was never married.

533   II.   Charles Franklin Miles, born Sept. 14, 1836. He was drowned in Erie Bay, July 20, 1848.

534   III.   George Washington Miles, born Nov. 25, 1838. He is unmarried and resides in Buffalo, N. Y. Conductor on Canada Southern Division of Michigan Central Railway.

535   IV.   Thomas Henry Miles, born in Erie, Pa., Dec. **969** 5, 1840. When a boy he was taken to Lafayette, Ind., to live with his uncle, E. II. Halliday, remaining there three years; then returned to Erie, and at the age of 15 shipped on the Lakes and followed them as a sailor for several years. He subsequently became a telegraph operator in the employ of the Lake Shore & Michigan Southern Railroad, and served in this capacity at Conneaut, Painesville, and Cleveland, being promoted to be superintendent of telegraph and chief train dispatcher. After eight years of this service he removed in 1872 to Portsmouth, N. II., remaining there seven years as chief train dispatcher of the Eastern Railroad, and then removed to Boston, where he holds the same position. He married, Nov. 30, 1865, Teresa Maria Finn, daughter of Anthony and Catharine Ann (Shooma) Finn of Erie, Pa. She was born in New York City, Oct. 10, 1843. They reside at 30 Pinkney Street, East Somerville, Mass.

536   **V. William Pitt Miles,** born June 18, 1844. Resides in Erie, Pa., unmarried. He is a sailor on the Lakes.

537   **VI. Mary Augusta Miles,** born Sept. 21, 1846. Resides in Erie, Pa.

538   **VII. Charles Edward Miles,** born in Erie, May 9,   **975** 1850. He married, Aug. 6, 1873, Ellen Rice Harton, daughter of John and Catharine F. (Vanansdol) Harton of Seymour, Ind. She died July 20, 1874. He married (2d), Dec. 10, 1879, Anna Louise Harton, daughter of John and Millison (Sparks) Harton of Seymour. He is a conductor on the Ohio & Mississippi Railroad, and resides in Seymour.

CHILDREN OF THOMAS HENRY AND HENRIETTA MINER **214**
(BROWN) MILES.

539   **I. George Washington Miles,** born Dec. 25, 1856.

540   **II. Willie Bryan Miles,** born May 25, 1868; died July 18, 1868.

CHILDREN OF ELIAS HANDY AND SUSAN STORER (MILES) **215**
HALLIDAY.

541   **I. Samuel Miles Halliday,** born in Massillon, Ohio, April 25, 1842; died in Erie, Pa., Aug. 11, 1843.

542   **II. Mary Adelaide Halliday,** born in Lafayette, Ind., April 25, 1844. Resides in Cleveland, Ohio.

543   **III. Sarah Francis Halliday,** born in Lafayette, Ind., Aug. 14, 1846; died there, July 21, 1849.

544   **IV. George Miles Halliday,** born in Lafayette, Ind.,   **977** Aug. 16, 1848. He became a telegraph operator, and in this capacity entered the employ of the Lake Shore & Michigan Southern Railroad, being stationed principally

at Madison, Ohio. He married there, Dec. 29, 1870, Fleta
Alvira Allen, daughter of Abner and Serene (Kemp) Allen of Madison. After his marriage he removed to Collamer, Ohio, where his mother was living, and worked
upon the farm for a time; then obtained a clerical position in Cleveland, but his employers failed in business
and he resumed his old occupation of operator, and is
now stationed at Cleveland, serving the Lake Shore &
Michigan Southern Railroad as train dispatcher. He resides at 48 Putnam Street.

545   V.   Susan Halliday, born in Lafayette, Ind., Aug.   978
26, 1850. She married, Jan. 24, 1872, Darwin Brainard
Beers, son of Benjamin Pitney and Evalina Beers of Collamer, Ohio.   He was born in East Cleveland, Sept. 21,
1849.   For eight years he held positions of trust in the
First National Bank of Cleveland, and in 1881 entered the
employ of the Ohio Building and Grindstone Company,
but subsequently (1883) changed to the Cleveland National Bank, where he holds the position of teller. Mrs.
Beers died in Cleveland, Dec. 31, 1872. He married (2d),
Jan. 26, 1875, Laura Marion Phillips of Ravenna, Ohio.
They have two children.

546   VI.   Edward Handy Halliday, born in Lafayette,
Ind., March 6, 1853; died there, June 29, 1853.

547   VII.   Elias Handy Halliday, Jr., born in Lafayette,
March 4, 1854; died there, April 14, 1859.

548   VIII.   Samuel Halliday, born in Lafayette, Jan. 12,
1857; died in Cleveland, Ohio, Aug. 28, 1877.

CHILDREN OF GEORGE WASHINGTON AND MARIA 217
LOUISE (KENDRICK) MILES.

549   I.   George Miles, born March 25, 1859; died March
16, 1860.
25

550 II. Warren Miles, born March, 1861; died Nov. 8, 1881.

CHILDREN OF FREDERICK BORIE AND SUSAN (STORER) 221
HEDGE.

551 I. John Storer Hedge, born Aug. 17, 1841. He resides in Westville, Conn., where he is clerk in a hardware manufactory.

552 II. Abbie Hedge, born Jan. 8, 1843. She married, 979 Aug. 2, 1865, John Seaman of Brookhaven, L. I., a painter. She died Aug. 13, 1879.

553 III. Frederick Blydon Hedge, born March 6, 1844. He is a clerk in a restaurant in New York.

554 IV. Hannah Augusta Hedge, born Oct. 2, 1846; died Sept. 9, 1847.

555 V. David Harvey Hedge, born Aug. 1, 1848. He is a hotel clerk in Chicago, Ill.

556 VI. Charles Timothy Hedge, born Nov. 14, 1854; died March 30, 1856.

CHILDREN OF JAMES MERRITT AND CAROLINE (CLARK) 223
IVES.

557 I. Chauncey Ives, born July 28, 1847. He married, 986 Nov. 18, 1868, Elizabeth Taylor Van Baskerk, daughter of Abraham Taylor and Mary (Birdsall) Van Baskerk of Brooklyn, N. Y. He is an importer of diamonds and precious stones, at 26 Maiden Lane, New York.

558 II. Augusta Beulah Ives, born July 29, 1849.

559 III. James Merritt Ives, Jr., born Aug. 21, 1851; died Feb. 8, 1853.

560   IV.   Caroline Clark Ives, born Dec. 29, 1854.

561   V.   Elizabeth Mary Ives, born Jan. 16, 1857.   She   988
married, Sept. 13, 1876, Hobart John Park, who is engaged in the grocery business at 917 Broadway, New York.
They reside at 10 West Forty-ninth Street.

562   VI.   Jenny Strong Ives, born Aug. 17, 1859.

563   VII.   Frederic Dana Ives, born Aug. 16, 1862.

CHILDREN OF GEORGE HENRY AND MARGARET (GIB-   225
BENS) IVES.

564   I.   Henry Ives, born in Brooklyn, N. Y., April 21,
1852.   He married, Jan. 14, 1885, in Grand Rapids, Mich.,
Abbie Rebecca Nelson, daughter of James Madison and
Abba Gray (Bridge) Nelson of that city.   He is a real-
estate broker.   They reside in Grand Rapids.

565   II.   James Ives, born in Brooklyn, N. Y., June 10,
1853; died Oct. 14, 1853.

566   III.   Alonzo Ives, born in Philadelphia, Pa., Oct. 6,
1854; died Sept. 20, 1859.

567   VI.   George Ives, born in Philadelphia, Dec. 19,
1855.   He married, July 3, 1883, Blanche Watson, daughter of John Davis and Caroline (Wilkins) Watson of
Philadelphia.   They reside at Grand Rapids, Mich.   He
is a hotel clerk.

568   V.   Edward Ives, born in Philadelphia, Nov. 6, 1857.
He resides at 2127 Aubrey Place, Philadelphia, and is a
salesman.

569   VI.   Charles William Ives, born in Philadelphia,
Nov. 1, 1860.   He is a salesman, and resides at 2127
Aubrey Place.

570   VII.   Emma Margaret Ives, born in Philadelphia, Sept. 4, 1863.

571   VIII.   Merritt Walstrom Ives, born in Philadelphia, Feb. 16, 1865 ; died at Hainesport, N. J., Aug. 18, 1865.

572   IX.   Katie May Ives, born in Philadelphia, Sept. 10, 1866 ; died there, May 24, 1867.

573   X.   Chauncey Ives, born in Philadelphia, Sept. 18, 1867 ; died there, March 4, 1882.

574   XI.   Clara Augusta Ives, born in Philadelphia, March 15, 1870 ; died in Hainesport, N. J., July 20, 1870.

CHILDREN OF EDWARD AND GRACE CAROLINE (BISHOP)   232
BULKELEY.

575   I.   Jane Bontecou Bulkeley, born May 24, 1868.

576   II.   Lucy Mansfield Bulkeley, born March 19, 1870.

577   III.   Grace Chetwood Bulkeley, born Nov. 26, 1872.

578   IV.   Edward Bulkeley, born March 12, 1875.

579   V.   Sarah Chauncey Bulkeley, born May 7, 1878.

CHILDREN OF WILLIAM WHITTEMORE AND EVELINA   233
(PECK) LOW.

580   I.   Geraldine Whittemore Low, born Aug. 9, 1862.

581   II.   Grace Bontecou Low, born Jan. 3, 1867.

582   III.   William Whittemore Low, Jr., born May 19, 1869.

583   IV.   Theodore Henry Low, born Aug. 26, 1870.

CHILD OF JAMES MADISON AND JOANNA BONTECOU **234**
(PECK) WHITTEMORE.

584   I. **Grace Bontecou Whittemore**, born Feb. 14,
1865; died at West Point, N. Y., Feb. 24, 1865.

CHILD OF CHARLES TIMOTHY AND ADELLA J. (BARNES) **237**
TOWNSEND.

585   I. **Charles Edwin Townsend**, born July 1, 1867.

CHILDREN OF MARCUS HENRY AND HARRIET (GUNN) **240**
TROWBRIDGE.

586   I. **Adelaide Trowbridge**, born March 7, 1855. She   **989**
married, June 2, 1875, Rev. Algernon Sidney Crapsey.
He was born in Cincinnati, Ohio, served in the army during the Civil War, and afterward settled in New York
city, where he became a book-keeper. Later he became a
student at St. Stephens College, Annandale, N. Y., and
after graduation passed a three-years' course in the General Theological Seminary in New York. He was ordained to the diaconate and priesthood in St. Paul's Church, of
which he became assistant minister; afterwards removed
to Rochester, N. Y., and took charge of the Episcopal
Church of St. Andrew's, which under his ministry has
grown into and maintained a very flourishing condition.

587   II. **Arthur Hunt Trowbridge**, born Oct. 24, 1858;
died in Catskill, N. Y., Aug. 3, 1883. " Arthur H. Trowbridge was a young man of good character and abilities,
and of fine promise for the future. As local editor and
business assistant in the *Examiner* office for the past five
years, his services had contributed materially to the increasing business of the office, and his loss there will be
severely felt. Always courteous, honorable, and even-
tempered, he made and held friends of all political
parties." — *Catskill Recorder.*

CHILD OF HOBART AND KATHARINE V. W. (MILLER) **245**
TROWBRIDGE.

588   **I.** **Cornelius Miller Trowbridge,** born Jan. 21, 1869.

CHILD OF CHARLES, JR., AND MARY (JOESBURY) TROW- **246**
BRIDGE.

589   **I.** **Frank West Trowbridge,** born Sept. 20, 1874.

CHILDREN OF REED BROCKWAY AND SUSAN (NORTHRUP) $\begin{cases} 249 \\ 263 \end{cases}$
BONTECOU.

590   **I.** **Joanna Bontecou,** born April 13, 1850; died Jan. 11, 1852.

591   **II.** **Anna Louise Bontecou,** born May 5, 1851; died Jan. 19, 1872.

592   **III.** **Josephine Bontecou,** born Nov. 17, 1856.

593   **II.** **Horatio Brinsmade Bontecou,** born Nov. 17, 1861; died April 19, 1862.

594   **V.** **Reed Brinsmade Bontecou,** born Dec. 1, 1864.

CHILDREN OF JAMES KEELER AND SEMANTHA BROCK- **251**
WAY (BONTECOU) SELLECK.

595   **I.** **Reed Bontecou Selleck,** born in Troy, N. Y., Oct. 4, 1854; died there, Nov. 19, 1856.

596   **II.** **Frederick Dabney Selleck,** born in Troy, Aug. **994**
7, 1856. He married, Sept. 19, 1878, Nellie Egan of Chicago, Ill. They reside in Chicago.

597   **III.** **Charles Bontecou Selleck,** born in Troy, Jan. 24, 1859. He married, Dec. 27, 1879, at Port Chester, N. Y., Isabel S. Hanford. He is a stock broker in New York.

598   IV.   James Keeler Selleck, Jr., born in Troy, Aug. 19, 1861; died in Bergen, N. J., Aug. 30, 1865.

599   V.   Wilson Waddingham Selleck, born in Bergen, Dec. 8, 1864; died at North Bergen, Nov. 23, 1873.

600   VI.   Clara Frances Selleck, born in Bergen, Jan. 11, 1867.

601   VII.   Florence Thompson Selleck, born in Bergen, March 12, 1869.

602   VIII.   Josephine Keeler Selleck, born in North Bergen, Feb. 18, 1871; died there, Sept. 18, 1871.

603   IX.   Eugenia Selleck, born in North Bergen, Feb. 18, 1871; died there. Sept. 9, 1871.

604   X.   Jonathan Howard Selleck, born in North Bergen, Nov. 7, 1872.

CHILDREN OF WILBUR F. AND JULIA (BONTECOU) GOSS.   253

605   I.   Alice Bontecou Goss, born June 26, 1858.

606   II.   Isabel Newlands Goss, born July 14, 1860.

607   III.   George Goss, born April 23, 1862; died March 17, 1864.

608   IV.   Peter Bontecou Goss, born April 11, 1867.

CHILDREN OF JOHN W. A. AND ELIZABETH (BONTECOU) CLUETT.   256

609   I.   Robert Cluett, born June 12, 1865.

610   II.   Jessie Cluett, born May 28, 1867.

611   III.   Minnie Cluett, born May 28, 1867.

612   IV.   David Edmond Cluett, born Oct. 7, 1868.

613   V.   Stanley Bywater Cluett, born Feb. 4, 1871.

614   VI.   Louise Bontecou Cluett, born Sept. 25, 1873.

615   VII.   Joseph Mulford Cluett, born Dec. 19, 1876.

CHILDREN OF JOHN AND LOUISA ABIGAIL (GREGORY)   259
NORTHRUP.

616   I.   George Huntington Northrup, born Nov. 16,   996
1845; married, Jan. 18, 1872, Adelaide Bruice, daughter
of Mathias D. and Martha (Van Vleck) Bruice of Danby,
Tompkins County, N. Y.   He is engaged with his father
in the spring-bed and sewing-machine business, at Ithaca,
N. Y., and is also Treasurer of Tompkins County, having
been twice elected to that office.

617   II.   Mary Elizabeth Northrup, born Sept. 9, 1848; { 657
married, Oct. 10, 1872, Gardner Landon Bontecou (289), { 998
son of Francis (108) and Clarissa Maria (Landon) Bontecou.   They reside in Eureka, Kan.

618   III.   Harriet Louisa Northrup, born July 6, 1852.   999
She married, Oct. 8, 1874, Lewis Kelmond Thurlow, who
is a wholesale chandler and grocer at 38 South Street,
New York.   They reside at 152 Gates Avenue, Brooklyn.

619   IV.   Henry Gregory Northrup, born Aug. 19, 1854.

620   V.   Jennie Northrup, born April 20, 1863.

CHILDREN OF JAMES AND ELSINA S. (BENNETT) NOR-   260
THRUP.

621   I.   Mary Stella Northrup, born Sept. 3, 1849; died
March 1, 1870.

622   II.   Ellen Maria Northrup, born June 7, 1851; died
March 9, 1869.

623   III.   Charles Bontecou Northrup, born May 12, 1853; died July 18, 1864.

624   IV.   Elizabeth Northrup, born May 2, 1855; died May 2, 1875.

625   V.   Charlotte Kidder Northrup, born May 25, 1857; died Aug. 31, 1873.

626   VI.   Sarah Eliza Northrup, born July 15, 1859. 1002 She married, Aug. 4, 1880, Augustus A. Lines.   He is a wagon maker and carriage trimmer.   They reside in Homer, N. Y.

627   VII.   Cephas Moses Northrup, born April 20, 1862.

628   VIII.   Alfred Bennett Northrup, born April 3, 1864; died Nov. 29, 1884.

629   IX.   Edward James Northrup, born Nov. 1, 1867.

CHILDREN OF REED BROCKWAY AND SUSAN (NOR- $\begin{cases} 249 \\ 263 \end{cases}$
THRUP) BONTECOU.

630   1.   Joanna Bontecou, born April 13, 1850; died Jan. 11, 1852.

631   II.   Anna Louise Bontecou, born May 5, 1851; died Jan. 10, 1872.

632   III.   Josephine Bontecou, born Nov. 17, 1856.

633   IV.   Horatio Brinsmade Bontecou, born Nov. 17, 1861; died April 19, 1862.

634   V.   Reed Brinsmade Bontecou, born Dec. 1, 1864.

CHILD OF JOSEPH CONNABLE AND MARIA PRISCILLA   264
(OVEN) BONTECOU.

635   I.   Margaret Celia Bontecou, born in Jackson, Mich., Feb. 27, 1871.

CHILD OF GEORGE BYWATER AND SARAH BONTECOU   **269**
(GOLDEN) CLUETT.

636   I. George Golden Cluett, born in 1864; died, aged
11 days.

CHILDREN OF IRA GLAZIER AND MARY HANNAH (BON-   **273**
TECOU) BIDWELL.

637   I. Charlton Bontecou Bidwell, born May 13, 1863.

638   II. Lydia Kate Bidwell, born Feb. 27, 1865.

CHILDREN OF FREDERICK WEBSTER AND SUSAN (BON-   **275**
TECOU) PICKERING.

639   I. Frederick Bontecou Pickering, born Jan. 8,
1864.

640   II. William Pickering, born Nov. 19, 1866; died
Sept. 9, 1867.

641   III. Edith Annie Pickering, born Dec. 29, 1867.

CHILDREN OF WILLIAM WRIGHT WHIPPLE AND FLOR-   **276**
ENCE C. (NEALE) BONTECOU.

642   I. Infant, not named, born Jan. 23, 1871; died Feb.
21, 1871.

643   II. Charles Neale Bontecou, born Nov. 18, 1871.

644   III. Clara Lydia Bontecou, born July 23, 1873.

645   IV. Mary Edith Bontecou, born April 1, 1879.

CHILDREN OF ELIJAH WHIPPLE AND CLARA (HOLLAND)   **277**
BONTECOU.

646   I. Charles Holland Bontecou, born Aug. 1, 1874;
died April 7, 1875.

647   II. Mary Lillian Bontecou, born Nov. 8, 1875.

CHILD OF GEORGE HENRY AND ANNA (NEVINS) BON- **278**
TECOU.

648   I.   George Nelson Bontecou, born March 25, 1872.

CHILDREN OF GEORGE HENRY AND EMMA (MASE) BON- **278**
TECOU.

649   I.   Howell Bontecou, born Jan. 23, 1877.

650   II.   Edna Bontecou, born Feb. 27, 1881.

650a   III.   Pierre Bontecou, born Oct. 18, 1884.

CHILDREN OF PHILIP DORLON AND ADA FLORENCE **279**
(EWING) BONTECOU.

651   I.   Frank Foster Bontecou, born in Spring Valley,
Minn., Jan. 27, 1877; died in Armstrong, Minn., Sept. 12,
1878.

652   II.   Athol Reed Bontecou, born July 26, 1879; died
in Armstrong, Sept. 10, 1879.

653   III.   Gladys Achsah Bontecou, born in Spring Valley, Nov. 12, 1881.

CHILDREN OF JAMES COVIL AND SARAH MARIA (BON- **285**
TECOU) ARCHIBALD.

654   I.   Grace Bontecou Archibald, born Feb. 19, 1879.

655   II.   Frances Gertrude Archibald, born Sept. 6,
1880.

656   III.   James Wentworth Archibald, born Dec. 29,
1882.

CHILD OF GARDNER LANDON AND MARY ELIZABETH { **289**
(NORTHRUP) BONTECOU.   { **617**

657   I.   Frederick Finch Bontecou, born in New York,
July 29, 1873.

CHILDREN OF AMBROSE RYDER AND MARY KATE (BON- **290**
TECOU) ADAMS.

658   I.   Mabel Estelle Adams, born Nov. 18, 1880.

659   II.   Ella Adams, born April 11, 1882; died same day.

CHILDREN OF GILMAN AND CHARLOTTE CAROLINE (BUR- **296**
RITT) FAY.

660   I.   Edward Prescott Fay, born in Westborough,
Mass., Nov. 27, 1852; died in Washington, D. C., July 9,
1873.

661   II.   Arthur Burritt Fay, born in Westborough, Oct.
12, 1860; died July 23, 1871.

662   III.   Miriam Starr Fay, born in Westborough, Aug.
17, 1862; died Aug. 11, 1871.

CHILDREN OF JOHN MENZIES AND HARRIET MUIR (KNAPP) **299**
BURRITT.

663   I.   Ida Florence Burritt, born in New York, March
21, 1860; died May 30, 1860.

664   II.   Elinor Louise Burritt, born in Stoughton, Wis.,
March 3, 1864.

CHILDREN OF FRANK DUFFLE AND HARRIET MUIR (BUR- **300**
RITT) BURRITT.

665   I.   Jessie Allyn Burritt, born Nov. 27, 1868.

666   II.   Harry Rayner Burritt, born May 12, 1874.

CHILDREN OF BENJAMIN STUART AND JULIA MARIA **301**
(HARDEN) RAYNER.

667   I.   Ida Louisa Rayner, born March 31, 1861.

668   II.   Clinton Leicester Rayner, born July 22, 1862.

669   III.   Stella Gertrude Rayner, born Feb. 7, 1864.

CHILDREN OF WILLIAM HENRY AND SARAH EMMA (RAY-
NER) LONG. **308**

670   I.   Florence Pauline Long, born in Bordentown,
N. J., May 3, 1865.

671   II.   Henry Carrick Long, born in Bordentown, Nov.
14, 1868.

672   III.   Lulu Hester Long, born in Janesville, Wis.,
Dec. 29, 1871; died in Trenton, N. J., Nov. 25, 1879.

673   IV.   Sarah Emma Long, born in Burlington, N. J.,
April 2, 1880.

CHILDREN OF WILLIAM HENRY AND SUSAN REBECCA **309**
(RAYNER) CARRICK.

674   I.   Thomas Carrick, born in Philadelphia, Pa., Sept.
16, 1874.

675   II.   Vernon Rayner Carrick, born in Philadelphia,
Jan. 1, 1879.

676   III.   Allyn Barclay Carrick, born in Philadelphia,
Jan. 21, 1881.

CHILDREN OF WILLIAM RAYNER AND ELLEN MARIA **311**
(HENRY) WARNER.

677   I.   Charles Henry Warner, born in Westborough,
Mass., June 18, 1868.

678   II.   George Menzies Warner, born Feb. 3, 1870.

CHILDREN OF WILLIAM AUGUSTUS AND ELIZABETH GIL- **312**
MAN (WARNER) PRICKITT.

679   I.   Jennie Warner Prickitt, born in Westborough,
Mass., March 8, 1868.

206   BONTECOU FAMILY.

680   II. **William Augustus Prickitt, Jr.**, born in Trenton, N. J., May 2, 1871; died in Westborough, Mass., Sept. 19, 1871.

681   III. **Lizzie Alice Prickitt**, born in Trenton, May 2, 1871; died there, July 24, 1871.

682   IV. **Annie Gilman Prickitt**, born in Farmingdale, N. J., Dec. 23, 1873.

683   V. **Louise Eugenie Prickitt**, born in Farmingdale, Oct. 11, 1875.

CHILDREN OF GEORGE BLISS AND ELIZABETH (LATHROP)   313
MORRIS.

684   I. **George Bliss Morris, Jr.**, born in Springfield, Mass., Nov. 5, 1843. Graduated from Harvard College, 1864, and Cambridge Law School, 1867. He is unmarried, and resides in New York City, where he is engaged in the practice of his profession.

685   II. **Robert Oliver Morris**, born in Springfield, Oct. 18, 1846. He is a lawyer, and succeeded his father as Clerk of the Courts of Hampden County in 1872, which office he still holds. He married, Nov. 27, 1872, Elizabeth Cadwell, daughter of George G. and Pamelia (Ball) Cadwell of Springfield, who was born March 27, 1850. They reside in Springfield, at 72 Temple Street. They have no children.

686   III. **Caroline Morris**, born in Springfield, Sept. 18, 1848. She resides in New York City, and conducts a private school.

CHILDREN OF JAMES AND HARRIET ANGELINE (DAY)   314
LATHROP.

687   I. **Edward Flint Lathrop**, born Sept. 16, 1849. He 1003 married, Oct. 13, 1873, Nancy Lane, daughter of Benja-

min and Maria L. (Powell) Lane of Queens, L. I., who was born May 31, 1851. He is a railroad contractor, and resides at 632 Willoughby Avenue, Brooklyn, N. Y.

688   II.   **James Bontecou Lathrop**, born July 4, 1855; died Feb. 5, 1870.

CHILD OF OLIVER ELLSWORTH AND CATHARINE BON-   **315**
TECOU (LATHROP) WOOD.

689   I.   **Winthrop Wolcott Wood**, born Jan. 27, 1865; died Sept. 14, 1871.

CHILDREN OF RICHARD BONTECOU AND MARY (RIPLEY)   **319**
MORRIS.

690   I.   **Richard Hunt Morris**, born in Adrian, Mich., April 4, 1860. He received his education at Racine (Wis.) College. He married, Feb. 16, 1885, Nellie Brown of Atchison, Kan., and is engaged in the wholesale hardware business in Atchison.

691   II.   **Edward Ripley Morris**, born in Springfield, Mass., Nov. 20, 1861. He is employed as a clerk in the post-office at Atchison.

692   III.   **John Bakewell Morris**, born in Atchison, Dec. 17, 1868.

693   IV.   **Mary Lee Morris**, born Oct. 6, 1870, in Atchison.

CHILD OF RANSOM WILLIAMS AND HARRIET BONTECOU   **321**
(MORRIS) DUNHAM.

694   I.   **William Dunham**, born Oct. 13, 1865.

CHILDREN OF FRANK AND CATHARINE SYBIL (MORRIS)   **322**
REED.

695   I.   **Raymond Reed**, born July —, 1871.

696   II. Kitty Reed, born Dec. 31, 1875.

697   III. Charles Bliss Reed, born Feb. 1, 1882; died July 30, 1882.

CHILDREN OF JOHN EMERY AND MARY PAMELIA (FELT)   **323**
MORRIS.

698   I. Henry Lincoln Morris, born in Hartford, Conn., Feb. 6, 1868.

699   II. Edward Bontecou Morris, born in Hartford, Aug. 16, 1875.

700   III. John Felt Morris, born in Hartford, Oct. 29, 1877.

EIGHTH GENERATION.

CHILDREN OF JAMES AND HARRIET ELIZABETH (BONTE- **327** COU) HOOK.

701   I. **Martha Esther Hook,** born June 22, 1851; died Oct. 12, 1860.

702   II. **George Henry Hook,** born Oct. 21, 1852: died Jan. 28, 1853.

703   III. **Mary Emma Hook,** born Sept. 3, 1855. Resides in Dunkirk. N. Y.

704   IV. **Ida Anna Hook,** born Oct. 11, 1857. She mar- **1006a** ried, Nov. 29, 1883, Frank E. Williams, son of Ebenezer B. and Hannah Mary (Clark) Williams of Hartford, Conn. He was born in New London, Conn., Aug. 1, 1860. They reside in Hartford, where he is engaged in the clothing business.

CHILD OF EUGENE OSCAR AND JOSEPHINE (BONTECOU) **329** WARRING.

705   I. **George Bontecou Warring,** born Oct. 15, 1855.

CHILDREN OF WALTER HENRY AND MARY (MOSHER) **330** BONTECOU.

706   I. **Walter Wright Bontecou,** died Dec. 5, 1863.

707   II. **Augustus Van Rensselaer Bontecou,** born April 14, 1866.

708   III. **Mary Emma Bontecou,** born Jan. 2, 1869.

27

CHILDREN OF ROBERT JOHN AND ELLEN JANE (SULLI-　332
VAN) HAMILTON.

709　　I.　Harriet Bontecou Hamilton, born April 1, 1859.　1007
She married, June 15, 1882, Charles Henry Jones of Dunkirk, N. Y.　He is a temperer of steel tools, and is employed in the locomotive works at Dunkirk.

710　　II.　William Henry Hamilton, born Feb. 6, 1861.

711　　III.　Infant, not named, born Dec. 29, 1864; died
Jan. 18, 1865.

712　　IV.　Agnes Jane Hamilton, born Feb. 7, 1866.

713　　V.　Robert John Hamilton, Jr., born May 12, 1868.

714　　VI.　James Hamilton, born Aug. 25, 1870; died May
8, 1875.

715　　VII.　Mary Louisa Hamilton, born Oct. 11, 1872.

716　　VIII.　Arthur Wilson Hamilton, born Aug. 4, 1875.

717　　IX.　Bontecou Hamilton, born March 5, 1878.

718　　X.　Samuel Hamilton, born Feb. 23, 1881.

CHILDREN OF CHARLES FREDERICK AND AGNES JANE　333
(HAMILTON) CHAPMAN.

719　　I.　Charles Frederick Chapman, Jr., born Nov. 13,
1862.　He is a clerk, and resides in New York City.

720　　II.　Frank Gerard Chapman, born Jan. 3, 1868; died
Sept. 6, 1877, in New York.

CHILDREN OF ARTHUR AND MARY LOUISA (HAMILTON)　336
WILSON.

721　　I.　Ida May Wilson, born Feb. 27, 1866.

722　　II.　Margaret Anna Wilson, born April 27, 1868.

CHILDREN OF CHARLES BENHAM AND LOUISIANA SUSAN **341**
(COCKE) HAYDEN.

723   I. **Irene Hayden,** born Aug. 1, 1841.

724   II. **Louisiana Cocke Hayden,** born June 10, 1843.

CHILDREN OF CHARLES BENHAM AND MARY ELIZABETH **341**
(KILBY) HAYDEN.

725   I. **Mary Susan Hayden,** born Jan. 5, 1846.

726   II. **Julia White Hayden,** born Sept. 18, 1847.

727   III. **Ann Thompson Hayden,** born Sept. 25, 1848; died June 19, 1850.

728   IV. **Norman Bontecou Hayden,** born Sept. 8, 1849. He was for a number of years assistant librarian of the Public School Library of St. Louis, Mo., but left that position to attend upon his father during his last sickness, and later was engaged in teaching at Randolph Depot, Charlotte County, Va.

729   V. **Nancy Jones Hayden,** born Nov. 9, 1854.

730   VI. **Charles Benham Hayden, Jr.,** born Dec. 10, 1856. He is a book-keeper, and resides in Smithfield, Va.

CHILD OF CHARLES BENHAM AND JULIA ANN (WILSON) **341**
HAYDEN.

731   I. **Eliza Virginia Hayden,** born March 15, 1871.

CHILDREN OF WILLIAM AND JULIA REBECCA (SALTER) **344**
HOMES.

732   I. **Frederic Cleveland Homes,** born May 18, 1844. **1008** He married, July 5, 1871, Myra A. Wadhams, daughter of Orlando and Martha J. (Pickett) Wadhams of Waverly, Ill. They reside in Waverly. He is a farmer.

733   II.   William Francis Homes, born Aug. 1, 1846; died Sept. 23, 1857.

734   III.   Henry Bullard Homes, born Oct. 18, 1848; died Sept. 7, 1850.

735   IV.   Francis King Homes, born Sept. 30, 1850; died Jan. 14, 1857.

736   V.   Julia Bacon Homes, born Nov. 29, 1854; died Dec. 15, 1856.

737   VI.   Mary Louise Homes, born Aug. 7, 1857.   She 1012 married, Aug. 7, 1879, Horace Rollin Boynton of Waverly. He is proprietor of a large mill, elevator, and lumber-yard.

738   VII.   John Charles Homes, born Sept. 27, 1861; died March 10, 1862.

CHILDREN OF CHARLES ROGER AND MARY LOUISA (SAL- 345 TER) WELLES.

739   I.   Julia Norton Welles, born May 30, 1842; died Jan. 22, 1857.

740   II.   Thomas Mather Welles, born June 17, 1844; died Aug. 31, 1845.

741   III.   Charles Salter Welles, born Sept. 13, 1846. 1014 He married, Oct. 19, 1871, Susannah Parrish, daughter of Dr. Joseph and Lydia (Gaskill) Parrish of Burlington, N. J.   She died March 4, 1883.   Mr. Welles resides at Elwyn, Pa., near Philadelphia, and is not engaged in business.

742   IV.   Mary Frances Welles, born Jan. 4, 1849; died Jan. 28, 1857.

743   V.   Helen Susan Welles, born Feb. 8, 1851; died Jan. 11, 1857.

744 VI. John Martin Welles, born Feb. 4, 1853; died Aug. 22, 1854.

CHILDREN OF WASHINGTON HOLMES AND SUSAN (BEN- **346**
HAM) BARDWELL.

745 I. Frank Edgar Bardwell, born Sept. 1, 1853. He is a machinist and resides in Hatfield, Mass., unmarried.

746 II. Fred Homer Bardwell, born Oct. 24, 1856; died Feb. 21, 1864.

747 III. Elmer Ellsworth Bardwell, born July 29, 1861; died Oct. 9, 1862.

CHILDREN OF RALPH AND LOUISA WATERS (BENHAM) **347**
CHILDS.

748 I. Erastus Ralph Childs, born Aug. 11, 1845. He **1015** married, Oct. 24, 1866, Julia Mary Stevens, daughter of Robert and Mary Elizabeth (Merwin) Stevens of New Haven, Conn. They reside in Norwich, Conn., where he conducts an advertising and newspaper business.

749 II. Charles Henry Childs, born July 17, 1847; died April 25, 1853.

750 III. Homer Benham Childs, born Aug. 7, 1850; died April 27, 1853.

751 IV. Ida Louisa Childs, born May 11, 1854; died July 20, 1858.

752 V. Isabella Julia Childs, born Nov. 13, 1856; died July 22, 1858.

753 VI. Charles Henry Childs, born Nov. 12, 1858. He **1016** married, Jan. 4, 1880, Julia Louisa Wolford, daughter of August A. and Christiana Wolford of Providence, R. I. They reside in Providence. He is a printer.

754 **VII. Homer Benham Childs,** born June 11, 1862. **1017** He married, Nov. 5, 1881, Lillian Estella Hopkins, daughter of William and Hannah (Torry) Hopkins of Providence. He is a carpenter. They reside in Providence.

755 **VIII. Julia Louisa Childs,** born in Coleraine, Mass., **1017a** Feb. 7, 1865. She married, May 1, 1880, Albert Ellsworth Martin of Attleborough, Mass., son of Lewis and Casdeallia (Bornar) Martin of Plainville, Mass. He is a jeweler. Mrs. Martin died in Providence, R. I., April 13, 1884.

CHILDREN OF FRANCIS KIMBERLY AND EMILY JANE **348** (LEEK) BENHAM.

756 **I. Emily Frances Benham,** born in New Haven, **1018** Conn., June 5, 1851. She married, Dec. 30, 1868, Herman Everett Smith. He is engaged in the grocery business, at No. 7 Broadway, New Haven. They reside at 324 George Street.

757 **II. Leverett Hayden Benham,** born in New Haven, Feb. 27, 1853; died Nov. 22, 1853.

758 **III. William Webster Benham,** born in New Haven, **1019** Nov. 23, 1854. He married, Nov. 17, 1878, Jessie Eugenia Roberts, daughter of William E. and Phœbe (Hutchinson) Roberts of New Haven. They reside at 82 Elliott Street, New Haven. He is a clerk.

759 **IV. Frank Edward Benham,** born Nov. 23, 1854; died Nov. 23, 1854.

760 **V. Lillian Martha Benham,** born March 24, 1861. Married, March 24, 1880, William Henry Turnbull of New Haven. He died April 27, 1881. She resides with her father at 324 George Street, New Haven.

761 **VI. Alice Mary Benham,** born March 24, 1861; died March 24, 1861.

CHILD OF ROBERT ALEXANDER AND DELIA DELIGHT **349**
(LEEK) BENHAM.

762 I. **Ellen Martha Benham,** born Nov. 17, 1862. She 1019a
married, Oct. 3, 1883, John Greenwood, son of William
and Agatha Greenwood. He was born in Walsden, Lanca-
shire, Eng., Sept. 16, 1855. They reside in New Haven.
He is a salesman.

CHILD OF WILLIAM EDWARD AND ROSE LINDA (CLARK) **350**
BUSHNELL.

763 I. **William Edward Bushnell, Jr.,** born July 5, 1874.

CHILDREN OF DOUGLAS RITCHIE AND EMILY J. C. (ED- **351**
SON) BUSHNELL.

764 I. **Emma Louise Bushnell,** born June 21, 1850. She 1020
married, Oct. 12, 1874, John Howard Lawrence, a native
of Burlington, Vt. They reside in Sterling, Ill., where he
is engaged in the hardware business.

765 II. **William Francis Bushnell,** born Sept. 26, 1854;
died Oct. 27, 1855.

766 III. **Grace Edson Bushnell,** born Oct. 22, 1860. 1023
She married, Jan. 22, 1880, Charles Noble Clark, who was
born in Rutland, Vt. He is a jeweler. They reside in
Sterling, Ill.

767 IV. **Cora Douglas Bushnell,** born Nov. 1, 1861.

CHILD OF REV. FRANCIS HAYDEN AND MARY VIRGINIA **352**
(BREEDEN) BUSHNELL.

768 I. **Mary Louisa Bushnell,** born in Louisville, Ky.,
June 3, 1859. She married at Beechland, Ky., Sept. 15,
1880, Richard T. Coleman, a merchant, who was born in
Frankfort, Ky., March 4, 1850. They reside in Louisville.

CHILDREN OF RICHARD WELLS AND MARY B. (TANNER) **354**
BUSHNELL.

769   **I.   William Henry Bushnell,** born Sept. 27, 1854.

770   **II.   Frank Walter Bushnell,** born in Chicago, Ill., **1024**
Nov. 8, 1856.   He married, Jan. 22, 1878, Ellen Darney.
They reside in Iowa Falls, Iowa.   He is a locomotive engineer on the Burlington, Cedar Rapids & Northern Railroad.

771   **III.   James Tanner Bushnell,** born May 25, 1859;
died Dec. 17, 1859.

772   **IV.   Douglas Ritchie Bushnell,** born Aug. 18, 1861 ;
died Sept. 5, 1861.

773   **V.   Mary Gertrude Bushnell,** born Aug. 18, 1861.

CHILDREN OF RICHARD WELLS AND MARY SOPHIA **354**
(THOMAS) BUSHNELL.

774   **I.   Charles Richard Bushnell,** born May 11, 1870.

775   **II.   Edward Wells Bushnell,** born Aug. 2, 1876.

CHILDREN OF ANSON MUNSON AND CAROLINE URETTA **355**
(PRITCHARD) DURAND.

776   **I.   Caroline Augusta Durand,** born June 19, 1846. **1025**
She married, Nov. 17, 1866, Thomas Bond Haughawort.
They reside in Carthage, Jasper County, Mo.   He is a lawyer, and prosecuting attorney for Jasper County.

777   **II.   Charles Anson Durand,** born April 1, 1850;
died Feb. 4, 1863.

778   **III.   William Rufus Durand,** born in Brunswick, **1032**
Medina County, Ohio, May 13, 1852.   He was brought up
on a farm, and afterwards learned the printer's trade.   His
boyhood was passed in Wisconsin; in 1870 he removed to

Carthage, Mo., and in 1880 to Des Moines, Iowa, where he is now engaged as clerk in the grocery trade. He married, June 6, 1874, Mary Frances McCulloch, daughter of William II. and Nancy Adaline (Lewis) McCulloch of Carthage.

779   IV.   **Sarah Eliza Durand,** born May 17, 1858. She **1035** married, Jan. 22, 1874, Albert Wells Carpenter, who was born in Girard, Pa., Nov. 9, 1846. He resided in Carthage from 1870 to 1882, when he removed to Des Moines. He is a job printer and publisher.

780   V.   **Addie Louise Durand,** born Aug. 18, 1860; died Jan. 24, 1863.

781   VI.   **George Ernest Durand,** born Dec. 18, 1863.

782   VII.   **Mary Louise Durand,** born Oct. 6, 1866.

783   VIII.   **Henry Harrison Durand,** born May 13, 1869; died Sept. 10, 1872.

784   IX.   **Frederick Albert Durand,** born April 13, 1873.

CHILDREN OF WILLIAM WICKS AND MARY CLARINDA **356** (STEBBINS) PRITCHARD.

785   I.   **Frederick Pritchard,** born Oct. 3, 1853. Resides in Brunswick, Ohio, unmarried.

786   II.   **Clarence Robinson Pritchard,** born Sept. 12, 1858. He is unmarried, and resides in Brunswick.

787   III.   **Mary Ellen Pritchard,** born Dec. 23, 1861; resides in Brunswick.

788   IV.   **Lyman Wiliston Pritchard,** born July 27, 1864; resides in Brunswick.

28

CHILDREN OF CHARLES FREDERICK AND MARY SUSAN 357
(WESTCOTT) PRITCHARD.

789   I. **Ella Bell Pritchard,** born Jan. 27, 1857. She 1040
married, Aug. 16, 1879, Congrave Jackson Tyler, a farmer.
They reside in Lake City, Jackson County, Mo.

790   II. **Lewis Henry Pritchard,** born Aug. 27, 1859;
died Oct. 10, 1860.

791   III. **Sarah Eliza Pritchard,** born July 14, 1864.

792   IV. **Jennie May Pritchard,** born May 10, 1866.

793   V. **Mary Susan Pritchard,** born March 20, 1872.

794   VI. **George Anson Pritchard,** born March 10, 1881.

CHILDREN OF GEORGE ANSON AND JANE ELIZABETH 358
(FREESE) PRITCHARD.

795   I. **George Edwin Pritchard,** born Sept. 2, 1855;
died March 29, 1865.

796   II. **Frances Elizabeth Pritchard,** born in Bruns- 1041
wick, Ohio, Nov. 27, 1858. She married, May 27, 1879,
Frederick Donaldson Parker, who was born in Birmingham, Erie County, Ohio, Sept. 1, 1850. He is the son of
Dr. William Tell and Ann (Denman) Parker, and grandson of John Denman, one of the pioneers of the Western
Reserve of Connecticut; on the paternal side grandson of
Rev. Daniel Parker, founder and for many years pastor
of the First Restorationist Church in Cincinnati. He removed with his parents to Tennessee, and engaged in
farming and teaching; returned to the North in 1872 and
in time settled in Des Moines, Iowa. After marriage, in
1879, they removed to Denver, Col., where he is engaged
in the produce and general commission business. Mrs.
Parker is a graduate of the High School of Des Moines,

and was salutatorian of her class. She was afterwards engaged in teaching school and music in Des Moines and adjacent towns.

CHILDREN OF HENRY HARRISON AND CORNELIA (HAR- **359**
RISON) PRITCHARD.

797   I.   **Willis Lawson Pritchard,** born March 8, 1871.

798   II. **Ida Pritchard,** born June 3, 1872.

799   III. **Josie Pritchard,** born Sept. 11, 1873.

800   IV. **George Henry Pritchard,** born Nov. 30, 1876.

801   V.   **Nellie Pritchard,** born June 30, 1878.

CHILDREN OF JOHN FRANKLIN AND ELIZABETH ADE- **360**
LAIDE (PRITCHARD) ROLLINS.

802   I.   **Katie Rollins,** born Aug. 1, 1864.

803   II. **Marion Rose Rollins,** born May 12, 1867.

804   III. **Alonzo William Rollins,** born Oct. 16, 1874.

805   IV. **Ruth Rollins,** born March 16, 1882.

CHILDREN OF OSCAR CORNELIUS AND SUSAN HENRIETTA **361**
(PRITCHARD) ROSE.

806   I.   **William Cornelius Rose,** born Oct. 6, 1875.

807   II. **Charles Henry Rose,** born June 17, 1878.

CHILDREN OF WILLIS CHARLES AND ELIZABETH (HEAT- **365**
LY) HALL.

808   I.   **Charles Edward Hall,** born March 7, 1858. He **1042**
married, Sept. 11, 1879, Janette Elizabeth Warren, daughter of Franklin and Elizabeth (Budrow) Warren of Waterbury, Conn. He is book-keeper and partner in the dry-

goods business in Waterbury, also captain of the Chatfield Guards, Company A, 2d Regiment Connecticut National Guard.

809   II. **Walter Heatly Hall,** born Aug. 8, 1861; died Aug. 6, 1864.

810   III. **Gardner Irving Hall,** born Nov. 27, 1868.

CHILD OF WILLIS CHARLES AND ORINDA (DANIELS) 365
HALL.

811   1. **Joseph Bontecou Hall,** born April 12, 1882.

CHILDREN OF SETH ELIADA AND ELLEN MARY (HALL) 366
FROST.

812   I. **Minnie Carrie Frost,** born Dec. 1, 1861.

813   II. **Adelaide Lourene Frost,** born Feb. 8, 1866.

814   III. **Louise Amy Frost,** born Dec. 4, 1872.

CHILD OF ELMER WILLIAM AND EMMA CELIA (HALL) 367
HITCHCOCK.

815   I. **Edson Wilbur Hitchcock,** born Feb. 2, 1869.

CHILDREN OF GARDNER MOSS AND GEORGIANA ELIZA- 368
BETH (MULLINGS) HALL.

816   I. **Willis Mullings Hall,** born April 23, 1873.

817   II. **Elizabeth Amy Hall,** born Dec. 8, 1874.

CHILD OF FRANKLIN AMOS AND ADELAIDE ULISSA (MUN- 369
GER) HALL.

818   I. **Frank Edward Hall,** born April 3, 1870.

CHILDREN OF GEORGE BRITAIN AND ADELAIDE ELIZA 371
(HALL) LAWTON.

819   I. **May Hall Lawton,** born May 19, 1873.

820   II.   Harold Carlyle Lawton, born Nov. 2, 1875.

821   III.   Lefa Elizabeth Lawton, born Oct. 2, 1879.

821a   IV.   Amy Moss Lawton, born March 4, 1884.

CHILD OF WARREN LEANDER AND ETTA LOUISA (AN-   372
DREWS) HALL.

821b   I.   Lamont Andrew Hall, born Dec. 16, 1884, in
Naugatuck, Conn.

CHILD OF ALMER BRONSON AND LOUISA ELIZABETH   374
(HALL) HITCHCOCK.

822   I.   Gaius Arthur Hitchcock, born May 8, 1876.

CHILD OF GEORGE AND NANCY ORILLA (HALL) HAUX-   376
HURST.

823   I.   Wilbur Clarence Hauxhurst, born Feb. 3, 1879.

CHILD OF JOHN DAVID AND NANCY ORILLA (HALL)   378
BENHAM.

824   I.   Frederick Benham, born Nov. 15, 1872.

CHILD OF WILLIAM AND EMMA E. (LIVINGSTON) PEEBLES.   379

825   I.   Elwin Livingston Peebles, born Feb. 4, 1865.

CHILD OF HORACE AND EMMA E. (PEEBLES) CARPENTER.   379

826   I.   Etta Bontecou Carpenter, born July 14, 1882.

CHILDREN OF AMOS AND CARRIE (RETTEG) LIVINGSTON.   380

827   I.   Donna Romaine Livingston, born June 26, 1872.

828   II.   Susan Gay Livingston, born May 3, 1874.

CHILD OF HIRAM EDWARD AND HATTIE CURTIS (ELLIS)   383
LIVINGSTON.

829   I.   Clara Ellis Livingston, born Feb. 5, 1882.

CHILDREN OF ISAIAH ALEXANDER AND MARY ELIZA- 384
BETH (TERRELL) UFFENDALE.

830   I.   Edward Terrell Uffendale, born Sept. 14, 1879.

831   II. Harry William Uffendale, born Feb. 2, 1882.

831a   III. Frank Isaiah Uffendale, born Dec. 25, 1883.

CHILDREN OF CHARLES LAURENS AND JULIA ADELAIDE 386
(LUSK) BENEDICT.

832   I.   Charles Allen Reed Benedict, born Dec. 20, 1857.

833   II. Jessie Maud Benedict, born Oct. 1, 1859.

834   III. Florence Emily Benedict, born Jan. 31, 1861.

CHILDREN OF GEORGE RICE, JR., AND SARAH ISABEL 387
(HART) BENEDICT.

835   I.   Mary Laurinda Benedict, born Jan. 8, 1870.

836   II. George Rice Benedict (3d), born Aug. 14, 1875.

837   III. Emily Isabel Benedict, born Nov. 26, 1879.

CHILD OF DANIEL AND MARGARET ELIZABETH (THOMP- 391
SON) BENEDICT.

838   I.   Olive Sarah Benedict, born May 4, 1876.

CHILDREN OF JULIUS AND HARRIET (MUNGER) BENE- 392
DICT.

839   I.   Charles Sidney Benedict, born July 7, 1861.

840   II. George Curtis Benedict, born Oct. 2, 1865; died
Sept. 18, 1866.

CHILD OF DANIEL PALMER AND EUNICE (ELDERKIN) 397
UTLEY.

841   I.   Jedediah George Utley, born June 2, 1872.

CHILDREN OF GEORGE WASHINGTON AND EMILY ELIZA **399** (UTLEY) VAN VALKENBURGH.

842   **I. Ella Montresor Van Valkenburgh,** born April 12, 1856; died in 1860.

843   **II. Maria Montresor Van Valkenburgh,** born March 14, 1861.

CHILDREN OF MORRIS EUGENE AND DESDEMONA (STIM- **402** SON) UTLEY.

844   **I. Ida May Utley,** born Jan. 17, 1867.

845   **II. Frank Utley,** born Dec. 9, 1876.

CHILD OF ALMER W. AND ALMA AUGUSTA (UTLEY) **403** MITCHELL.

846   **I. Donnie Lou Mitchell,** born Aug. 3, 1877.

CHILDREN OF GEORGE BENEDICT AND EMMA JANE **404** (LARAWAY) UTLEY.

847   **I. Lottie Cordelia Utley,** born Dec. 17, 1877.

848   **II. George Joseph Utley,** born Feb. 20, 1880.

CHILD OF JULIUS FRANCELO AND AMY (GALLUP) CREGO. **405**

849   **I. Leona Crego,** born March --, 1854. She married **1044** George Conant, a jeweler, and resides in Hudson, Lenawee County, Mich.

CHILDREN OF JULIUS FRANCELO AND CAROLINE M. **405** (CHANDLER) CREGO.

850   **I. Julius Crego,** born Nov. 18, 1863.

851   **II. Fannie H. Crego,** born Aug. 31, 1865.

852   **III. William G. Crego,** born March 26, 1869.

CHILDREN OF HARRISON AND MARTHA ANN (CREGO)   406
OSTRANDER.

853   I.   Harrison Clinton Ostrander, born May 2, 1863; died March 14, 1864.

854   II.   Harrison Clinton Ostrander, born Oct. 24, 1864.

CHILDREN OF GEORGE CLINTON AND MARY ELEANOR   408
(LAWRENCE) CREGO.

855   I.   George Elmer Crego, born Aug. 16, 1869.

856   II.   Lavinnie Crego, born April 7, 1874.

CHILDREN OF JAMES HENRY AND ANNA (SCOTT) CREGO.   409

857   I.   Verna Crego, born June 20, 1871.

858   II.   Vine Crego, born April 10, 1873; died Oct. —, 1873.

CHILDREN OF JAMES NOAH AND NANCY ELIZABETH   414
(RICE) FINCH.

859   I.   Charles Silas Finch, born Sept. 2, 1850.   He married, May 12, 1879, Mrs. Dora M. Pool, widow of Samuel Pool of Tyrone, Mich., and daughter of Isaac Walker of Tyrone. She died Jan. 4, 1883. They had no children. Mr. Finch is a farmer, and resides in Solon Township, Kent County, Mich.

860   II.   James Delbert Finch, born July 27, 1852. He 1045 married, Nov. —, 1874, Harriet Randall, daughter of Joseph and Jane (Dusenberry) Randall of Grand Rapids, Mich. They reside in Solon Township, Mich.

861   III.   Eben Eugene Finch, born Nov. 3, 1856.

862   IV.   Edgar Mead Finch, born Sept. 11, 1861; mar-

ried, Oct. 4, 1883, Ann Jane Bloomfield, daughter of Henry and Ellen (Johnson) Bloomfield of Solon Township, Mich.

863   V.   Perry Finch, born Sept. —, 1865.

CHILDREN OF CHARLES BENHAM AND LOIS MARIETTE   415
(SHEAR) RICE.

864   I.   Carrie Rice, born Sept. 8, 1864.

865   II.   Daniel Rice, born Feb. 9, 1866.

866   III.   Emma Belle Rice, born Feb. 8, 1869.

CHILDREN OF EBEN SMITH AND CINDERELLA (BURT)   416
RICE.

867   I.   Ella Elmetta Rice, born Jan. 14, 1859. She 1047
married, Oct. 1, 1876, Louis Napoleon Cole, a farmer, son of David Cole of Ada, Kent County, Mich. They reside in Ada.

868   II.   Adelaide Adelia Rice, born Feb. 6, 1862. She 1048
married, June 25, 1880, John James Wheeler of Grand Rapids Township, Mich., farmer.

CHILDREN OF JOHN AND THEODOSIA PHEBE (RICE)   417
CONLEY.

869   I.   Mary Conley, born May —, 1865.

870   II.   William Conley, born March 6, 1866.

871   III.   Daniel Conley, born Oct. —, —— ?
[There were other children in this family who died young.]

CHILDREN OF JOHN DOUGREY AND ELIZABETH (VAN   422
ZANDT) NICHOLS.

872   I.   Carrie Nichols, born Dec. 21, 1859.
29

873   II.   James Nichols, born June —, 1862; died Aug. 3, 1863.

874   III.   Samuel Nichols, born March 27, 1867.

CHILDREN OF JOHN AND ISABEL MARY (MONTGOMERY)   424
DOUGREY.

875   I.   George Moulton Dougrey, born Sept. 16, 1859. He married, May 3, 1881, Margaret Gates, daughter of William and Elizabeth (Pier) Gates of Cohoes, N. Y. She was born Oct. 17, 1859. They reside in Lansingburg, N. Y., where he is engaged with his father in a local express business.

876   II.   John Montgomery Dougrey, born June 20, 1861; died Nov. 30, 1861.

877   III.   Emma Isabel Dougrey, born July 15, 1863.

878   IV.   John Brown Dougrey, born April 17, 1867.

CHILDREN OF JAMES (3D) AND JANE AMANDA (JONES)   425
DOUGREY.

879   I.   James Cragen Dougrey, born Sept. 14, 1860. Assists his father on his stock-farm, in Stillwater, N. Y.

880   II.   Elizabeth Moulton Dougrey, born July 7, 1868.

881   III.   Howard Chandler Dougrey, born Feb. 24, 1870.

CHILDREN OF CHANDLER HEZEKIAH AND CLARISSA BON-   429
TECOU (DOUGREY) LOOMIS.

882   I.   Frances Elizabeth Loomis, born Sept. 12, 1870.

883   II.   Sarah Harriet Loomis, born Jan. 20, 1874.

CHILDREN OF DAVID REEVES AND JUANA (CARRASCO)   430
SMITH.

884   I.   Alva Clara Smith, born in Copiapo, Chile, May 4, 1862.

885 II. **Charles Boutecou Smith**, born in El Cobota, Mexico, Jan. 9, 1864.

886 III. **Anna Inez Smith**, born in Enriquita (Arizona), Feb. 21, 1866.

887 IV. **David James Smith**, born in Benicia, Cal., Jan. 10, 1868; died there, Jan. 31, 1868.

888 V. **David Reeves Smith, Jr.**, born in San Francisco, Cal., March 19, 1869.

889 VI. **Henry Day Smith**, born in San Francisco, April 8, 1870; died there, May 18, 1870.

890 VII. **Henry Day Smith**, born in San Francisco, April 14, 1871; died there, May 29, 1871.

891 VIII. **Stella Maria Smith**, born in Peoria, Ill., June 4, 1872.

892 IX. **Day Wallace Smith**, born in Cali-Cauca, United States of Colombia, Jan. 21, 1875.

893 X. **Vida Kellogg Smith**, born in New York, May 7, 1878.

894 XI. **A daughter**, born in West Troy, N. Y., Aug. 17, 1880; died same day.

CHILDREN OF ALBERT JACOB AND ANNA MARY (SMITH) 432
MITCHELL.

895 I. **Winifred Dongrey Mitchell**, born Aug. 16, 1862.

896 II. **Clarissa Isabel Mitchell**, born March 3, 1866.

897 III. **Paul Albert Mitchell**, born Jan. 20, 1868.

898 IV. **Charles Day Mitchell**, born April 19, 1870; died Jan. 2, 1872.

CHILDREN OF DAY KELLOGG AND MARGARET VIRGINIA   **433**
(DONLEVY) SMITH.

899   **I.   Day Kellogg Smith, Jr.,** born in Peoria, Ill., Nov. 24, 1871.

900   **II.   Winifred Louise Smith,** born in Peoria, Nov. 13, 1872.

901   **III.   Frederick Donlevy Smith,** born in Peoria, Oct. 16, 1874.

902   **IV.   Robert Ormsby Smith,** born in Chicago, July 27, 1878.

903   **V.   Clara Helen Smith,** born in St. Paul, Minn., May 11, 1882; died there, July 22, 1882.

CHILDREN OF EDGAR W. AND CLARA FRANCES (SMITH)   **434**
NYE.

904   **I.   Bessie Loring Nye,** born Feb. 6, 1878.

905   **II.   Winifred Louise Nye,** born May 25, 1879.

CHILDREN OF CALVIN JOHN AND CELIA FRANCES (CUR-   **435**
RAN) BARKER.

906   **I.   Calvin Curran Barker,** born April 19, 1864; died May 6, 1864.

907   **II.   Irene Frances Barker,** born Jan. 16, 1868.

908   **III.   Edward Gorham Barker,** born Dec. 14, 1871.

909   **IV.   Clara Burbank Barker,** born June 17, 1878.

CHILD OF JAMES ALBERT AND ALICE MAGDALENE   **440**
(CORY) WHITTAKER.

910   **I.   Julia Whittaker,** born July 11, 1882.

CHILDREN OF FREDERICK NORTH AND MARIA DICK- **442**
INSON (FRENCH) PAGE.

911   I. **Frederick West Page,** born in Athens, Pa., July 1049
6, 1855. He removed to Williamsport, Pa., in 1869, and
at one time was engaged in the retail furniture trade,
but is now secretary of the Williamsport Furniture Manufacturing Company. He married, Sept. 2, 1875, Sarah
Virginia Weise, daughter of Henry and Sarah (Sellers)
Weise of Hagerstown, Md.

912   II. **Mildred Anne Page,** born March 26, 1857. She 1052
married, June 15, 1880, James Wesley Maynard of Williamsport, who was born there March 24, 1844. He is
not engaged in business.

913   III. **Ellen Maria Page,** born Aug. 12, 1859.

914   IV. **Martha French Page,** born May 2, 1861. She
married, Feb. 6, 1883, Clarence Eugene Else of Williamsport, born there May 24, 1857. He is a clerk.

915   V. **Sylvester John Page,** born Sept. 15, 1863.

916   VI. **Joseph Albert Page,** born Jan. 23, 1866; died
Jan. 26, 1868.

917   VII. **Andrew Thomas Page,** born March 15, 1868.

918   VIII. **Louis French Page,** born Aug. 16, 1870;
died June 26, 1879.

919   IX. **Ethel Page,** born Oct. 7, 1872.

920   X. **Percy Rheinhold Page,** born March 27, 1875;
died Sept. 16, 1875.

CHILDREN OF JOHN M. AND MARY GLENNEY (FRENCH) **443**
ACKERMAN.

921   I. **Carrie Golden Ackerman,** born Aug. 27, 1866.

922   II.   Mary French Ackerman, born Sept. 16, 1870.

CHILDREN OF FOUNTAIN THOMAS AND JULIA CAS-   **444**
SANDANA (FRENCH) PAGE.

923   I.   Robert Fountain Page, born Oct. 28, 1867.

924   II.   Walter Thomas Page, born Dec. 5, 1869.

925   III.   Bertha Alice Page, born March 29, 1872.

926   IV.   Louis Page, born Feb. 11, 1880.

CHILDREN OF JOHN FERDINAND AND SARAH (BUCK   **445**
INGHAM) SANFORD.

927   I.   Albert Latham Sanford, born May 9, 1872;
died July 12, 1872.

928   II.   Arthur Ferdinand Sanford, born Jan. 4, 1875.

CHILDREN OF LUCIEN WHITE AND JULIA ALICE   **450**
(BRISTOLL) STILWELL.

929   I.   Mary Irene Stilwell, born Sept. 26, 1874.

930   II.   Hugh Alvin Stilwell, born April 30, 1881.

931   III.   Donald Louzon Stilwell, born Dec. 7, 1883, in
Deadwood, Dak.

CHILD OF ARTHUR HENRY AND MARY HANFORD   **453**
(BRISTOLL) DAVIDSON.

932   I.   Florence Hope Davidson, born March 7, 1880.

CHILDREN OF HENRY AND ELLA (BRISTOL) DUNHAM.   **454**

933   I.   Ida Dunham, born Jan. 18, 1870.

934   II.   Harry Bristol Dunham, born Jan. 31, 1872.

935   III. Emma Hunt Dunham, born Aug. 20, 1873; died April 3, 1874.

936   IV. Arthur LeRoy Dunham, born July 10, 1880.

CHILD OF HUGH BRADFORD AND IDA (BRISTOL) 456
JACKSON.

937   I. Hugh Bradford Jackson, Jr., born Nov. 1, 1872; died Jan. 3, 1874.

CHILDREN OF CHARLES SAMUEL AND KENTUCKY ANN 461
(THOMAS) NEWTON.

938   I. Willie Newton, born July 29, 1867; died Oct. 3, 1867.

939   II. Eddie Charles Newton, born Sept. 11, 1869.

CHILDREN OF CHARLES SAMUEL AND MARY ELIZABETH 461
(JONES) NEWTON.

940   I. Harry Newton, born July 20, 1872; died Aug. 28, 1873.

941   II. John Becker Newton, born Oct. 20, 1874; died May 10, 1878.

942   III. Merta Newton, born April 16, 1876.

943   IV. Carl Newton, born Feb. 2, 1878.

944   V. Clay Newton, born Dec. 23, 1879.

CHILDREN OF WILLIAM FREDERICK AND NANCY ELIZA- 463
BETH (KENDAL) NEWTON.

945   I. Walter Kendal Newton, born March 17, 1878.

946   II. Florence Reufina Newton, born Sept. 29, 1879; died Sept. 3, 1882.

CHILDREN OF EDWARD ALEXANDER AND JANE ELIZA **465**
(NEWTON) BULLOCK.

947   I.   Lew Nora Bullock, born Nov. 9, 1870.

948   II.   Orastus Bullock, born May 2, 1873; died Oct. 31, 1873.

949   III.   Charles Lester Bullock, born Dec. 30, 1874.

950   IV.   Willie Edward Bullock, born March 29, 1880; died Aug. 20, 1880.

CHILD OF WILLIAM GAY AND EMMA (JESUP) SHELDON. **487**

951   I.   Mary Louise Sheldon, born June 7, 1867; died Aug. 10, 1868.

CHILD OF EDWARD HENRY AND LOUISA HANFORD **489**
(JESUP) CUDDY.

952   I.   Louisa Jesup Cuddy, born April 14, 1868.

CHILD OF FRANCIS WRIGHT, JR., AND EFFIE (CROOK) **490**
JESUP.

953   I.   Florence Marguerite Jesup, born Aug. 10, 1881.

CHILD OF HANFORD AND ANNIE MARIA (TATOR) DAY. **491**

954   I.   Henry Hanford Day, born July 5, 1868.

CHILD OF CHARLES GUSTAVUS AND LILLIA FRANCES **501**
(SMITH) WILSON.

955   I.   Flora May Wilson, born Feb. 9, 1881.

CHILD OF CHARLES HENRY AND MARTHA HENRIETTA **504**
(STRONG) FOWLER.

956   I.   John William Fowler, born Dec. 27, 1881.

CHILD OF GEORGE FRANCIS AND CLARA M. (MATTHEWS) MUNSON. **505**

957   I.   **Jennie Tyler Munson**, born Nov. 9, 1880.

CHILDREN OF TOURO AND MARIA ELIZABETH (SANFORD) ROBERTSON. **508**

958   I.   **Lizzie Edna Robertson**, born Nov. 26, 1868.

959   II.   **Jessie Sanford Robertson**, born April 16, 1870.

960   III.   **William Touro Robertson**, born Nov. 18, 1871.

CHILDREN OF JOHN EDWARD MENEMON AND MARTHA CLARK (TAYLOR) SANFORD. **510**

961   I.   **Mary Sanford**, born March 20, 1871.

962   II.   **Huntington Sanford**, born Dec. 4, 1882.

CHILD OF CHARLES EDWARD AND KATE (LAIMBEER) SANFORD. **511**

963   I.   **Richard Laimbeer Sanford**, born in Brooklyn, N. Y., Dec. 17, 1877.

CHILDREN OF SHERMAN E. AND MARY HUTTON (RICE) FOOTE. **518**

964   I.   **Arthur Ellsworth Foote**, born Jan. 3, 1874.

965   II.   **Henry Lyman Foote**, born March 11, 1881.

CHILDREN OF THOMAS, JR., AND MARY ALASEBIA (BENNETT) McCONKEY. **531**

966   I.   **Mary Augusta McConkey**, born March 16, 1862.

967   II.   **Hattie Bennett McConkey**, born May 6, 1864.

968   III.   **Grace Miles McConkey**, born Jan. 21, 1874.

CHILDREN OF THOMAS HENRY AND TERESA MARIA 535
(FINN) MILES.

969   I.   Catharine Rebecca Miles, born in Erie, Pa., Oct. 15, 1866.

970   II. Maud Miles, born in Cleveland, Ohio, Oct. 22. 1868; died in Portsmouth, N. H., June 3, 1873.

971   III. Richard Benton Miles, born in Cleveland, Aug. 24, 1870; died in Portsmouth, N. H., May 22, 1873.

972   IV. Maud Mary Miles, born in Portsmouth, April 12, 1875.

973   V.   Harriet Teresa Miles, born in East Somerville, Mass., Feb. 21, 1880.

974   VI. Marion Miles, born in East Somerville, Feb. 9, 1882.

CHILDREN OF CHARLES EDWARD AND ANNA LOUISE 538
(HARTON) MILES.

975   I.   Millison Louisa Miles, born Dec. 18, 1880.

976   II. Thomas Harton Miles, born Aug. 17, 1882.

CHILD OF GEORGE MILES AND FLETA ALVIRA (ALLEN) 544
HALLIDAY.

977   I.   Susan Fleta Halliday, born in Cleveland, Ohio, March 30, 1872.

CHILD OF DARWIN BRAINARD AND SUSAN (HALLIDAY) 545
BEERS.

978   I.   Benjamin Pitney Beers, born in Cleveland, Ohio, Dec. 24, 1872; died in Cleveland, July 10, 1873.

CHILDREN OF JOHN AND ABBIE (HEDGE) SEAMAN. **552**

979   I.   **Charles Seaman,** born Sept. 22, 1866.

980   II.   **Edgar Seaman,** born Nov. 26, 1867.

981   III.   **Gussie Seaman,** born July 7, 1870.

982   IV.   **Frederick Seaman,** born Aug. 27, 1872.

983   V.   **Mabel Seaman,** born Sept. 19, 1874.

984   VI.   **Isaac Seaman,** born Jan. 1, 1877.

985   VII.   **Ada Abbie Seaman,** born June 30, 1879.

CHILDREN OF CHAUNCEY AND ELIZABETH TAYLOR (VAN   **557**
BASKERK) IVES.

986   I.   **Augusta Cromwell Ives,** born Sept. 22, 1869.

987   II.   **Harold Ives,** born Nov. 13, 1871.

CHILD OF HOBART JOHN AND ELIZABETH MARY (IVES)   **561**
PARK.

988   I.   **Maud Ives Park,** born Dec. 22, 1877.

CHILDREN OF REV. ALGERNON SIDNEY AND ADELAIDE   **586**
(TROWBRIDGE) CRAPSEY.

989   I.   **Philip Trowbridge Crapsey,** born March 7, 1876.

990   II.   **Emily Margaret Crapsey,** born March 1, 1877.

991   III.   **Adelaide Crapsey,** born Sept. 7, 1878.

992   IV.   **Paul Crapsey,** born Aug. 24, 1880.

993   V.   **Rachel Morris Crapsey,** born Aug. 11, 1882.

CHILDREN OF FREDERICK DABNEY AND NELLIE (EGAN)   **596**
SELLECK.

994   I.   **James Keeler Selleck,** born in Chicago, Ill., July
3, 1879.

995   II.   Edna Selleck, born in Chicago, Oct. 30, 1881.

CHILDREN OF GEORGE HUNTINGTON AND ADELAIDE   616
(BRUCE) NORTHRUP.

996   I.   John Bruice Northrup, born July 21, 1873; died
Feb. 28, 1876.

997   II.   Jessie Louisa Northrup, born Oct. 23, 1879;
died June 2, 1881.

CHILD OF GARDNER LANDON AND MARY ELIZABETH { 289
(NORTHRUP) BONTECOU.   { 617

998   I.   Frederick Finch Bontecou, born in New York,
July 29, 1873.

CHILDREN OF LEWIS KELMOND AND HARRIET LOUISA   618
(NORTHRUP) THURLOW.

999   I.   Mark Belcher Thurlow, born Oct. 12, 1875.

1000   II.   George Huntington Thurlow, born June 30,
1878; died May 28, 1881.

1001   III.   Edith Acelia Thurlow, born Sept. 6, 1880.

CHILDREN OF AUGUSTUS A. AND SARAH ELIZA (NORTH-   626
RUP) LINES.

1002   I.   James Roy Lines, born Aug. 26, 1881.

1002a   II.   Alfred Northrup Lines, born Feb. 2, 1885.

CHILDREN OF EDWARD FLINT AND NANCY (LANE)   687
LATHROP.

1003   I.   Harriet Angeline Lathrop, born Nov. 1, 1874;
died Oct. 3, 1878.

1004   II.   Benjamin Lane Lathrop, born Dec. 7, 1877.

1005   III.   James Lathrop, born Feb. 27, 1880.

1006   IV.   Edward Flint Lathrop, Jr., born Dec. 8, 1883.

NINTH GENERATION.

CHILD OF FRANK E. AND IDA ANNA (HOOK) WILLIAMS.   704

1006a   I.   Henry Raymond Williams, born June 2, 1885.

CHILD OF CHARLES HENRY AND HARRIET BONTECOU   709
(HAMILTON) JONES.

1007   I.   Daughter, not named, born May 15, 1883.

CHILDREN OF FREDERIC CLEVELAND AND MYRA A.   732
(WADHAMS) HOMES.

1008   I.   Charles Ives Homes, born July 3, 1872.

1009   II.   Susie Welles Homes, born May 18, 1876.

1010   III.   Frederic Cleveland Homes, Jr., born Nov. 5, 1879.

1011   IV.   Myra Wadhams Homes, born Feb. 16, 1882.

CHILDREN OF HORACE ROLLIN AND MARY LOUISE   737
(HOMES) BOYNTON.

1012   I.   Mary Louise Boynton, born March 20, 1881.

1013   II.   Julia Salter Boynton, born Jan. 6, 1883.

CHILD OF CHARLES SALTER AND SUSANNAH (PARRISH)   741
WELLES.

1014   I.   Susie Homes Welles, born Jan. 1, 1881.

238 BONTECOU FAMILY.

CHILD OF ERASTUS RALPH AND JULIA MARY (STEVENS) 748
CHILDS.

1015 I. Robert Joseph Childs, born Sept. 12, 1867.

CHILD OF CHARLES HENRY AND JULIA LOUISA (WOL- 753
FORD) CHILDS.

1016 I. Ida May Childs, born Jan. 3, 1882.

CHILD OF HOMER BENHAM AND LILLIAN ESTELLA (HOP- 754
KINS) CHILDS.

1017 I. Estella Lillian Childs, born July 30, 1882.

CHILD OF ALBERT ELLSWORTH AND JULIA LOUISA 755
(CHILDS) MARTIN.

1017a I. Clarence Albert Martin, born Feb. 13, 1884.

CHILD OF HERMAN EVERETT AND EMILY FRANCES (BEN- 756
HAM) SMITH.

1018 I. Minnie Cristine Smith, born in New Haven,
Conn., Dec. 1, 1876.

CHILDREN OF WILLIAM WEBSTER AND JESSIE EUGENIA 758
(ROBERTS) BENHAM.

1019 I. Alice Mabel Benham, born Sept. 23, 1881.

1019a II. Agnes Louise Benham, born May 10, 1885.

CHILD OF JOHN AND ELLEN MARTHA (BENHAM) GREEN- 762
WOOD.

1019b I. Edith Agatha Greenwood, born Nov. 19, 1884;
died Dec. 17, 1884.

CHILDREN OF JOHN HOWARD AND EMMA LOUISE (BUSH- 764
NELL) LAWRENCE.

1020 I. Louise Howard Lawrence, born Nov. 23, 1875.

1021   II.   Ethel Douglas Lawrence, born March 27, 1880.

1022   III.   Son, not named, born March 25, 1883.

CHILD OF CHARLES NOBLE AND GRACE EDSON (BUSH- 766
NELL) CLARK.

1023   I.   Virginia Norman Clark, born June 17, 1881.

CHILD OF FRANK WALTER AND ELLEN (DARNEY) 770
BUSHNELL.

1024   I.   William Frank Bushnell, born ——.

CHILDREN OF THOMAS BOND AND CAROLINE AUGUSTA 776
(DURAND) HAUGHAWORT.

1025   I.   Willie Haughawort, born Oct. 12, 1867; died
Oct. 28, 1867.

1026   II.   Grant Haughawort, born Oct. 17, 1868; died
Dec. 1, 1868.

1027   III.   Caroline Haughawort, born Nov. 10, 1869.

1028   IV.   Henry Haughawort, born Dec. 23, 1870; died
Jan. 20, 1871.

1029   V.   Edith Haughawort, born April 15, 1875.

1030   VI.   Nina Haughawort, born Jan. 23, 1878.

1031   VII.   Bond Haughawort, born Jan. 13, 1881.

CHILDREN OF WILLIAM RUFUS AND MARY FRANCES 778
(McCULLOCH) DURAND.

1032   I.   Fountain Edgar Durand, born March 7, 1875.

1033   II.   Charles Durand, born Oct. 22, 1876; died
March 25, 1877.

1034   III.   Daughter, not named, born July 25, 1881.

CHILDREN OF ALBERT WELLS AND SARAH ELIZA (DU- **779** RAND) CARPENTER.

1035   I.   Agnes Carpenter, born Aug. 23, 1874; died Dec. 16, 1875.

1036   II.   Edith Carpenter, born July 4, 1876; died Dec. 23, 1877.   ✕

1037   III.   Kittie Carpenter, born Dec. 20, 1878; died May 16, 1879.

1038   IV.   Louise Beatrice Carpenter, born April 4, 1880.

1039   V.   George Albert Carpenter, born July 14, 1882.

CHILD OF CONGRAVE JACKSON AND ELLA BELL (PRITCH- **789** ARD) TYLER.

1040   I.   Charles Lewis Tyler, born Jan. 23, 1881.

CHILD OF FREDERICK DONALDSON AND FRANCES ELIZA- **796** BETH (PRITCHARD) PARKER.

1041   I.   Bertha Marguerite Parker, born July 2, 1880.

CHILDREN OF CHARLES EDWARD AND JANETTE ELIZA- **808** BETH (WARREN) HALL.

1042   I.   Orinda Elizabeth Hall, born Oct. 31, 1880.

1043   II.   Charles Warren Hall, born June 13, 1882.

CHILD OF GEORGE AND LEONA (CREGO) CONANT.   **849**

1044   I.   One child, born about 1876.

CHILDREN OF JAMES DELBERT AND HARRIET (RAN- **860** DALL) FINCH.

1045   I.   Mina Finch, born July 6, 1876.

1046   II.   James Edgar Finch, born March 7, 1878.

CHILD OF LOUIS NAPOLEON AND ELLA ELMETTA (RICE) 867
COLE.

1047 I. Raymond Burt Cole, born July 9, 1883.

CHILD OF JOHN JAMES AND ADELAIDE ADELIA (RICE) 868
WHEELER.

1048 I. Henry Norman Wheeler, born May 2, 1881;
died Oct. 5, 1881.

CHILDREN OF FREDERICK WEST AND SARAH VIRGINIA 911
(WEISE) PAGE.

1049 I. Robert Weise Page, born April 15, 1877.

1050 II. Maxwell Frederick Page, born May 29, 1879.

1051 III. Faith Page, born Jan. 24, 1883.

CHILD OF JAMES WESLEY AND MILDRED ANNE (PAGE) 912
MAYNARD.

1052 I. Lawrence Maynard, born Feb. 19, 1882.

ADDENDA.

Subsequent to the passage of the earlier pages of this book through the press, and the distribution of the type, a discovery was made most unexpectedly; namely, that Timothy Bontecou (9) was from 1741 to 1748 a *resident* of Stratford, Conn., and that four of his children were born in that town, viz.:

Peter (12), born June 9, 1741; baptized July 12, 1741.

David (14), born January 6, 1742–3; baptized March 13, 1743.

James (15), born March 10, 1743–4; baptized March 18, 1744.

Mary (16), born September 13, 1747; baptized Sept. 27, 1747.

There is no record that shows him to have been the owner of property there, but he probably removed thither from New Haven, on account of greater convenience in the enjoyment of his church privileges. In 1848 he was again a resident of New Haven.

It will be observed that the order of arrangement of his children, in this work, is disturbed by this discovery. Peter, instead of being the eldest son, gives place to Daniel, who was born in *New Haven*, Sept. 9, 1739; and in each succeeding generation the descendants of the latter should take precedence of those of the former.

It will also be noticed in the case of these children, except Daniel, that the *year* of birth only was given by the compiler. No record of births having been found, this was determined by the age at death, and owing to a misstatement of the year of *Peter's* (12) death, a wrong conclusion reached regarding the time of his birth, resulting in his being considered the *eldest* son. The compiler now considers it most probable that he died in 1781, the year in which his estate was admitted to probate, instead of in 1779.

It will be seen also that we now have the given name and date of birth of *Mrs. Lathrop* (16).

The compiler greatly regrets that he did not earlier learn these facts and record them in their proper place, but is pleased that the discovery was not made too late to be made use of even in this imperfect and somewhat unsatisfactory manner.

ERRATA.

———

Page 152. No. 354: for Mary B. Turner, read Mary B. Tanner.

Page 164. No. 405: Julius Francelo Crego, right-hand reference number should be 849, instead of 850.

Page 215. No. 762: Ellen Martha Benham, right-hand reference number should be 1019b, instead of 1019a.

INDEX

Of Descendants and their Relatives.

(REFERRED TO BY NUMBER.)

32

256   INDEX.

33

INDEX

Of all Other Names Mentioned in this Work.

(REFERRED TO BY PAGES.)

270 INDEX.

www.ingramcontent.com/pod-product-compliance
Lightning Source LLC
Chambersburg PA
CBHW020346030726
47496CB00007B/2027